Also by Carole Walker Carter

Aztarian Series
AZTARA, The Mastel Kingdom
SURTEES, Science Rules
AZTARA, A Galactic Love Story
AZTARA, Secrets Revealed

Evers and MacFarlan Detective Series
Final Alumni
Shadowy Faces
Nine Points of a Circle

Fantasy Books
The Child Rowanda, Little Dragon
The Child Rowanda, Return to Arolsen
The Child Rowanda, Underworld
The Child Rowanda, Dragon Princess

Children's Books on www.walkercarter.com
Tinker Robot
Grandma's Magic Scarf
Granny Nell
Alec the Astronaut

Carole Walker Carter

Surtees

Science Rules

Vol. I

Aztarian Series

Carole Walker Carter

WALKER CARTER PUBLISHING, LLC

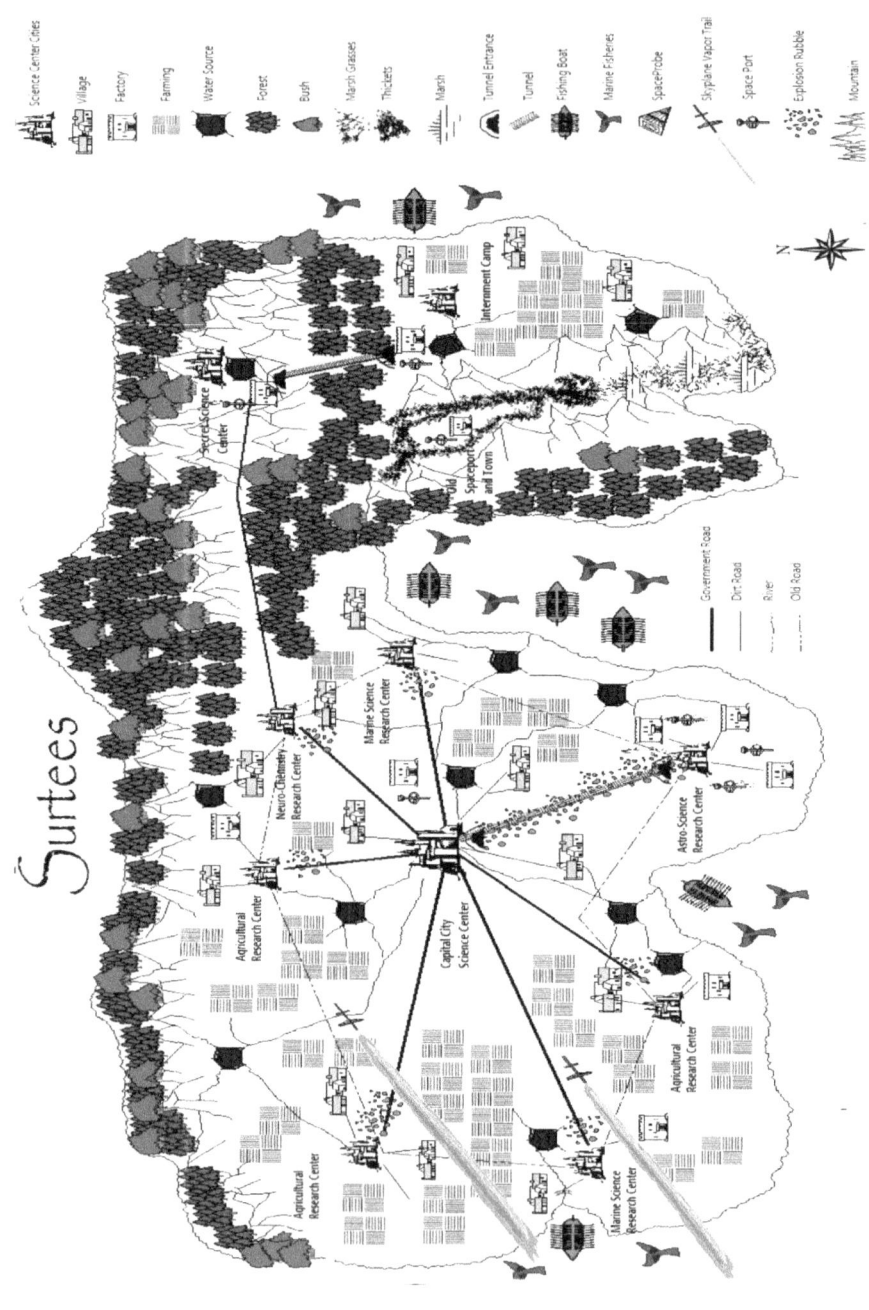

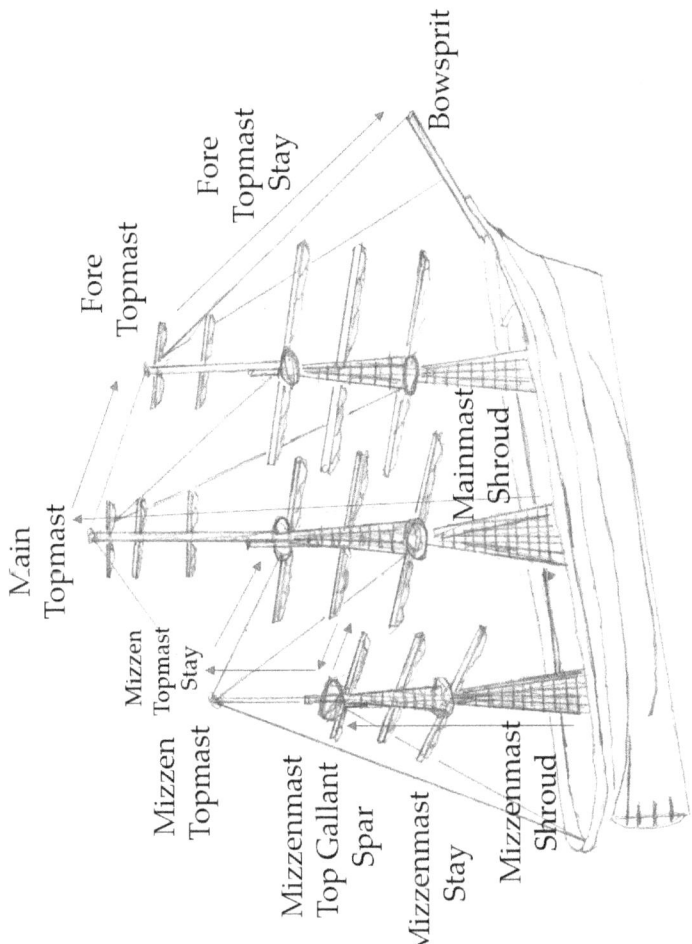

Carole Walker Carter

Cover Design by Donald E. Carter
Cover artwork © Fotolia by Adobe

SURTEES, Science Rules / by Carole Walker Carter
ISBN 978-1-947734-18-0

9 8 7 6 5 4 3 2 1 17 18 19 20 21

[1 Immortality, 2. Genetically Modified, 3. Vapor Trails, 4. Anti-Aging]

WALKER CARTER PUBLISHING, LLC

Carole Walker Carter

Please check out my website at www.walkercarter.com

To my girls Jennifer and Lisa, my grandson Nixon, my granddaughter Alex and my husband, Don.

In memory of my mother and dad, Elda and Dean Walker.

I will always love you!!!

Carole Walker Carter

ACKNOWLEDGEMENTS

I wrote this book in cooperation with my best friend and husband, Donald E. Carter, author of _Concurrent Engineering, Product Development Environment_ business books. Don's inspiration helped to create characters for the Evers and McFarlan Series and researched all the technical information.

Volume I <u>Surtees, Science Rules</u>, is the first book in the _Aztarian Series_. <u>Aztara, The Mastel Kingdom,</u> is the prequel to the _Aztarian Series_.

Janis Lane supported me with my writing by cheering me on to tell my stories. Don and I worked diligently to edit this book over the past year.

My girls, Jennifer and Lisa Coyle, provided several useful resource books. Without their support and prodding, this book may still be in draft form. Jennifer, with a keen eye for graphics, helped with the cover art.

Janel Walker, my younger sister, provided encouragement by always asking for the next chapter while providing excellent suggestions. Without my mother, Elda Walker, and older sister Linda Sturgill, giving me love, support, and resources, I would not be able to write.

Special thanks to all those that donated to my GoFundMe page, Linda Sturgill, Elda Walker, Janel Walker, Judy Mathiesen, Linda Maddex, Afsaneh Fowler, and Carol Royce Davidson. These donations kick-started my venture by allowing me to acquire editing and review tools, ISBN numbers, audio equipment, and final publication costs.

Table of Contents

CHAPTER ONE

Watching the children playing down below his third-story window, Ananaya wracked his memory for when he was young. 'Why can't I remember ever being young?' he thinks to himself. The children are running from each other and laughing, obviously playing some sort of game that requires speed and endurance. With no grass or shrubs and nothing but white walls surrounding hard ground, the children create games that can be played in the desolate courtyard. Ananaya smiles forlornly. 'How I long to be young again. Maybe I mean how I longed to be young…once.'

Ananaya was trained from very little to be a scientist like his mother and father. He was not allowed to play with other children for fear he may contract viruses that would jeopardize his developing brain. As a child, he often stood at this same third story window watching the children below playing similar styles of games. When caught by his nanny, he was chastised and returned to his tutoring sessions, where he received extra studies for being distracted. Painful slaps on the palms of his hands to keep the young child-focused were included as a reprimand.

With a head that seemed a bit too large for Ananaya's frail body, he walked unsteadily back to his desk. Tall and thin with long thinning hair that falls flat to his head without softening the sharp facial features: a jutting jawbone, pronounced brow, high cheekbones, and demoralizingly deep piercing grey eyes, Ananaya recalled his parents' philosophy about exercise. 'Developing body muscles is a waste of time,' according to his parents. 'The only muscle that matters is the brain.' His father's words ring in his mind even as he rubs his broad temples to assist his cognizance in returning to the present.

Reflecting, Ananaya realized that all his studies and tutoring paid off. He developed superhighways throughout his brain, creating hyper-areas of intelligence. Where most people use fifteen percent or less of their brain, Ananaya could use twenty-five percent for storing information and thought processing.

He knew that he should get back to work in his lab since there are many projects to oversee across multiple disciplines. Being the head scientist of one of the many science centers is an honor, bestowed on few. It confirmed his dedication and brilliance.

Ananaya marvels at being chosen to be on the Council of Scientist. He can't help but wonder if his mother and father had anything to do with it, but then he recants that thought with, 'I deserve the position. I am brilliant, and I have worked hard to obtain this seat in the council. I sometimes wonder if any of the council members have brains, or they would have put me in a position of power long before this. I know more than all of them combined.' He let his thoughts flow freely as he returned to the task at hand, feeling angry that it had taken this long for him to be promoted.

Ananaya's wife, Kaycee'na, belly swollen with twins, waddled into the lab, interrupting his thoughts. Before she can speak, she is greeted rudely with "What? What do you want now?"

She fights the desire to turn around and flee. She knows what that harsh greeting means. Ananaya is in a foul mood, and no matter what she came to tell him, essential or not, he will dismiss her and send her scurrying out the door with nasty remarks.

She meekly answers his question. "I have come to tell you that we have the test subjects that you directed us to obtain from the internment center."

Surprisingly, Ananaya's mood lifts. "Great! I have been waiting far too long for these test subjects, and I am pleased that they are here at last. Were there any complications? Did the parents sign the necessary papers giving us permission to do the tests? I hope that you compensated the parents adequately?"

Kaycee'na knows better than to tell Ananaya the truth. 'Let him think that everything is as he directed. It is better for all the subordinates if he is in a good mood. What he doesn't know won't hurt him, but if he finds out the truth, we could all be in terrible trouble,' Kaycee'na thinks to herself, hoping her remarkable husband will not be able to read her mind.

"The parents will not cause any trouble. They are excited that their sons may serve the Council of Scientist in any capacity," Kaycee'na lies. As quickly as a late-term pregnant woman could turn, Kaycee'na pivots to leave Ananaya's lab and quietly closes the door.

Outside in the hallway, Kaycee'na releases the breath she was holding while inside the room with her husband. She knows she has work to do to cover her tracks. Holding her aching back, Kaycee'na toddles quickly down the hall and out of sight. She does not notice the door opening as Ananaya walks out several steps behind her.

Bellowing, Ananaya shouts a command to his guard to have Hexyeb brought to his lab. Knowing the Center for Genetic Studies is many k-rods from the Capital Science Center, and it will take time for Hexyeb to be brought to him, Ananaya returns to his work. Hexyeb will come promptly. He would not dare refuse to come when commanded.

Biogerontology, Ananaya's specialty, was a science imposed upon Ananaya from childhood to the present. His own father, Ryndor, now old and feeble, was counting on his son to find the cure for aging. With Zyla, Ananaya's mother, now dead and cremated, Ryndor was pressing his son daily for news of a treatment. Approaching death, now a pressing reality after his wife's death, seemed to weigh heavily upon the old man, and Ananaya was finding his father's presence annoying and disruptive to his own agenda.

Almost on cue, Ryndor entered without knocking. "Ananaya, time is not something I have on my side. You are not working hard enough to find a cure to reverse the aging process. I am growing weaker each and every day. Why haven't you found a cure? Are you stupid or just incompetent? I raised you to be a thinking man. You should have found a cure for my decaying body seasons before now. I want to know why you have not done what you were bred to do?"

Not even looking up for one moment, Ananaya says in a monotone, "Old man, get out of my lab. I don't have time for your prattle today. I have important work to do. Now get out!"

"What could be more important than keeping me alive? Breaking down into a fit of coughing, Ryndor continues through his spasm. "I gave you life. Now it is your chance to return the favor. I want to hear by tomorrow that you have found the key to my longevity. This world needs my genius, and it is up to you to make sure that I stay alive."

"Let me help you out of the door and down the hall, Father." Ananaya unceremoniously grabs the old man by his thin arm and fast walks him into the hallway past his attending staff. Reaching the stair landing, Ananaya pushes his father down the stairs and smiles when he heard the unmistakable sound of old bones cracking like eggshells.

"I don't think he will bother me again, do you, Guyzar? Now, get rid of his remains. The furnace in the basement will do just fine." Ananaya returned to his lab without a backward glance to see if Guyzar is doing what has been asked of him. He knows Guyzar's loyalty is without question.

Guyzar is not surprised to see a lack of remorse in Ananaya's eyes as the scientist passed by him. Summoning his fellow guard, Guyzar descends the stairs where blood splatters can be seen. He knows one of his duties will be to make sure the maintenance crew is summoned without haste. Guyzar knows that Ananaya would be displeased if Hexyeb should arrive and see the blood upon the stairs. One does not question the Head Scientist. Guyzar knows his duty and will carry out the orders with efficiency.

Ananaya was briefly disturbed. 'Why did I tolerate that stupid old man to interrupt my work for so long? Luckily, my brilliant mind will be able to return to what I was doing…but, what if my mind would not have been so finely tuned?' Chuckling at the absurdity of his thought, Ananaya refocused on the task at hand.

Irritation surfaced again when a knock at his door announced an intruder until Ananaya remembered he was expecting Hexyeb. In a booming voice, Ananaya said, 'Come in and close the door behind you."

Hexyeb stood at the door opening. Taller than Ananaya and considerably better looking with iridescent, raven-black hair and hazel eyes, Ananaya resisted an inner desire to throw acid in the man's face. "I said to come in and close the door behind you!"

Hexyeb closed the door and walked stately towards Ananaya. "Why did you want to see me? What is so important that it could not wait until our general meeting tomorrow?"

Ananaya stiffened at the arrogant words spoken to him. "I have a project that must be started today. Kaycee'na informed me that the test subjects are ready for your genetic testing. I want it started immediately. Go find Kaycee'na, and she will tell you where the subjects are being housed. I am quite sure she had the forethought to send them to your facility."

Hexyeb bristled. "Why should I go find Kaycee'na? Don't you have the staff to do your bidding? Tell them to inform me when they find Kaycee'na. In the meantime, I am returning to my lab. This interruption has put me behind schedule. When I return, I will give my technicians the first vial to inject into the subjects."

Ananaya found his blood turning cold. Menacingly, he said, "YOU will find Kaycee'na yourself...NOW, and YOU will personally give each and every injection. Do you understand? I will have no mistakes made by your incompetent technicians. If anything goes awry, it will be your head on the chopping block. You do understand me, don't you?"

Without a word of acknowledgment, Hexyeb turned and left the lab with Ananaya's eyes boring deep holes into his back. 'That one has to go!' Ananaya thought to himself but returned to his work, knowing his command would be carried out precisely as dictated. 'Hexyeb is an arrogant man, but he is not stupid,' Ananaya thinks as a way to calm his anger.

Hexyeb followed the same path as Ryndor had earlier, but on his feet. There was no sign of blood on any of the stairs, and Hexyeb would not have even noticed if there was any. He was steaming mad, but he was not a fool. He knew he needed to find Kaycee'na and start Ananaya's project immediately. It galled him that he needed to put his own work on the back burner. He was so close to isolating the gene that caused polymyoextremis, a crippling disease that plagued many residents of Surtees. Why Ananaya always felt his projects were more important than Hexyeb's own was becoming a major problem. Hexyeb made the decision to bring up this point at the general council meeting tomorrow. He knew the ramifications would be horrific for him if the other scientists were not in agreement with himself. 'I don't care! I am tired of my work being interrupted by that pompous jerk. I am quite sure the other scientists must feel the same way.' Seeing Kaycee'na in the distance, all other thoughts, but the importance of catching up with her left his head.

"Kaycee'na! Wait!" Hexyeb yelled, feeling embarrassed that he was reduced to an errand boy.

Kaycee'na turned and waited for Hexyeb to catch up to her. "Hexyeb, what can I do for you?" Kaycee'na asked in all earnest.

Icily, Hexyeb answered, "Your husband sent me to find you. His directives were for you to take me to the test subjects. I am to stop everything I am working on and start Ananaya's pet project. You are to take me immediately to the subjects."

Kaycee'na was visibly shaken. This could be the moment of truth for her. Would Hexyeb realize the subjects were not consensual subjects? Would he complain to the Council of Scientists that children were being abducted for experimentation, or would he realize it was in his own best interest to turn a blind eye? All these thoughts raced through Kaycee'na's mind as she tried to compose herself.

"Will we take public transport to your center, or do you have a personal skyplane waiting for us?" Kaycee'na said as casually as her jumbled and fearful mind could muster.

Hexyeb indicated his skyplane was waiting on the second level, and he took Kaycee'na gently by the elbow to lead her to the flight deck. Not missing the fact that Kaycee'na seemed irritable, Hexyeb escorted her into the skyplane and started small talk, hoping to draw out why Kaycee'na seemed unusually nervous. He knew living with Ananaya would make even a rock crumble; he sensed

Kaycee'na's nervousness went even beyond her normal state of anxiety.

"So, tell me, Kaycee'na, have all the test subjects been selected with the desirable genetic traits required for this trial? You know it will be risky if any of them do not possess the necessary genetic makeup," Hexyeb pried.

Kaycee'na lied, "I have been assured that each and every one of the test subjects possesses the necessary genetic code to make them the best possible candidates for this research."

Kaycee'na visibly squirmed in her seat, and the unconscious movement was not lost on Hexyeb. "So how were the candidates picked? Did you personally supervise the selection?"

Looking out the window of the transporter at the hazy air, Kaycee'na felt trapped. If she said she personally supervised the selection and anything went wrong, it would be the end of her career. If she said her team selected the subjects and anything went wrong, her staff would be exiled to the internment camp or worse. Putting herself first, she responded, "My team is quite capable. I put my trust in them. I am sure they made good choices."

Hexyeb said with a steely voice, "You are betting your life on your team. You better hope they are capable; Ananaya is not a forgiving man."

CHAPTER TWO

With growing panic, Hexyeb watched as several boys died horrible deaths, writhing in pain as limbs developed into grossly distorted versions of arms and legs. Facial features contorted and finally relaxed as death took each young life. There was no recognizing the dead children as the same ones who recently received the first injection.

Hexyeb was furious at Kaycee'na's incompetence, and Ananaya's lack of compassion for life, in general, decided he had enough. The General Council would meet in the afternoon, and Hexyeb would not be deterred. He would announce to each and every member of the council that Ananaya must be stopped. 'Ananaya is a monster!' thought Hexyeb. 'He has no ones' interest except his own self-interest at heart. He cares nothing for the people of Surtees. He must be dismissed from his position!' Hexyeb quickly planned out the speech he would prepare for the Council of Scientists as he stared down at the faces of the children lying dead on cots in his lab.

An enormous room in the Capital City central research center was set aside for the Council of Scientist. Ananaya made sure the meeting hall was at his own facility. He was not about to spend valuable time on a transporter. He also liked the idea that all the other scientists needed to come to him. He reasoned that he was the most valuable of all the scientists, and he should never be inconvenienced.

Guyzar and several other staff members accompanied Ananaya into the gathering. He leaned heavily upon his trusted guard as his weak legs failed him occasionally when he walked any distance. Even though the central meeting hall was not actually far, Ananaya shrewdly used his disability to be surrounded by trusted staff.

The larger, padded chair awaited him at the round table. Ananaya often felt he should rid the room of a round table. Sitting at the head of a table would convey his importance and minimize the other scientists from feeling they were just as valuable as himself. Mental note: 'Get rid of the round table,' Ananaya inscribed into his mind.

Escorted to his chair, Ananaya indicated that his staff should remain standing behind him. None of the other scientists had a team in the room with them. It was evident from the start of the meeting, who was in charge.

"I have gathered all of you to this meeting because I have disturbing news to share. My father is dead. I will conduct this meeting. It has come to my attention that Hexyeb has failed completely with the task at hand. It is my opinion, and I am sure it will be shared by all of you, that Hexyeb needs to complete retraining at the internment camp. His experiment has cost the lives of twelve boys, whose parents put their trust in the hands of science. We cannot and will not let our young people come to harm at the hands of incompetent research. Kaycee'na, my wife, will take over the research."

As Hexyeb stood to object, Ananaya's staff members immediately came behind him with an injection to subdue the man. Hexyeb's legs buckled. Guards at each side of Hexyeb grabbed him as he started to fall and dragged him from the room.

"Does anyone have any objection to Kaycee'na continuing the research?" Ananaya asked. Ananaya looked from one assembled scientist to another.

Hoygazor, the lead scientist of Astro Science, obsequiously commented. "I believe Kaycee'na will be the perfect person to continue the trials. I vote that we accept her appointment."

With his penetrating eyes, Ananaya looked at Eyutho, lead Marine Science Director. "Do you also confirm my appointment, as well?"

With a nod and no verbal response, Eyutho added to the vote. Rigid in his chair, it was understandable, Eyutho was frozen with fear. He knew the internment camp was not a retraining program, but a place from which no one ever returned. At least, not the same person they were when they entered.

Doyfear, the head scientist at the Agricultural Research Center, braved one question. "Will more test subjects be required to replace the twelve young men who perished?"

Ananaya looked to Kaycee'na for a response. Visibly unraveling before his gaze, Kaycee'na lost her voice. "Are you prepared to answer the question put before you, Kaycee'na?" Ananaya said with no hint in his voice of the malevolence in his eyes.

Kaycee'na jolted upright as if a prod was used to get her to her feet as Ananaya's eyes pierced into her own. "We have already picked alternate test subjects. We will inject them yet today. They should be ready for the second injection tomorrow along with the other subjects who survived the first injection today."

Leaving Kaycee'na shaking, Ananaya dismisses her with a wave of his hand, and she sits down clumsily burdened by the extra weight from her pregnancy. Turning to Doyfear, Ananaya directs his next question to the scientist. "Doyfear, how is research proceeding with genetically modified seeds? I want crops growing next season. It is imperative, our food source must enhance our microchondrial metabolism (OXPHOS). Once our new test crops are flourishing, you must release your UberBugs to destroy all existing heritage crops. Do you have everything under control?"

Doyfear knew Ananaya was expecting a definite answer. Knowing it is in his best interest to say all is well, Doyfear remarks, "All is going well. The seeds will be planted in several locations next month when the growing season is optimal. The UberBugs are currently under development. Entayta, who is in charge of the robotic engineering team, has two models from which to choose. We are leaning towards using the model which can destroy existing pests as well as the heritage crops."

Ananaya listened intently and nodded his assent. Turning toward Eyutho, who seemed distracted, Ananaya shouted his name. Eyutho jumps when he hears his name. He knows he is next in the hot seat.

"Eyutho, your question is twofold. First, our drinking water should be enhanced with xanthothinphyll (XTTPL). It takes seasons to reap its benefits. Time is wasting. If you don't already have the chemical at the water refining plant, do so immediately. Secondly, XTTPL should be in the irrigation system, providing the necessary antioxidants that can be absorbed by the seeds once planted. That gives you one month to have the chemical ready for in-situ hybridization. Get it done."

There was no need to reply. Eyutho, who could not find his voice anyway, just nodded. He was still shaking from the scene being played over and over in his mind, of Hexyeb being dragged from the round table.

Hoygazor knew he was going to be next to be questioned. His skyplanes continuously seen leaving vapor trails as they traveled across the sky, were visible indicators to all concerned that his team was already doing what was expected. Monochloride and nucuobromine were oxidized and sprayed into the air at high altitudes for the benefits of anti-aging. Hoygazor waited to be praised.

"I want an update on our Starprobe research and deployment," Ananaya demanded.

Caught off guard, by the unexpected question, Hoygazor's face drained of color. Expecting praise for his accomplishments, Hoygazor was off balance to answer the question put to him. "Hmmm…hmmm, we will launch a dozen intergalactic Starprobes in search of alternate viable planets within five seasons."

Looking Hoygazor directly in the eyes, Ananaya said, "I will give you two seasons, and it better be done right. I want to make sure we capture molecular genetics down to the individual nucleic acid molecules from species as well as finding livability of several of the selected planets."

Hoygazor gulped. He wanted praise for all the work completed to date; instead, a daunting task remained ahead. Knowing he had best appear sure, he bolstered his confidence and said it would be done in the time assigned.

Ananaya, feeling he wasted enough of his precious time, ended the meeting. Looking to Guyzar for assistance, he rose from his chair and exited with his staff on his heels. Aside, he remarked to Guyzar, "Hexyeb will be dealt with promptly. Correct? I want a directive to all the scientists and their staff that I am now the Chief Scientist, and all activities will be run past me for approval from this time forward. And get rid of that round table. I want my seat at the head of the table by the next meeting."

The rest of the scientists stalled before leaving. No one wanted to encroach on Ananaya and his entourage as they left the hall. Slowly and silently, each scientist left the room, leaving Kaycee'na and

Eyutho as the last two to vacate. Sharing a feeling of impending doom, Eyutho, a diminutive and balding man, gathered his wits and commented in a low voice to Kaycee'na. "We can no longer report any failures to Ananaya, or we will meet the same fate as Hexyeb."

"What will we do? We are bound to have failures. Ananaya demands too much from us. He doesn't allow us time to do proper research. It is unrealistic what he wants us to accomplish. " Kaycee'na said in a whisper, knowing she could trust her childhood friend more than her husband.

"I will set up an underground system where the failures will be hidden and treated. You will need to find a discreet medical team that can research and create antidotes for our failures. We need to watch each other's backs if we are going to survive Ananaya's reign."

Realizing they overstayed their time alone together in the conference room, it was understood, by both, that they leave quickly so as not to draw attention from Ananaya's network of spies. Kaycee'na was sure Ananaya had not placed listening devices in the meeting hall, but she was also sure he would do so now that his father was no longer in charge. This would be the last time she and Eyutho could talk in this room ever again.

Walking down the hall, Kaycee'na was gripped by intense pain. She doubled over, holding her enormous belly. The twins would be arriving soon. She knew Ananaya would allow only time for her to give birth before he would expect her back to work. As the pain subsided, Kaycee'na raced to the landing to catch a skyplane to the genetics lab. The alternate patients were being tested and prepped for their first injections. Kaycee'na knew it was important that these subjects survived their initial dose. No more failures would be tolerated today, and Ananaya knew precisely how many subjects were available to date. Keeping his spies from the lab was not going to be easy, but necessary to hide any further failures. Hopefully, there would be no more.

CHAPTER THREE

The babies were demanding to be born. Kaycee'na breathed deeply, trying hard not to scream out in pain. She wondered if the boys she injected were in as much pain as she was as they underwent the physical changes the drugs induced. A moment of empathy crossed her mind but drifted away as she prepared herself for the next onslaught of cramping muscles, which were forcing the first twin into the hands of the waiting nurse.

No doctor was spared for the birth of the twins. Ananaya said childbirth was natural, and he was not going to summon a doctor from his essential job just to placate Kaycee'na. Kaycee'na pleaded with Ananaya, saying twins were riskier than a single birth, but her pleas fell on deaf ears.

"You will have a midwife with you. What more do you want? Women all over this planet give birth at home with no one to assist. You seem to think you deserve more. Well, you don't!" Kaycee'na remembers Ananaya's words before the next contraction eradicated all thoughts from her mind.

Pushing with all her might, Kaycee'na waited for the brief rest between contractions, but none came. A second spasm grabbed her immediately before the first subsided, feeling as though wave after wave of on-going pain would never stop. Wanting desperately to be in control of her body, Kaycee'na stifled the cry and dug her fingernails into her palms. Finally, unable to contain her moans any longer, she let the noise flow from her throat in guttural screams of agony like a wounded animal.

A cry was heard as the baby dropped into the waiting hands of the nurse. "It is a girl," the cheerful nurse said as she wrapped the baby in a blanket and took her to be weighed and cleaned. "You have a second child to push out. Try to relax. The contractions will start again soon."

Dreading the renewed contractions, Kaycee'na, exhausted from the delivery of the first baby, lay back on the birthing table. Drifting into a momentary sleep, she was suddenly awakened with an intense tightening of her belly. She knew there would be no rest between the births as the second child was shoved into the opening.

Again, wave after wave of intense pain ripped through Kaycee'na's body. This time, Kaycee'na's back was in spasm more than her stomach muscles. She thought birth could not be any worse, but the pain in her back was so intense, she could not get comfortable in any position. Kaycee'na rolled from side to side, whimpering. Moments felt like days as she found it impossible to relax even for a second. She thought, 'what I wouldn't give for just one moment without pain.'

Relief came only when she heard the second baby cry. There was enough time between births for the nurse to care for the first and place her in a safe crib. She was ready to take the second baby as it was pushed from the birth canal.

"It is a little girl, too! How exciting…identical twins. They are perfect and beautiful, Kaycee'na. You must be very proud. What will you call them?"

Kaycee'na didn't want to name them or even see them. She knew she would not be allowed to mother them in any way. Ananaya already told her she would need to return to work shortly after the birth. It would be too painful to connect on any level with her babies. "You name them. I have to get dressed and go back to work."

The nurse understood what Kaycee'na was going through. Already, Ananaya summoned the nanny who took care of him when he was little. The ancient old woman was no-nonsense and would direct all aspects of the twin's care and future studies. Sadly, the nurse gazed down at the darling little girls with pity and concern.

"If you are serious about my naming them, I would suggest Yyemara and Tawtanya after my own sisters. Would you like me to put those names on their birth certificates?" The nurse kindly asked.

"Those names are as good as any. If they please you, go ahead and put them on the papers. Someone should think kindly of my babies when they hear their names. It may as well be you," Kaycee'na said while struggling to sit up.

The nurse rushed to her side. "You can't leave yet. You still need to deliver the afterbirth, and we must reduce the size of your fundus, or you could bleed to death."

Kaycee'na, feeling depressed and tired, almost welcomed bleeding to death. Her world was pressing in on her. She could not be a good mother, she tortured the children of other mothers, and she needed to watch her back at all times. 'Maybe tomorrow I will feel better,' she hoped. Reclining back on the table, she knew she was lying to herself.

Kaycee'na was finally given permission to dress and leave. Syonne, the delivery nurse, was retained until Ananaya's own childhood nurse was found and reinstated. Delighted with the newborn twins, Syonne cared for the twins, day and night. She cuddled and cooed to them as well as sang lullabies Syonne, young and energetic, worked happily to care for the two little girls. Wishing she could sweep them away, never to be found by the

31

scientific world, she guarded them fiercely until the day the old matron arrived.

Zoolyol announced her arrival immediately. "Put that baby back in her crib. We don't spoil babies while I am in charge. If you want to retain your position as my assistant, you will do as I say without question. Is that understood?"

Syonne sized up the old matron. Everything about her sagged, yet she appeared daunting and unyielding. Her gray hair was thin and tied back from her face. Bald spots were evident through her tightly brushed bun. Her eyes lacked color or kind expression. Skin hung from her body as if she had once been fat, and now the overstretch skin folded around her fragile frame. Her bony fingers were long and almost appeared as claws. She pointed one of them at the crib and repeated her command. "Did you hear me, girl? Put that baby down!"

Syonne scampered to her feet and gently laid the baby in her crib. Tawtanya immediately started to cry. The baby was comfortable and happy in Syonne's arms, and now she was angry for the unexpected betrayal. Looking down at the tiny infant, Syonne felt the infant's feelings of disloyalty at unceremoniously being put down flat on her back. The nurse's tender heart ached to pick the crying baby up in her arms to comfort her.

Standing back, Syonne knew she must appease the old woman, or she would be ripped away from the two babies she had grown to love. Knowing the only hope, the babies would have for any love would come from her…when she was alone with them. She would need to bide her time.

"Now, this is the list of your duties. You will change diapers, bathe the babies, and feed them. Once they are clean and fed, they will be returned to their cribs. Aural exciters for brain manipulation will be played when they are awake to start their education. The aural exciter uses harmonics to reward the ion pathways while at the same time saturating the higher-level brain areas with new information. You will find my case in the corner, has all the exciters labeled as to when and what order they will be played. The babies will be allowed a half-day of sleep a day and no more. The rest of the time will be spent developing and manipulating their cognitive processes."

Syonne was appalled, "What about developing their large motor muscles and eye-hand coordination?"

"What do scientists need with muscles? The only organ worth developing is the brain. That is our task and nothing else. From now on, don't ask questions. Just do as I say," barked Zoolyol

Shrinking back from the harsh words, Syonne vowed on the spot that her babies would be nurtured if it was the last thing she did. The trick would be to find time to do so without the prying eyes of the old bat watching her. She knew Zooyol was old and would need rest periods. Syonne also knew she, herself, would not need near as much sleep as the aging woman. She would give the babies the care they needed when it was safe.

"We will work in shifts. You will have the early morning shift and the night shift. I will relieve you in the midmorning and leave again for evening mealtime. You can expect me to check on you at any time day or night," Zoolyol said in a dry, demanding tone.

The routine was set. When Zooyol was in the room, everything was as she dictated. Syonne took the precious moments to soothe the babies when she bathed and fed them before the morning routine Zooyol dictated. It was her moment to cuddle and caress each as Zooyol was distracted with which aural exciter would be played next.

As time passed, it became apparent that Tawtanya's ion pathways were connecting to her upper motor neurons as she kicked and cried more in her crib, wanting to be out and held. Yyemara was more content to listen to the exciters and relaxed and cooed as the aural exciter played. Zooyol found herself more detached from the physical twin and concentrated all her energies on Yyemara. Syonne found even more time to be alone with Tawtanya.

Every opportunity Syonne was given when Zooyol was out of the room or asleep, the young nurse would allow the twins to play with each other. They delighted in being free to crawl and explore but never let the other twin out of their sight. Frequently, they would return from exploring to play with a mutual toy, which was stored discreetly out of sight from Zooyol. Toys were not allowed under the old matron's watch.

Watching the twins grow was exciting for Syonne. She delighted in Tawtanya's strength and prowess even as a toddler. Yyemara found more delight in sedentary games. Each, however, would partake in the other's playtime just to be together. Syonne felt much satisfaction from the growing attachment each twin felt for the other.

TaTa, as Yyemara called Tawtanya, dominated the physical world of play. She would race around the room with Yyemara following clumsily, as best as she could. Climbing upon the sparse furniture in the education center was always fun for Tawtanya. Pulling her sister upon the chairs and tables was TaTa's favorite game. Yyemara struggled to follow, but TaTa would lend a helping hand. Syonne never grew tired of hearing the little voices. "TaTa, help." Yyemara would howl when Tawtanya would be out of her reach.

Yyemara was far better at language, so TaTa would mimic YaYa, as Yyemara was called by her twin. "Say please, TaTa." And Tawtanya would answer with "pweas." Laughing, Yyemara would repeat the word, "please." Yyemara's verbal games increased with more and more words for Tawtanya to imitate. Objects in the room all had names, and Yyemara would howl with laughter when Tawtanya would mispronounce many of them.

Tawtanya, however, continued to be king of the mountain and ran circles around her twin sister. Tag-to-be-king was TaTa's favorite game. Yyemara was a willing partner to each and every game invented by her stronger, willful sister.

Exhausted by the physical games, the twins would fall on the floor in an intertwined heap of little bodies, and fall asleep, content in each other's company. Syonne was always there to carry each to their separate beds to make sure they were where Zooyol expected them to be each morning.

The middle of the night, while Zooyol would sleep, became the most wonderful time of the day for the twins. With Syonne by their side to keep them safe and relatively quiet, days passed into seasons. The twins' bonds grew stronger and stronger until Syonne grew fearful that the children's increasing speech would give a hint to the playful nights. There was no way Syonne could tell the children not to tell Zooyol that they played every night with each other. The twins just would not understand why Syonne was giving them a warning.

During the day, each child was within their isolated bubble. Zooyol concentrated most of her energies on Yyemara. Puzzled why Yyemara kept repeating the word TaTa, Zooyol became increasingly suspicious.

Unfortunately, Zooyol returned early one day from an outing to find the twins on the ground playing together. "What are you doing, Syonne? You know this is forbidden. How dare you go behind my back. Ananaya will hear of your deceit! Now, put those babies back in their individual pedagogic learning bubbles!" Zooyol said angrily as she stomped out of the room to inform the Chief Scientist.

Ananaya was busy and was furious when his old matron entered his lab unannounced, but he stopped out of respect for the old woman. "What brings you to my lab, Zooyol? You know I am busy."

"I wouldn't bother you, but this is important. The twins are not developing in the same way as you supposed they would be developing as identical twins. I wish to dismiss Syonne. I feel she is a bad influence on the one called Tawtanya. I actually found the twins on the floor playing while in Syonne's care. Will you give me permission to dismiss her immediately?" Zooyol said with indignation.

Ananaya listened and paused. "You say the twins are not developing in the same way? How old are they now?"

"No, Syr, they are not developing the same way, and now that they are three seasons old, it is noticeable. Tawtanya seems only interested in being physical. Yyemara is cerebral and developing as she should. I hold Syonne responsible for Tawtanya's delays in cognitive development. I want her dismissed immediately!"

"Interesting," Ananaya said, "I think I have a better suggestion. I would like to see how the twins develop in different settings. If they are identical, I would think they would develop at the same rate, but you say they are not. I want to push this experiment even further. Yes, you may dismiss Syonne, but she is to take Tawtanya with her. The one you call Yyemara will remain with you, and you will continue her studies in the same way you instructed me when I was a child. I want a behavioral scientist to secretly watch Tawtanya and report back on her development without Syonne being aware that she is being watched. Take care of this."

Turning his back on Zooyol, Ananaya returned to his work. Zooyol was not satisfied with the decision Ananaya just made, but she knew better than to question him. Zooyol could not help but feel Syonne had won a significant battle, and Zoolyol did not like it one bit. 'Oh well, at least, I get to keep the smart one. Syonne can keep the dumb one,' Zoolyol rationalized to keep her annoyance tamped down.

Returning to the colorless education center, Zooyol announced that Syonne would be leaving, and she should take the stupid baby with her. "You have exactly five clicks of the clock to be out of this building, or I will have the guards take both of you to the internment camp!" Zooyol threatened.

Syonne quickly gathered Tawtanya and rushed from the building. Hating to leave Yyemara in the sole care of the hateful old woman, Syonne knew she should count her blessings to save at least one of the twins. Finding a place to stay would not be hard. Syonne had a loving family who would gladly take her and the baby into their home.

Zooyol smugly watched as Syonne ran from the education center. "Good riddance to you and that horrible child. I don't want to ever see your face again!" Zooyol flung insults at Syonne's retreating backside.

'Now, I will concentrate on Yyemara. She will make me proud and keep me in good graces with Ananaya. I know Yyemara will be the brightest scientist in the galaxy.' Zooyol daydreamed. Picturing Yyemara ruling beside her first prodigy, Ananaya, gave Zooyol a feeling of accomplishment and purpose. Her world was in order, and all was well…except for the one disappointment in her career, Tawtanya.

CHAPTER FOUR

The modified crops grew well in the chemically enriched soil with the chemically enhanced water. One thing though, there was an overabundance of thorny weeds that were scarce before the modified crops. The farmers were told the UberBugs were designed to eat the weeds; instead, they devoured the heritage crops leaving nothing but the genetically modified crops to feed the Surtees population. Farmers were concerned when the decree was posted that no seeds should be planted other than those supplied by Doyfear.

Harvest time found bushels of baskets loaded with various crops packed in cartons to take to the markets. Animals grown for food were more substantial initially than previous stocks, but the animals were unable to breed successfully. It seemed fewer offspring were born to genetically modified livestock. More baby animals were born dead or with defects, and the ones who managed to grow to adulthood were often confiscated by the agricultural research department for further studies. No one seemed to know why fewer of the animals thrived.

The scientists assured the farmers they would return the healthy adult animals, and their stock would be even stronger and more prolific than before the genetically modified feed became mandatory. So far, that promise was not fulfilled.

Noryan lived on his family farm. He was born on this piece of Surtees, and he figured he would die on this same piece of land. Married to Merlynn, the two were raising their families. The past season was particularly hard for the family. Their eldest son disappeared from school, and no one had any idea what happened to him. The authorities were informed, and a search conducted, but it seemed their son just vanished off the face of Surtees. Noryan's heart was broken, as was his wife's.

The remaining two younger children were guarded and not allowed to go to school. Noryan felt all they needed to know could be taught from home. Merlynn was responsible for teaching reading, writing, and math, while Noryan showed the two how to manage a farm.

With the boys being too young to help with the farming, Noryan found himself extremely busy. In the past, his eldest son supplied much of the needed labor to keep the farm running smoothly. The younger two children were able to help with minimal chores, but the hard job of farming was still beyond their capabilities. Merlynn was recruited to do more manual work as she did when the couple was first married and before the children started to arrive. Her duties to educate the boys as well as being a farmhand left the woman exhausted by evening and often irritable.

After the children were fed and tucked into bed, the couple would sit down and discuss the day. "I don't know how we are going to make it," Noryan announced quietly so as not to wake the children. "The herd is not very hearty. The animals grow too quickly at the beginning, which breaks down their legs. Most of the animals can hardly get around in the field. They are losing weight rapidly instead of gaining like they should. By the time the market comes around, I am not sure they will weigh enough for us to break even."

Sadly, Merlynn shook her head in agreement. This was not the first season with the new stock provided by the scientists. The promise for better and larger livestock was not happening. The opposite seemed to be true.

"What makes things worse," Merlynn complained, "is the fact that the agriculture department takes our best animals to study. How are we supposed to improve our stock if they constantly take the very best ones? Why can't we refuse to let them have the best animals when they come?"

"Merlynn, you know about the internment camps. You and the two children would never survive if they came for me. We are not living well, but at least we are living. I just don't want to say anything and end up dead or whatever happens in that camp. Please don't complain to anyone—not even Lyryca," Noryan asked.

"Lyryca is my best friend. She would never say anything to anyone if I told her not to," Merlynn protested.

With fear creeping into Noryan's voice, he asked, "You haven't already told her what we talk about at night, have you? If she says anything to anyone, I fear the Chief Scientist's new guards will come for me in the night. Please tell me you have not said anything to her."

"She won't say anything to anyone. I have to talk to someone about my fears. It was hard enough when our son disappeared. Who do you think got me through that crisis? It was Lyryca. I would not be functioning today if I didn't have her to talk with," Merlynn said emphatically.

Noryan shook his head. "I hope not…for your sake. We have no savings for you and the children to live on. What will you do if they come for me?"

"Stop saying that! No one is going to come for you. Why do you keep saying that? Do you know someone who has been taken away by those hideous guards? And where in the world did those horrible guards come from in the first place? What do they call them…Enforcers? We never had Enforcers before. Why does the Chief Scientist need guards? This is just crazy!" Merlynn's voice escalated as she became more and more excited.

"Shh, you will wake the children," Noryan admonished. "We need to go to bed. We have crops ready to pick tomorrow."

"Don't shush me. This is serious. We never had trouble making a living before the Chief Scientist took control over all the scientists. We could depend on Doyfear before this. Now, our heritage crops are destroyed by those awful robotic UberBugs, and we are only left with the seeds the agricultural research center has given us to plant and not for cheap, I might add. We have to pay dearly for those seeds and sure, they grow, but they taste terrible. I would rather eat dirt. In fact, it won't be long, and that is all we will have to eat. Those UberBugs could go out of control at any time and eat everything. Then what would we do." Merlynn ranted on about the plight of the plants and switched immediately to the livestock. "And, while we are on the subject, how are we supposed to make trade-chips on those pathetic beasts out in the field? "

"Please, Merlynn, I am tired. I need to go to sleep. Your ranting is not going to help. It can only get me thrown into the internment camp. You must keep your opinions to yourself. Doyfear may be a reasonable man, but I hear Ananaya even killed his own father. He is without conscience."

"You really heard that the Chief Scientist killed his own father? That is horrible. Why isn't he in the internment camp?" asked Merlynn in a shocked whisper. "Who did you hear that from?

"Please, Merlynn, don't say anything about Ryndor being killed by his own son. I can't tell you who told me. If you would slip and tell Lyryca, my friend would be killed. Things are so much worse than you realize. Just stay close to home and keep the boys in sight at all times."

Noryan turned over in his bed and faced the other side of the room. He hoped Merlynn would have the good sense to stop asking questions and go to sleep. Noryan, even though exhausted, was going to find it very difficult to sleep. He was not sure how he was going to feed his family. Farming was never this difficult. The scientists said they were going to improve everyone's' lives, but so far, it was just the opposite. Surtees seemed to be imploding around its citizens.

The next morning came early as it did to every farm. Chores needed to be done even before the morning meal. Merlynn was up and helping with the chores. Going back inside of the tiny farmhouse to make a sparse meal, she woke the boys and told them to dress and go help feed the livestock before the morning meal. When Merlynn went out to the barn to retrieve her family to come and eat, she heard the familiar sound of her two boys playing.

"Look, Mom, I can fly," came the familiar voice of her now eldest son, Khrelyn. Following the sound, Merlynn, with her hair tied back in a knot at her neck, looked up and saw her sons in the loft of the barn. Taking a running start, Khrelyn launched himself off the loft beam, spreading his arms full length outstretched in the air, he landed in the mound of hay at her feet.

"Khrelyn!" Merlynn yelled, "that was dangerous. Don't you ever do that again! You could break your neck. Promise me you will never, ever do that again."

"Aww, Mom, I just wanted to fly. That is all I ever think about," Khrelyn whined.

Disgusted at her son's dangerous antics, Merlynn imprinted, "You are a farmer's son. That is all you will ever be. Now get your head out of the clouds and get your brother and father to the house for the morning meal." Angry at her son's foolishness, Merlynn turned sharply and retreated to the house in a huff.

Josyah timidly came down from the loft by the ladder. He was nervous. He was used to his mother being irritable, but she rarely got so angry.

"Khrelyn, why did you make Mommy so mad? You know she has been upset lately. Now, she is going to burn our meal," Josyah said as he left the barn and raced to catch up with his mother before she reached the shabby front porch.

"Big baby! Mommy's little baby!" Khrelyn yelled after his retreating brother. Under his breath, Khrelyn made one more comment. "I will show you. I will fly."

Noryan rounded the corner just about that time. "Son, I heard your mother yelling at you all the way from the pens. What was that all about?"

"Oh, Dad! Mom has no vision. She got mad at me when I tried to fly from the loft. She said I was the son of a farmer, and that would be all I would be for the rest of my life."

Noryan approached his son and put a comforting hand on Khrelyn's shoulder. "Mom can't read the future. No one knows for sure whether we will even have this farm forever. Who knows, you may need to learn to fly…. One thing for certain, if you work hard at your studies, pass all your exams with high grades, your dreams just might come true. Come on, we need to get some food in our stomachs."

Noryan guided Khrelyn towards the house. Noryan hung his head as he headed in for the morning meal. Khrelyn noticed the changes in his parents and felt confused and afraid. Something was happening, but Khrelyn didn't know what it was. He knew better than to ask.

At the meal, Noryan made an announcement. "Merlynn, I want you and the boys to go to live with your sister for a while. The journey to the Astro Science Center will be long, but if you take the old road, you can be there in less than five days. I don't want you to take the main road through the Capital City Central Science Center and then go on to the Astro Science Center. This trip must be as secret as possible. Take the smaller ryke and one trydox. You will need to sell the ryke and trydox before you reach your sister's house. The trydox would be too conspicuous at the Astro Science Center. Any farmer outside of the city would probably buy both for a fair-trade chip."

Merlynn started to protest, but Noryan cut her off. "I am not arguing about this. You will do as I say. When I feel it is safe for you to return, I will come for you myself. Is that understood?"

Merlynn sadly nodded her head that she understood what Noryan had said. Wanting to argue, Merlynn started to open her mouth to speak, when Noryan pounded his fist on the table.

"I said I was not arguing about this. Pack clothes for you and the boys. Make sure you have enough food and water for several days. I will put together a temporary shelter and blankets for the few nights you will need to sleep out on the road. I want you ready to leave before the sun is high." Noryan got up from the table and left the house. The two boys and Merlynn stared at the closed door where Noryan just vacated.

"Mother...?" Khrelyn started to question.

"Go pack now, and don't ask any questions." Merlynn snapped at her eldest son. "Take Josyah with you and make sure he packs enough clothes, clean underwear, socks, and two pairs of shoes."

Merlynn started to clear the dishes from the small wooden table. Noting that her sons were still sitting, she scolded, "I mean now!"

Both boys jumped from the table and ran to pack clothes. Bewilderment set in, but fear made the boys remain silent.

With the ryke hitched to the trydox and camping supplies already in place, Noryan waited for his family to appear with bags of clothes and other provisions. His heart was heavy. Noryan did not want to part from his family, but deep down, Noryan knew the Enforcers would come for him within one full moon, knowing his private complaints to his wife were disclosed. He only hoped his family would be safe with Merlynn's sister. Noryan had little knowledge as to whether or not the new Chief Scientist kept records of all citizens and their family trees. He doubted seriously that Ananaya had the resources to track every person on Surtees. At least, he was betting his family's life on that assumption.

After hugging each son and giving them commands to help their mother, he lifted them each into the ryke. Turning to his wife, Noryan said, "I know you think I am overreacting. I hope that is true and I can come for you soon. In the meantime, do what you must to survive in the city. You will need to find a job to help pay for your stay. I am sure your sister can help you. If...if I don't come for you, you will know that I am in the internment camp. You will not be able to find me, so don't try. The farm will be lost, so don't come back. Do you understand? I am counting on you to raise our two sons and keep them safe. I love you and the boys very much."

Embracing, Merlynn kissed her husband. Tears were streaming down her cheeks. Noryan brushed her tears away and lifted his wife up onto the seat. He handed her the reins and gave the trydox a slap on the rump to get him moving.

"Remember to stay on the old roads. It will be rough going with most of the road being in disarray. With the trydox, you should be able to navigate it without needing to leave the path. I put in two spare wheels just in case of breakage. Khrelyn is old enough to help you change the wheel if it should break. If all else fails, pack what you can on the trydox and continue on foot. Merlynn, please do all that you can to support Khrelyn's desire to become a pilot. And Khrelyn, help your mother and brother," Noryan shouted these last instructions as the trydox plugged down the road.

With his emotions in check showing a stern demeanor, the ryke, with his family, moved further and further away. Knowing when his family could no longer see him, Noryan let his shoulders slump. He realized he may never see his family again. With that gut-wrenching thought, Noryan finally broke down into tears.

CHAPTER FIVE

Syonne allowed Tawtanya much freedom in the city. At first, Syonne guarded her with her life, but as seasons passed with no one coming to take her away, Syonne relaxed. Tawtanya went to the science center school in the middle of the city with all the other children. She excelled in her studies, but spent every spare moment outdoors, physically playing with the other children. Syonne worried a bit about Tawtanya spending so much time outdoors with the air quality becoming poor. She could hear the children frequently coughing as they ran and played.

Tawtanya became obsessed with the Zrymyr Games ever since Syonne had taken her to competition during the school break. Tawtanya marveled at how the athletes could be so strong and agile, and she wanted nothing more than to be one of them. Watching how they were able to run and flip in midair, Tawtanya imitated their actions. She found she was able to do some of the simpler movements without any training. Building her strength was important, so Tawtanya lifted anything available that would build her muscles.

"Tawtanya, put that down!" Syonne said continuously while laughing at her mischievous daughter. She had no idea why Tawtanya was driven to exercise all day long, but she felt it was better to be strong and healthy than not, so she left her to her own devices. Besides, Syonne minded several small children in her care.

She had little time to check on Tawtanya. Daycare for the smaller children brought in needed trade-chips.

Several of the older children in the neighborhood were working with a coach after school each day. The coach said Tawtanya was not old enough to be in the group when she stood quietly observing and finally got the courage to ask if she could train, too. Tawtanya took that as a challenge and demonstrated what she could do. The coach was amazed at what the small child could already do on her own, and decided she could join in his afternoon class.

Most of the older children welcomed her since she was cute, but two of the older boys resented the small child being allowed to participate. They felt it diminished their accomplishments to have such a young girl allowed into the training.

"Coach, we worked hard to get a place in your class, so why are you letting this little girl come in before she is even the correct age. It really isn't fair to any of us," V'zeyuk complained.

"This is not a reflection on any of you. I see raw talent in this little girl. She has an inner drive that is unusual for her age. I wish to develop her talents. That does not mean I will take away any time from you or the others, V'zeyuk. Besides, I don't want you questioning my motives. I am the coach, and I will make the decisions as to whom I train and who I won't. If you want to continue your training with me, I suggest you get back to work and stop worrying about one little girl!" The coach ended his statement emphatically, and V'zeyuk, said not one word more to the coach; however, he continued to complain to his friends.

"It galls me that the coach is allowing that baby into our sessions. That means less time that he will spend with us. We are the ones who will be competing soon, not that little runt. We need all of his attention right now with competitions approaching." V'zeyuk made sure the coach did not hear him as he sowed the seeds of discontent to his group of followers.

Myana kept close to Tawtanya. She heard the grumblings of V'zeyuk and a couple of his buddies and knew it could be bad for the little girl. There was no way any harm was going to come to Tawtanya as long as she was around.

Tall, athletic, and willowy, Myana towered over some of the boys. Having lived on the streets all her life, Myana knew how to fight. V'zeyuk, a spoiled boy from a wealthy family, knew better than to cross Myana. His friends often said that she could kick anyone's butt if she were mad. V'zeyuk didn't want to be one of the butts being kicked. He knew there were other ways to achieve his goals other than being physical.

"Tawtanya, let me show you how to do that movement. You are a natural, but there is a thing or two I can show you to improve your technique. Watch as I climb up this rope. Pay close attention to how I use my legs. Later, when you are stronger, I will show you how to climb without using your legs. Now watch." Myana demonstrated her rope climbing abilities. She climbed twenty rods in less than a blink of an eye, or so it seemed to Tawtanya. "Now you try it," Myana encouraged.

Tawtanya scrambled up the rope using her legs and arms but soon felt the sting in her arm muscles as she struggled to reach the top. Tawtanya was resolute to reach the very top where there was a large, shiny bell hanging for the athletes to ring, declaring to all their victory. Struggling, but determined, Tawtanya clamped her feet around the rope and continued to pull until she had the satisfaction of hearing the gong of the bell.

"Wonderful!" boomed the voice of the coach as Myana danced around at the bottom of the rope, cheering. "Myana, you are going to be a good coach someday. Keep up the good work."

Myana beamed at the coach's praise. Encouraged, Myana found another reason to spend time with the little girl. Realizing the little girl was a prodigy, Myana envisioned herself as the coach of Tawtanya as the future Champion of Surtees.

Coming out of her daydream, Myana realized Tawtanya was on the ground beside her awaiting instructions. "Okay, Tawtanya, go up the rope again."

Taking a deep breath and shaking out her arms, Tawtanya grabbed the rope and started the ascent one more time. The training continued with Myana beside Tawtanya for several moons developing speed, while showing off graceful style. Increasing the difficulty by climbing past twenty rods, Myana pushed Tawtanya to her limits. "Tawtanya," Myana called out, "now, I want you to do the same climb using just your arms."

Being graceful, as a dancer, Tawtanya climbed the ropes with her arms allowing her body to flow in a serpentine manner while keeping her legs horizontal and her toes pointed upwards. Three-fourths of the way up, Tawtanya spread her arms apart along the rope and lifted her body horizontally while slowly spinning herself in a giant circle around the rope. Continuing her serpentine climb to the top, she found Myana jumping up and down in uncontrolled exuberance. The coach approached Myana and told her to have Tawtanya to keep that maneuver in her routine for the event. The added difficulty and style points would offset any lack of speed.

As Tawtanya dropped back to the ground, Myana grabbed her into a hug. "The coach and I are your biggest fans. You lift our spirits with your innovation, agility, and perfect technique."

V'zeyuk watching Tawtanya's spiral display, fanned the fury inside of him. Petty jealousy and spite were his constant companions, and he plotted how he would take Tawtanya down.

Myana was not blind to V'zeyuk's childish behavior and continued to put herself between Tawtanya and V'zeyuk and his followers. For obvious reason, V'zeyuk seemed disinclined to hassle Tawtanya when Myana was near. With her guardian angel by her side, Tawtanya felt safe and happy.

Training continued night and day. All the students worked on tedious repetition while increasing the difficulty of a single event. No one could continue to the next event until all students mastered it. Beings Zrymyr Game events are a team competition where each member must master every event, or the team fails the competition. The coach was adamant about everyone passing each and every trial.

Besides being a team competition, each member receives individual points judged on speed, style, and the difficulty of the event as well as how easy the individual competitor makes the event look. The most accumulated individual points are the key factor for becoming the Champion of Surtees. Only the elite of each team has any possibility of ever reaching this coveted title. Many teams never even have a single member who accumulates enough points to compete, while other teams may have several with enough accumulated points. With rivalries amongst team members, often, the team aspect is completely forgotten as the ultimate prize becomes the only thing of importance.

After a particularly grueling day of practice, the coach gathered potential participants. "As you know, I have been keeping an eye on each and every one of you during this season of training. Competitions will be starting soon, and we have five teams participating. Many of you were not involved last season, so you may not be aware of the black mark this sport received when jealousy and poor sportsmanship wormed its way into one team. For you, that remember, bear with me while I tell our younger team members what transpired.

"Two members of the same team accumulated the same amount of points. When competing last season at the event at the Center for Marine Sciences, one of the participants craved personal winning beyond the success of his fellow teammates. He sabotaged the member of his team who was neck to neck with him in the competition. By doing so, he caused the death of this young man. When it became apparent, another team member was at fault, that young man was taken to the internment center immediately, without a trial or even a chance to say good-bye to his family. His team failed the event and is still on probation this season. This team will have penalties put upon them at the beginning of this season's competition, which will make it almost impossible for the team to win or for any single person on that team to accumulate enough points to compete for the Champion of Surtees title.

"I am telling you this because I expect more from each and every one of you. Our goal is to win as a team. Period! If we have members who excel and accumulate enough points to be taken as serious contenders for the Champion of Surtees title, I expect the team to be proud of his or her efforts and back them one hundred percent. If I get wind that anyone is planning to sabotage another member's efforts, I will drop him or her from this team immediately. I suspect rumors will be enough to send an Enforcer or two to your house. Is that clear? You have been forewarned. That is the last word I will say about the subject."

The coach continued on with a cheerier note. "I have the names of the members who will be competing as a team. I also have the names of three alternates who will be available to compete if any of the team members who feel they are not able to compete that day due to illness or injury. The alternates are available to fill in as needed if anyone event proves to be too challenging for a team member.

"It will not be held against any of you if you feel you cannot complete any event. You will lose personal points for that section of the event, but the team will still be able to win with the help of the alternate points. Those of you who have competed before know what I am saying. If any of the newbies have further questions, please seek one of the older members of the team for an explanation.

"Now, we have practice tomorrow. Our first competition of this season will be at the Marine Science Center next week. The following five days of practice will concentrate on shrouds and gymnastics on masts, spars and stays many rods above ground. Go home and get some rest. Be here on time tomorrow."

Myana noticed the puzzled look on Tawtanya's face. "What is wrong, Little One?"

"I guess I thought I would make the team. I am only an alternate?" Tawtanya said, rather dejected. "I thought I was doing well; at least, you and the coach said I was…."

"Oh, Sweetie, you are doing well. You are doing great. You are a natural at this. It is just that you are still quite young. The other competitors would be very angry if they got cut from the team so someone your age could compete instead. Be patient. You will be on the team for sure next season. I am certain. This season, you must stay ready at all times. Alternates play an important role in the team. At any time, without warning, you could be called upon to step in and compete when a team member feels inadequate for a particular event or is injured. The whole team fails if the alternate is unable to complete the task. It is a very important position." Hugging Tawtanya, Myana walked her down the street towards her aunt's house.

"Now, go home, do your studies, and get some rest. We have difficult practices the following days. The rope shrouds and masts are problematic to navigate. It takes a special technique, and the spars are very narrow with the added difficulty that they tilt."

Tawtanya tried to think positively. Everything Myana told her made sense, but Tawtanya was anxious to compete as a team member and not just as an alternative. Syonne sensed something was bothering Tawtanya, and she gave her a big hug. "If you want to talk about something, I would love to listen."

Just as Syonne said this to Tawtanya, one of the children in her care, fell and started wailing. Syonne rushed to the injured child to comfort him, and Tawtanya went to her room. She had studies to do, and besides, she needed to think about what Myana said. Tawtanya knew Myana was right, but disappointment is hard to get over. Tawtanya knew she would, though. Half of competing is being in the right mind-set. If it took all night to get into a positive attitude, Tawtanya would do so, and she would be ready for practice on the morrow.

CHAPTER SIX

Many seasons passed, and Merlynn resolved herself to the fact that she would never see her husband, Noryan, again. Her life on the farm with her boys was a past memory now. It didn't seem to bother Khrelyn at all that they lived in a city, but Josyah suffered more from leaving the farm life. Both boys missed their father, but no one asked any longer when Father would come to get them. It was obvious that their father would never return.

Merlynn worked all day at the electrical systems and instrumentation factory. Her younger sister managed to get her an interview in the same department where she worked. The trade chips were fair and steady, and they helped the two women with their combined income to live above the standards of most workers. Merlynn was grateful that she was able to keep her promise to Noryan to allow the boys to stay in school and to support Khrelyn's dream to become a pilot.

Khrelyn was selected to be one of the students to continue his training with aviation classes. Khrelyn was obsessed with his classes and spent every waking moment reading textbooks about the subject. He was acing his tests and was at the top of his class. Khrelyn knew if he continued to work hard, he would be picked for pilot training when he was older.

The few moments each day that he allowed himself to be outdoors with Josyah in play found him looking upwards to the sky. He saw the vapor trails and imagined being the one to make them. Josyah's insistence was the only thing that would draw his mind back to the ground. Josyah enjoyed rough play now that he was older and stronger, and Khrelyn found himself a willing wrestling partner once Josyah got his attention.

Khrelyn admitted to himself that the physical play was necessary for his health as most of his day was spent sitting and studying. If it were not for Josyah's reminder that pilots must be in top physical form, Khrelyn would probably have just stayed seated all day long.

Coming to grips with the fact that he was not in the best shape possible, Khrelyn looked for other outlets than just playing with his brother for physical exercise. He heard about Zrymyr courses and wondered if there was a chance that he may be allowed to work out with the serious students. Khrelyn decided to visit the local practice course, where he met with the district Zrymyr coach. He was surprised by the coach's attitude.

"I am not interested in anyone practicing with my team, who is not one hundred percent involved. You are going to the aviation school, correct? I am not sure you can spend the time required to be part of my group. However, I am friends with the duty training officer on the base. I will ask him whether he sees you as a prospect for his pilot training. If he does, he may ask you to spend most of the day with me each day. He has asked that of me in the past for some of his special students. It would mean double work on your part, though. Would you like me to make the request on your behalf?" asked the Zrymyr coach from Astro Science District, whose name was Nedstrym.

Khrelyn was taken aback. He was thinking of exercising for a short time—not half a day. However, if the exercise would help him to get into the pilot's training, he would be willing to work hard for as long as needed.

"Yes," Khrelyn said. "I would appreciate it very much."

"Then I suggest you add, Syr, to that request," Nedstrym said with a stern look on his face.

"Yes, Syr!" Khrelyn amended emphatically.

"Go join that group on the far left. They are all newbies. The tall boy is the elder of the group, so listen to him carefully and do what he tells you to do. Run along now," the coach said as he gave Khrelyn a gentle shove on the back in the direction of the boys.

Joining the group, Khrelyn watched to see what was expected and then joined in. He was ill-prepared for the strength and agility the exercise program needed, but he was determined to work twice as hard as everyone else if it would help to get him into the pilot's program. He knew his days would be long and stressful from here on out.

Working for weeks with the Astro Science Center Zrymyr team was proving to be more fun than Khrelyn anticipated when he joined to just get into better physical shape. Once his strength increased, Khrelyn was amazed at how easily the techniques came to him. His coach, on more than one occasion, asked Khrelyn whether he would like to join the team.

"You are a natural, Khrelyn. You have good balance, with excellent spatial orientation and great reflexes. Each of these traits would serve you well in the Zrymyr courses as they will in pilot training. It will take more time out of each day and will require travel, but I believe I could convince your duty training officer of the benefits to compete with my team," Nedstrym added.

Khrelyn was hesitant. "I guess I would gladly do so if my duty training officer agrees."

Khrelyn started thinking of the risks. If he became incapacitated in any way, he could kiss his pilot training good-bye. Fear loomed in his mind, and he wanted to recant what he just said to the coach. He wanted to fly, and nothing else was important.

CHAPTER SEVEN

Ananaya was finding his micromanagement style to be a double-edged sword. It was tedious to read each and every report that came across his desk. Making sure his detailed instructions were being followed precisely without question was necessary. It annoyed him that he needed to check up on each and every research center. If he could trust them to do exactly as he commanded, Ananaya would have more time to do his own research.

Zooyol retired long ago from her overseeing Yyemara. Kaycee'na now had the added responsibility to educate and train Yyemara. Yyemara was proving to be a genius with neurochemistry and especially as it related to genetics.

Ananaya followed the progression of each daughter with interest. Once Tawtanya was placed in a more standard setting, Ananaya made sure Tawtanya's life was reported to him every week as well. Fascinated that Tawtanya was developing her physical attributes while maintaining top scores in all her educational classes, made Ananaya more curious than ever why one academic subject had not taken precedence over another. Ananaya pondered whether the physical body, when overtly primed, superseded the cognitive lobes of the brain. A part of Ananaya wanted to dissect both of the twin's brains to see how their development deviated from the other. Knowing that it was too soon to experiment with the two girls,

Ananaya practiced patience to let the research trial continue. Both may prove more valuable alive than dead in time.

Kaycee'na enjoyed having Yyemara by her side. She was cheated from bonding with her infants, but Kaycee'na could not let Ananaya know she felt anything towards Yyemara other than being supervisor and teacher. Checking her desire to watch her daughter all day long, Kaycee'na made the decision to have Yyemara spend most of her day under the tutelage of a genetic scientist known as Fyyenen. Knowing he was more than capable of passing on the basic knowledge of genetic sciences. In so doing, Kaycee'na protected herself from the possibility of Ananaya's rage if he suspected her maternal feelings.

Yyemara knew Kaycee'na was her mother. She wondered why she didn't feel any strong feelings for her. Fyyenen was more special to the young lady than her own biological mother. Her time with Fyyenen was exciting as she learned more and more about a subject that occupied her waking thoughts. Being out from under the old matron's hand allowed Yyemara time to ponder her thoughts and not being driven to listen to aural tapes every waking moment, as was the case with Zooyol in charge. Fyyenen allowed Yyemara to stop and think through problems. Like the endorphins released after strenuous exercise, this concentrated learning excited and expanded Yyemara's mind.

Another freedom allowed now that Zooyol was retired and gone was that Yyemara could take walks in the early morning before her arduous study schedule. Never before had Yyemara been allowed outdoors for more than a fleeting moment. Feeling the cool wind on her face and hearing birds in the trees surrounding the concrete buildings was refreshing and stimulating. Yyemara actually felt she could think better after her walks and wanted to tell her mother, Kaycee'na that she should take walks, too.

Watching Kaycee'na from across the lab, Yyemara noted the woman's frenzied work ethics. Yyemara knew all the personnel worked determinedly under Ananaya's ever-watchful eye. Allowing a moment to ponder, Yyemara found it difficult to think of either Kaycee'na or Ananaya as her parents. Trying hard to picture how it would have been to sit at the dinner table with them and discuss topics of relevance made Yyemara briefly sad. She could barely remember her childhood at all, and her future was predestined. Shrugging off the thought that she never had any control over her life, she settled back into the book Fyyenen placed before her.

"Child, your mind is far away. You need to bring it back to your studies. One never knows when Ananaya might pop in. He does that when least expected," Fyyenen remarked.

As if on cue, the door opened quietly, and the thin, bent-over man walked in, leaning on the arm of his guard. Scanning the room, he noted everyone was working at tasks assigned except Yyemara and Fyyenen. Scowling, Ananaya tugged on his guard's arm to direct him to the two still in his sharp gaze.

"How are studies faring, Fyyenen?" Ananaya accusingly asked of the tutor.

"Yyemara has very unique gifts. When a solution is not obvious, she has a keen ability to break the problem down into smaller boxes while developing the processes needed to reach a positive solution. Soon, I believe she will be an asset to the genetic program. Yyemara has accomplished more than any other student under my tutelage," Fyyenen said with obvious pride in his student.

"I see," Ananaya said without looking directly at his daughter.

Ananaya continued his rounds, stopping briefly to make a comment to Kaycee'na. Yyemara noted Kaycee'na stiffen at the quiet comment Ananaya made to her. As Ananaya left the room,

Yyemara watched closely as Kaycee'na nervously returned to her work, visibly shaken by the words her husband whispered in her ear before exiting.

Yyemara didn't know her father. She noted that everyone wanted to please him desperately, even though Ananaya was frequently breaking science norms and rules. Still, she wondered why everyone was afraid of him. She turned to Fyyenen to ask.

Fyyenen shook his head quickly to let her know that she was to be studying and not asking questions. It was as if Fyyenen knew what she was about to ask and was afraid to answer.

Yyemara returned to her studies. She was determined to be the best scientist, and she would gain her father's favor. 'Everyone wanted to gain his favor. It may as well be me who sits at his right hand,' thought Yyemara. A smile crossed her face as she envisioned herself being elevated to Ananaya's favorite.

CHAPTER EIGHT

Preparing for the first competition that would be held at the Center of Marine Science was grueling on the team members. Getting footholds on the rope ladder, called a shroud, was difficult enough. Performing on the narrow, tilting spar that ran perpendicular to the mast took concentration and balance that was well beyond most of the newer team members. Tawtanya's smaller feet found it easier to stay balanced on such a narrow beam. Drawing confidence, the agile young girl found she was able to perform gymnastic feats her older team members were unable to do. Myana cheered enthusiastically as Tawtanya practiced well above their heads. V'zeyuk only scowled.

"At least, she is only an alternate. Not much chance she will be performing with the team," V'zeyuk said to a fellow teammate quietly so the coach would not overhear his remarks. "Tricks isn't the only thing the judges will be looking for. I can cross the spar in half the time it would take for that little showoff to do one of her balancing tricks. Time is more important than tricks any day."

"Maybe so, V'zeyuk," whispered to his friend, "but finesse and embellishments catch the judges' eyes. Someday, that little poser will be a threat to you. Mark my words."

"Shut up! I can take care of myself. Tawtanya will never be a champion. I will. Just wait and see," V'zeyuk shot back.

To begin the practice, Tawtanya laid back on the deck, grabbing ahold of a safety line that dangled from the Top Mizzenmast with both hands. At the sound of the starting bell, Tawtanya placed both feet on the Mizzenmast, using her arm strength, hand over hand up the line with feet pushing against the mast, she walked quickly, holding her horizontal position, up to the Mizzen Top Gallant deck. Wasting no time, Tawtanya began the next movement.

Myana's cheers became shrill whistles as Tawtanya did a handstand on the topgallant spar next to the mizzen mast. She began hand walking the whole distance of the teetering spar, which lowered drastically as she reached the endpoint. Tawtanya, with elegance, pivoted to return, still in the handstand position, up the spar to the mizzen mast where she started her feat.

"Absolutely incredible!" Myana said loudly to all who stood below watching.

"Maybe so, but let's see what she can do on the shroud," the coach added anxiously. "It will be interesting to see what she comes up with. She also has the thick sheets that pull the sails into a position to navigate. Remember, the obstacles we set up for our practice, simulate a real ship. However, in reality, it is nothing like the dynamics of an actual rolling and tilting ship on the water. The winds aloft and a pitching deck can ruin the best routines."

Tawtanya continued to have fun as she practiced. Before long, the coach called her down, so a select team member could get more practice. "You did well up there, Tawtanya. Someday soon, you will be an asset as well as a star for our team. Keep practicing."

Myana gave Tawtanya a hug and directed her to another area where she could train on the ground while the team took to the lines and poles erected for practice. V'zeyuk could not resist shoving Tawtanya out of the way as he proceeded to the smaller shroud. "Watch how a real man navigates the shroud and learn something!"

Myana high on her perch of the gallant spar caught a glimpse of V'zeyuk shoving Tawtanya. Seeing that no harm came to Tawtanya, she continued practicing her skills, with Tawtanya cheering her on from below, barely aware of the abuse V'zeyuk perpetrated upon her.

The competition was only a few days away. The team would be housed with families from the Marine Science village. It was considered an honor and privilege to host a member from another science center. If the families had room for more than one member of a team, they were given trade-chips from their science center to compensate for the extra mouth to feed.

Myana told Tawtanya that she would be housed with her when they arrived at the Marine Science Center. "It will be so much fun to room together. We have to make a promise to go to bed early and not stay up all night story-telling and giggling, okay? We want to be at our best for the competition. I heard that Ananaya may attend this first competition in person. I would love to receive top honors and be awarded a medal from the Chief Scientist. Maybe some season soon, you will be standing on the podium next to me."

"I will never be as good as you, Myana," Tawtanya said without envy in her voice. Pure admiration for the older girl who had taken the time to show her the ropes was evident.

"Come on, Tawtanya. I will walk you home," Myana said when she noticed V'zeyuk watching the two talking with malice glinting in his narrowed eyes.

Once home, Tawtanya rushed into Syonne's arms. "I had such a marvelous practice. The coach praised me, and guess what? Myana and I will be roommates when we are at the Marine Science

Center." Pausing briefly, Tawtanya added, "I wish you could go and watch…even though I probably won't get to compete."

"Sweetie, you are a champion even before you start competing. I have watched you since you were a tiny baby. No one has more determination than you. You will have more medals than you will be able to wear in your career. Just you mark my words," Syonne said as she held Tawtanya at arm's length to see the beautiful smile on her adopted daughter's face.

Hugging Syonne tightly, Tawtanya asked a question. "I know you are not really my mother. Do you know who my biological mother is?"

"I don't know, honey," Syonne lied." I was just lucky enough to get to raise you."

"But how did you get me?" Tawtanya pressed.

"I will tell you everything that I know when you are a little older. In fact, if you give me some time to do some research, I might be able to tell you more than I know now. Is it a deal? If you let me investigate more, I will let you know my findings?" Syonne said, hoping to stall Tawtanya for seasons to come. "Run along now. I need to get Bylly and Brytany ready to be picked up from daycare. Do you have studies?"

Cheerfully, Tawtanya agreed and went to her room to do her studies. It would soon be time for dinner, and Syonne had two more children to be picked up before she could start cooking. As she watched her growing girl leave the room. Syonne felt some despair. She had no idea how she was going to tell her who her parents were.

CHAPTER NINE

Improvising construction for the standard parts of a ship in the middle of the manufacturing district of the Astro Science Center was more difficult than it might have been at his old farm. Most factories were large, but the roof limited the size of what they could build. On the farm, there were fewer limitations. Khrelyn reminisced about the beams he walked upon and the rope hanging from the top of the barn's loft down to the floor that he and Josyah used to shimmy up and down. It was faster than the ladder that leaned against the hayloft and more fun to use. They could have used the fields around the farm to build a mast twenty times larger than the one in the warehouse. His father used to call them nedryls when he would watch them at play. Neither Khrelyn or Josyah knew what nedryl might be, but the word brought laughter to his father each time he used it about his two boys' shenanigans.

Those thoughts were bittersweet. Khrelyn didn't think about his father much these days. It was difficult for him to remember what his father even looked like. However, he could remember his laugh vividly as he recalled his father watching the scene in the barn. Khrelyn wondered whether his brother could recall what their father looked like? When he asked his mother, she always got depressed. Noryan's name became almost a forbidden word. It got to the point where no one spoke his father's name anymore. His mother would whisper that it was not safe to use his father's name. Khrelyn didn't understand why.

Khrelyn wondered whether his father was dead or at the internment camp. Secretly, he hoped that his father was at the camp, and he might escape someday and come home. The thought that his father would want the whole family to return to the farm never entered Khrelyn's head since he knew his father supported his desire to be a pilot. Josyah would be the farmer in the family if his father returned. Khrelyn relaxed, knowing his life would not change much even if his father did return. Maybe if he did return, his mother would smile again.

Most of Khrelyn's time was spent studying or practicing for Zrymyr games. He rarely had extra time to spend with his mother or brother these days. His mother, Merlynn, was too busy for much family time either since she worked half day shifts. Except for occasional late-night quiet family dinners, Khrelyn was alone in his room. His thoughts were ever on flying. If he excelled at Zrymyr games and Hoygazor was attending, Khrelyn believed he would be noticed. Once Hoygazor became aware of him, Hoygazor might investigate further and discover that Khrelyn's grades were exemplary and then, he might be accepted into pilot training immediately and put on the fast track towards his dream.

Driven to excel, Khrelyn spent days on the course set up in the large warehouse in the manufacturing district with his team members. All previous thoughts of his father vanished like early morning fog, as Khrelyn looked up at the pole that represented a mast. He visualized the course in his head. He knew greater heights might be a factor once his team boarded the real ship that would be used for the first Zrymyr competition of the season. His coach was aware of that fact, too, and erected beams and cross pieces as high as the building would allow. Even the smaller constructed practice ship was tall enough that it eliminated several team members who showed signs of being afraid of losing their balance at heights.

Khrelyn couldn't understand how those few boys or girls were ever chosen to compete since their district Zrymyr course used the rooftops of factories as part of the course. Khrelyn figured that the narrow beams or spars, as he thought the fisherman called them, were what made the difference. Jumping from building to building was done quickly, and no one had a chance to look down to the concrete below as they made the jumps from one ledge to another. One just measured the gap and made the leap to get to the next rooftop. On the flat part of the roof, one could tumble or do other gymnastic feats. When there were obstacles on the roof, the judges expected certain techniques and stunts to create degrees of difficulty. There could be high winds, and they often were a factor, but Khrelyn had never heard of anyone being blown off the rooftop.

"Khrelyn, you are up next," the coach yelled. "I want to see something spectacular out of you. Don't just race through the course. Make me excited to see you up there."

'Something spectacular?' thought Khrelyn. 'What can I do that hasn't been done before and still stay alive?'

Khrelyn mastered climbing shrouds early in practice. His strength served him well as he scampered up the rope ladder with ease. Time was still a major factor, so Khrelyn didn't want to do something at the beginning of the course. If he were going to do something that really caught the judges' eyes, it would need to be when he was at the very top when it would be very dangerous yet exciting. The difficulty level at that greatest height could get him extra points. The mainmast upper topsail deck was probably where he could make the most impact as he made his way to the mainmast.

Reaching the upper topsail deck, Khrelyn shimmied part way up, gripping the mast with his legs, letting go with his arms, he allowed his upper body to fall backward, appearing as though he was about to fall. As gasps were heard, Khrelyn knew he got the reaction he hoped for. Dangling for a moment, he pulled himself upwards towards his legs, pulling himself up with tightened core belly muscles and proceeded up to shimmy to the top where he planted his hands on the top of the mast and rose to a hand-stand with toes pointing towards the heavens. To make the feat more difficult, Khrelyn lifted his left hand, so he was balancing on only one hand. Returning to his starting position, Khrelyn continued his practice down to the end of the course.

Beaming at the coach when he reached the ground, he was disappointed when the coach said the one-handed handstand at the top was good, but it could be dangerous if there were a strong wind. "Your little display before your handstand where you faked a fall, looked just like that—a mistake. Leave that out of your routine and try to find some other place to make an impression."

Dejected, Khrelyn moved aside to watch his teammate make his run at the practice course. Not really focusing on the other contestant's run, Khrelyn watched his teammate only to see where he could apply some trick or feat that would impress the judges. There was not much time left before the day of the competition. Khrelyn knew he would need to be spontaneous.

The coach gave room assignments and told his team to be ready to leave the next morning early. The time and place for departure was written down for each contestant.

"Go home and get a good night's sleep. I will see you bright and early at the transporter. Make sure to eat breakfast before you leave. Nutrition snacks will be supplied by the Marine Science Center staff, but you won't be getting a meal until after the competition when you are housed with your host family. Please remember to be respectful since these families are spending their hard-earned trade-chips on meals for you. Now, go home," said the coach as he patted each contestant on the back as they left.

Grabbing Khrelyn by the elbow, the coach delayed his departure. "I have given some thought to one place you may add some embellishment to your routine would be at the ending on the fore topmast stay. I have seen your ability with gymnastics. At the top, the two stays are close enough together where you can straddle the two and use them to your advantage to flip between them to perform many different configurations in mid-air with minimal risk but maximum effect to the viewer. Think about it," the coach said as he gave him a pat on the back and sent him out of the huge double doors of the warehouse.

Khrelyn walked home, trying to imagine what he might be able to do with two lines running parallel but angling down rapidly with increased distance between the lines as they descended. It would only be possible to perform his feats when he just barely cleared the Fore Topmast.

Walking home by rote, Khrelyn's mind was in the clouds or as close to the clouds as the topmast allowed in his imagination. He pictured possible tricks in his head, trying to decide which gymnastic feat would leave the greatest impression. Allowing his mind to play out each technique time and time again, Khrelyn went to his room without dinner and fell asleep thinking about the competition the next day.

Khrelyn's mother did not need to wake him in the morning. Excited, Khrelyn was already packed and leaving his room when his eye fell on a model of a skyplane that he built earlier during free time. 'That would make a perfect gift to give to my host family,' Khrelyn thought as he tucked it carefully into his bag.

Josyah, still sleeping, was the only member of the household who was not at the door to wish Khrelyn well. "We wish we could come and watch the games," Khrelyn's aunt said while Merlynn nodded in agreement with her sister while dabbing at the tears in her eyes.

"You will make us proud, I know," Merlynn managed to say as she gave her son a kiss on his cheek. "Be safe…but win!"

Khrelyn knew his mother did not care if he won the games. She knew Khrelyn cared, and that was the only reason she added those final words as Khrelyn walked down the street to meet his team, where the transporter would be waiting.

Exhilaration met him at the meeting place near where they practiced in the old warehouse. The coach was already taking attendance and making seating assignments. The coach could barely be heard over the buzz of excitement as all the team members talked at once. Seeing every name check off his list, he barked a command for the members to get to their seats on the transporter.

"We don't have all day. I want us there early enough to be able to watch another team compete before us so I can tell you what those other team members do right or what they did wrong. I will expect you to watch carefully and listen to what I say."

As the team members took their seats, the buzz continued until about half-way to the Marine Science Center. Some of the team members took naps while others talked in whispers. Khrelyn's eyes seemed glazed as he tried to picture his routine over and over in his head, making small changes where needed.

Houses outside the city were the first sign they were getting near to the destination. Quickly, buildings sat on smaller and smaller lots until the shop walls became shared walls, and it was obvious, they were in the center of the city. The sea air drifted into the opened windows of the transporter with an aroma completely different from the manufacturing city they came from.

Khrelyn leaned out the window and filled his lungs with the air. It seemed fresh, salty, and damper than the air he normally breathed. He liked the breeze blowing gently across his face.

Looking at the dwellers walking the streets, he noted sun-burned faces or faces that had leathered from the constant contact with the damp winds. Even the children racing alongside the transporter had ruddy faces.

As the transporter started to descend slowly to the waterfront, Khrelyn caught sight of the ship that would be used for the games. Flags of all colors were flying near the harbor, and seating was erected for the prominent spectators while most others would stand to watch the games.

Tents were erected so merchants could sell their wares. Food rykes was all in one contained area for the ease of the spectators. They only needed to go to one area to purchase food or drink. The merchants complained that all the people would bypass their stands and go straight to the food section. Their concerns were for nothing since people came from all the science centers with trade-chips in their pockets to purchase items that they could not get at their home centers.

The spice tent was crowded, and Khrelyn breathed in deeply to smell the exotic aromas of spices that were never used in his aunt's kitchen. Feeling in his pocket, Khrelyn jingled a small handful of trade-chips and wondered if there was enough to buy his mother and aunt something unusual that they would never buy for themselves. Spices could be just the right gift until Khrelyn's eyes saw the tent filled with beautiful cloth and scarves.

As they drove past the merchant's tents and down to an area where other transporters were parked, Khrelyn asked the coach if they would have time to shop at the tents.

"Afraid not, unless your host family is willing to take you there. We need to stay together as a team the whole day. The host families know you are their responsibility once the games are over, so don't expect them to allow you any leeway," the coach said without even looking at Khrelyn.

"I will show you where we will be watching and waiting for our time to shine. Bring your bags. You will need to change into your uniform in a small building with toilet facilities over this way," the coach said as he led the team to a small building erected just for that purpose. The thin walls between the changing room for the males and females allowed only visual privacy. All comments could easily be heard, so the coach spent time checking the rowdier comments.

"The horn blared to signal the games would soon start.

CHAPTER TEN

The Marine Center was in a flutter. People would be coming to watch the Zrymyr Games from every science center. Tents were erected for vendors of all sorts. Food vendors were the most frequented. Everyone would be clamoring for fresh fish. Already it was well-known that the agriculture center was having problems with their food sources. Rumors of sickly animals and even sicker vegetation spread amongst the other centers of Surtees. Suppressed bickering was heard from sellers and buyers alike about the quality of the food since the genetically enhanced seeds were being used to produce the crops that farmers were now selling. At least, in the marine center, the fish was fresh from the seas, and the science experiments had not reached the great bodies of water. Fisherman feared that in time, even the lakes and oceans would bear the marks of the abhorrent science experimentation by Ananaya and his scientists. But for now, the fish was delicious.

As the competitors arrived at the city, host families gathered to find the athletes they would be housing. Signs held high with names and pictures of the individual athletes would make it easier for the families to find their guests at the end of the day.

Coaches, ever-present, allowed minimal time for some of the host families to make contact with their guests before ushering the team off to staging areas for preparation of the upcoming event. Many athletes traveled from greater distances than others, and if they were not able to sleep on their journeys in the transporters, they would be relying on adrenalin to get them through the course. Those living closer to the Marine Science Center were allowed to sleep longer in their own beds before heading out in the morning.

Tawtanya lived right in the middle of all the science centers since she lived near Capital City. She felt sorry for the participants who lived in the Agricultural Science Center since it was the greatest distance from the Marine Science Center, but she was sure they had all slept on the transporter. Having a fair and friendly competition was important to her.

Little did Tawtanya know how much nerves played in the competition. Many contestants' nerves would be frayed and not compete at their best due to stress. Those few who managed to keep calm under any circumstance were rare, but they often became the victors.

Tawtanya watched Myana. She was calm, collected, and composed. Tawtanya knew Myana was well-trained and in perfect physical condition. Myana's routine was practiced to perfection, and there was no room for error.

Tawtanya asked her earlier how she could be so confident. "What if a gust of wind blows violently just as you are about to start a difficult maneuver? Doesn't that make you afraid?"

"Not at all. There are things I have control of and things that I do not. If a wind blows at the wrong time, I will hold on tightly and wait until the gust diminishes, and then I will finish with the same finesse as I started. The judges will take into account that I have no control over the wind. They will judge me on how well I weathered the unexpected and persevered. Remember that, Tawtanya. You can only do your best. However, you must always do your best and anticipate the worst."

Tawtanya thought about Myana's words. Picturing a gust of wind in the middle of her routine, Tawtanya tried to anticipate what she might do to keep control of the situation. Any and every scenario that Tawtanya could imagine played out in her mind. Never apprehensive at practice, Tawtanya felt flutters in her stomach that she never felt before. 'Was this the stress everyone talked about?' Tawtanya wondered. She didn't like the feeling as the flutters turned to a sour stomach.

"There are times that it makes more sense to bypass a certain flourish that you intended to inject into your routine if the circumstances do not allow for it. It is always better to complete the routine and survive to compete another day than to doggedly continue to try to do something that will only get you hurt. Do you understand what I am telling you, Tawtanya?" Myana's words broke through to Tawtanya.

"Yes, Myana. I understand. You are saying not to be foolish, right?"

Myana smiled. "That is exactly what I am telling you."

The arena for the games was large but not nearly as large as the stadiums at the Capital City. The Marine Science Center only allowed seating on three sides as the ship used for the games was bobbing in the bay. A few spectators watched from small boats on the bayside of the ship. Occasionally, Tawtanya watched as one boat or another rowed to a more advantageous site before dropping their anchor. Noticing that several boats were close, barely keeping from rubbing against each other, she decided they were friends making a party of the games as they passed a jug of liquor back and forth, careful not to let it drop into the deep water.

At present, the weather was perfect. The winds were mild and out of the east. The flags on the topmast fluttered softly instead of whipping viciously about.

The first team would have an ideal situation to start. As the day progressed into the afternoon, the winds would pick up and blow in from the west, causing the bay water to churn, bouncing the ship like it was a toy boat. Predictions for dark clouds and even strikes of lightning were in the weather forecast. The judges were anxious to start the games so that each team had a chance at having equal conditions to participate.

Holding up the start was the fact that many of the head district scientists and the Chief Scientist had not yet arrived. It would be considered bad manners to start the games before the governing elite made their presence known. In the meantime, all participants waited, trying hard to keep their nerves in check.

The games were to commence shortly before the sun was straight overhead. It was already well beyond that point. Coaches were becoming visibly annoyed at the inconsideration to their athletes. Diets were balanced to give them the boost just when they would need it most. Now the coaches didn't know whether to give the athletes another snack that may weigh them down or not. Wrestling with problems that would seem insignificant to the scientists but essential to their team caused the athletes to become nervous as well.

Khrelyn's coach was about to go before the judges, announcing that his team would withdraw from the competition if the games did not begin immediately. The judges looked uncomfortable with making such a decision. Relief suddenly overwhelmed them when they saw the entourage of the Chief Scientist making their way to the seating left vacant for the prominent spectators.

The head judge, nodding towards the arrival of the Chief Scientist, knew that he could announce the first team. Even if the other head district scientists were not seated, it was known that the games could commence as long as Ananaya was seated.

The announcer went to the middle of the Starboard deck and announced that the first Zrymyr Game of the Season was about to begin. Announcing that the team from the Center for Genetic Studies was promenading onto the deck, the spectators cheered wildly.

The crowd became uncomfortable as they noted each competitor from the Center for Genetic Studies was notably larger than children their same ages. Whispers passed from spectator to spectator with suspicions that these children were genetically enhanced. Each stood at least a head taller than any of the other competitors from the other science centers. Muscles bulged on every aspect of their bodies, even on the females.

"Is it a fair competition if the children are genetically enhanced?" one man said a little louder than he intended. Looking around, he watched to see if he was receiving unwanted attention from guards that strangely appeared once Ananaya's entourage arrived.

"Be quiet, Lylan," hushed his companion. "You want to get us thrown into the internment center?"

As spectators turned and surveyed the crowd, the whispers stopped, and all eyes turned to the large three-mast ship. No one wanted to stand out in the crowd with Ananaya's new Enforcers milling around.

Body shudders could be visibly seen as one spectator after another caught a glimpse of an Enforcer moving through the crowds. The Enforcer's large bodies, distorted limbs, and facial features were monstrously out of place in this quiet fishing town. Even the burliest seaman seemed small in comparison.

The team from the Center of Genetic Studies ran the course, and the crowd was pleased to see that often their bulk slowed them down, and there was almost no finesse in the routines. They were able to climb the shrouds quickly by sheer strength. The teetering stays slowed the massive children as they awkwardly tried to navigate the small beams. One overly large contestant actually fell off but saved himself from injury by grabbing a sail line and swinging down to the deck.

Cheers were heard from the assembled crowd from the Center for Genetic Studies as if that mistake was part of the routine. The judges frowned and marked the score accordingly. They hoped they were in no danger from Ananaya since he was the Head Scientist over all the centers and would not show favoritism.

When the genetic team retired, Khrelyn knew the team's unified score would not be announced until all the center's teams participated. Khrelyn was sure the team from the genetic center would score low. There wasn't even one individual that he felt might score high enough to be considered a contender for the Champion of Surtees. Usually, but not always, the champion arose from the team with the highest score.

With some interest, Khrelyn watched the team from his birth town perform next. Khrelyn did not recognize a single contestant from the Agriculture Research Center and decided that the farm children were needed at home on their farms and did not try out for the team. Khrelyn knew that if his family remained on the farm, that would have been his fate. His father would have felt empathy for his son, who wanted to compete but would have needed to say no to the request. In fairness to his father, Khrelyn realized he would never have thought about trying out if he was still a farmer's son.

Khrelyn was disappointed in general as to how the Agriculture Research Center team performed. There were no burly farm boys on the team that he could see. They did seem to excel in gymnastics when it was allowed on the course. Those points alone would place them above the Center for Genetic Studies.

When the Capital City Team was due to gather on the deck, the announcer said an alternate would perform in place of one of the select team members. Khrelyn noted a small girl taking her place at the end of the line next to a tall, willowy female. Three young, but strong-looking boys of various ages rounded out the team. The boys took to the course first.

Khrelyn noted each boy seemed quite adequate on the course. One boy's time was quicker than the rest. Khrelyn watched with interest, hoping the faster boy would do something spectacular. He was disappointed, as well as the crowd when it was certain that the only points this boy would receive were for the quickest time set on the course.

The willowy teen took her place at the start. Flying up the mizzen mast shroud, the girl was destined to beat the best time if she continued her pace. Instead of racing through the course, Khrelyn watched with fascination as she twirled and twisted on the sail sheets, with her golden hair glinting around her spinning body. With perfect timing, she let loose of her hands and sailed through the air to the next sail sheet to continue gracefully on the course. Only slightly slower than the fastest time, but with grace and elegance, Khrelyn was sure the points mounted in her favor.

The last competitor raced up the mizzen mast shroud with little effort. Khrelyn was sure he was watching the mythological animal his father named the...nedryl. Scampering and leaping from rope square to rope square with her feet barely touching the shroud, the little girl walked out on her hands on the mizzen topgallant spar and turned around elegantly, and hand walked back to the mast.

Tight rope walking twenty yards above the deck, down the main topgallant stay, the girl began her climb down the mainmast topsail shroud. About the midway point, this young girl without hesitation leaped backward down to the lowest part of the mainmast shroud stopping herself less than one meter off the deck.

The crowd could be heard gasping in horror at this exciting maneuver. Spurred on by the sudden noise, the girl climbed up the edge most parts of the two shrouds, faster than anyone before her to the main mast top gallant deck. From here, she shimmied up the main topmast to the main royal stay. Holding her feet straight out, the girl grabbed the stay and walked hand over hand down the rope that connects the top of the mainmast to the foremast deck.

From the foremast deck to everyone's' surprise, she leaped through the air to the flying jib line and then to the upper bowsprit line. With feet outstretched, she continued her hand over hand to the bowsprit to finish with a handstand.

Khrelyn could not help himself from joining in applause with the spectators, the willowy girl, and her coach. Noting that the three boys stood brooding was not missed.

Realizing it was now his team's turn to participate in the competition, Khrelyn took deep breaths and calmed his nerves. He would be the last person to run the course for this competition, and then the points would be counted for teams and individuals alike. Khrelyn looked once more at the small alternate that just showed the older contestants how to perform. She was amazing. Khrelyn knew he would be following her career with interest.

CHAPTER ELEVEN

Khrelyn was not disappointed with his own routine. He kept in the handstand as the coach advised. Taking a cue from the little girl, Tawtanya's routine, Khrelyn added his own gymnastic style on the fore topmast stays where they split into descending angled lines. Sliding down on one line until the separation was great enough to allow his full body swing to turn the full 360 degrees, Khrelyn released his hold and found himself flying to the next stay where he was able to grab hold and use the momentum to flip another full circle around the stay. The rest of his routine was efficiently fast enough to land him close to the top times. Khrelyn hoped his embellishments would be enough to place him points ahead of the boy who had the quickest time.

So completely immersed in the competition, Khrelyn hadn't noticed when Hoygazor took his seat with the other head scientists. It was not until all the teams were standing on the deck to listen to the judges' announcement as to who the team winner would be and the winner of the over-all best individual competitor, that Khrelyn scanned the audience. At seeing Hoygazor's eyes meeting his own, Khrelyn felt his legs grow weak and his heart beating faster.

If he made an impression on Hoygazor, there was a chance that he may be placed into the pilot's program immediately. Standing with his shoulders back, taller, and straighter than he had before, Khrelyn tried to look official as he imagined a pilot would stand at salute. Trying hard to impress Hoygazor, Khrelyn was surprised to hear that the Astro Science team accumulated enough points to place in second place at the competition.

Tuning in to the judges, Khrelyn listened as it was announced that the Capital City team was first at the Marine Science Center. Turning his gaze towards the little girl named Tawtanya, he was pleased to see her jumping up and down while embracing the tall, willowy girl. For some reason, he felt oddly proud of the little girl, even if she was not on his own team.

The judges were now addressing the crowd to explain the point system for the individuals. The explanation included time, finesse, and difficulty as the individuals ran the course. The points obtained today would continue to add up if the contestants did as well in the next four competitions. The participant with the highest accumulated points at the end of all five competitions would be crowned the Champion of Surtees for this season.

Becoming impatient with the explanation, Khrelyn shifted his weight from foot-to-foot. The head judge continued his belabored speech but finally was at the point where he was ready to announce the top three contestants by points.

"The top three contenders for Champion of Surtees, at the start of the games, are in first place with 250 points is Myana Granyer from Capital City Team."

The applause was heard from the stands as Myana stepped forward and shook the judges' hands. Khrelyn watched Tawtanya proudly beaming sharing Myana's accomplishment. The crowd roared as Myana held aloft the Champion of the Astro Science Competition medallion.

"In second place, from team Astro Science is Khrelyn Lanyion with points accumulated to 248," the head judge was heard to announce over the applause dying down from Myana's fans.

Khrelyn frozen in place by surprise needed a push from a team member to get his body moving towards the judges to receive their congratulations. Letting his eyes momentarily land on Hoygazor, Khrelyn was not disappointed to see the scientist on his feet applauding loudly. Khrelyn was barely back in line when the judge announced the final and third place winner with accumulated points of 240 for holding the fastest time record on the course.

"V'zeyuk Jymnack time was faster than all competitors. Because the time was a new record for this course, V'zeyuk received high points even without noted added difficulty to his routine." The judge pointed out to the audience.

To V'zeyuk, it felt like a slap in the face. Basically, the judge said he only qualified for an award because he set a new time record. V'zeyuk looked to Myana to see if she was smugly looking down her nose at him and was relieved to see that she was still too excited about her own points to notice him. V'zeyuk vowed that Myana would notice him when he stood on the podium to receive the honor he deserved at the end of the season.

The judge continued with his speech to the audience. We have two notable mentions. The hometown team, Marine Science Center, was burdened with negative points from last season's competition. I am proud to say that despite having to overcome the obstacle, the team accumulated enough points to place them in third place in the team competition.

Cheers erupted from the townsfolk who felt the disgrace from the previous season. Feeling vindicated, exuberance was shared by the other spectators who cheered as well. They all knew that the team needed to overcome the stigma caused by one bad sportsman. Now the Marine Science Center team could move on and possibly received enough points to place them overall as the winners this season.

The judge calmed the audience to continue awarding one more Notable Mention. "The spectator newcomers to this game may not be aware of the fact that alternates' scores are added into the team score, but as alternates, they may not participate for the Champion title. Having said this, I want to announce that one alternate would have placed with a score of 246. Her score was added to her team's score to place them in first place at this competition. I would like to ask Tawtanya Hyden to step forward to receive the applause she so richly deserves."

As Myana pushed Tawtanya forward to the waiting judges, the crowd erupted, remembering the inspiring run; this young girl completed with flourishes that astounded even spectators who followed the games for many seasons. Khrelyn could not help himself as he hooted and whistled for the little girl who caught his eye. He found himself looking forward to the next game so he could watch this little sprite in action again.

Tawtanya's face colored with embarrassment. She felt as if she was living a fairy tale. She never dreamed she would even be able to compete as an alternate, and now she was standing next to the judges with every spectator on their feet.

In the crowd, Ananaya stood and clapped slowly and loudly. His guard stood beside him to balance the frail man. The attentive guard's eyes were only on the Chief Scientist. Ananaya's eyes squinted in concentration as he watched his daughter closely, wondering how her physical prowess would play out in the seasons to come.

CHAPTER TWELVE

As the teams started to celebrate before heading home with their host families, Khrelyn decided he needed to congratulate Tawtanya and let her know that she now had a fan. Rounding the food booths and heading towards the Capital City team, Khrelyn noted Myana was not by Tawtanya's side. Instead, Myana was deck side of the ship used for the competition with admirers encircling her. Tawtanya stood aside, eyes focused on her mentor.

V'zeyuk annoyed that Tawtanya beat his score, had his usual followers at his side. Narrowing in on the young girl, the three older boys moved to isolate Tawtanya from any other team member. Khrelyn quickened his pace so that he would reach the girl at the same time as V'zeyuk and his gang. Just as V'zeyuk was about to descend on the unsuspecting girl, Khrelyn stepped in between the boys and their target.

"I just want to let you know how impressed I was with your routine," Khrelyn said with an eye on the angry boys. Relieved to see them step aside and blend back into the crowd, Khrelyn concentrated on the young girl.

She was younger than she looked from a distance. The fact that she was tall and unusually proportionate in her build made her look seasons older than she actually was. Khrelyn guessed she was eleven or twelve, but no older.

"I should be the one to be telling you how impressed I was with your routine," Tawtanya said shyly. "Not only were your acrobatics on the sheets impressive, but your time was excellent. V'zeyuk may have set the record for the quickest time, but he didn't do anything but race through the course. You were marvelous. Your aerials were thrilling, graceful, and full of power. I hope you don't mind if I incorporate some of your moves into my routine."

"I would be flattered if you would," Khrelyn said as he continued to gaze at the girl.

Khrelyn wondered if it was wrong to be fascinated with a girl several seasons younger than himself. She was simply magnificent. Her eyes glittered with the excitement of the day. He couldn't decide if her large eyes were green or gold. Her dark lashes were lush and caused her eyes to be the first thing one noticed on her face. As he scrutinized her face, he found her features to be symmetrical. Her lips were full but not pouty. Her nose was ever so slightly upturned, which made her look impish but somehow regal. When she smiled, her full lips separated to allow her smile to spread even larger and friendlier.

Tawtanya cast her eyes down when she realized Khrelyn was studying her face. His attention made her uncomfortable…Tawtanya could not quite come up with the word she was feeling, flattered, maybe.

Realizing he was making the girl uncomfortable, Khrelyn looked to the ship. "Your friend was magnificent as well. She deserved every point that she received." Returning his eyes to Tawtanya, he added, "It isn't really fair that you cannot keep your points. It is also unfortunate that you are competing as an alternate. I think your coach was foolish not to put you on the team in the first place. You are too good to be an alternate."

"My coach knows what he is doing! He will put me on the team when I am seasoned and ready. Today was my initiation to the competition. I am glad that I passed. It means my coach will trust me to step in when I am needed," Tawtanya said, briskly feeling a need to defend her coach.

"I meant no disrespect to your coach. He is obviously an excellent coach, or your team would not be where you are in the competition so early," Khrelyn said, seeing Tawtanya stiffening. Adding in jest to lighten the moment, "Fair warning, the Astro Science Center team is one to be reckoned with."

"Tawtanya, come on. Our host family is here!" Myana yelled from across the crowd.

Without a goodbye, Tawtanya sprinted off to catch up with Myana. Khrelyn stood watching the girl wishing he had made a better impression on her. Scratching his head, Khrelyn wasn't sure why it was important for the girl to like him.

"Who were you talking to?" Myana asked as Tawtanya caught up to her.

"If you were closer, you would know he was the contestant from the Astro Science Center who came in second place. I am sure you will recognize him when you see him the next time. He was the one who did so well, almost besting V'zeyuk's time and still adding a lot of difficulty to his routine. Remember the guy who did the aerials from one line and jumped to the next line and then completed another aerial?"

"Oh yes, he was good," remarked Myana. "What did he want?"

"I am not sure. The contestant, I think his name is Khrelyn, told me how good I was and that I should be on the team and not just be an alternate," Tawtanya said as she looked back to search the crowd to see if she could see any sign of Khrelyn.

"He has a point," Myana said, rubbing the top of Tawtanya's head fiercely but lovingly as well. "You are good. However, you are only going to get better as you develop stronger muscles."

"I have muscles! Look," Tawtanya said as she flexed her arms to show off her arm muscles.

Myana only laughed as she flexed her own arm muscles, showing off the definition that most men would envy. "In a few seasons, your muscles will rival mine. Just wait."

The two girls melted into the crowd to the waiting host family. Khrelyn, stepping under the tarp covering one of the vendor's tents, still out of sight, continued to watch from afar, with fascination.

As he turned to leave to rejoin his own group, Khrelyn noticed that the Chief Scientist was pointing to Tawtanya and wondered why he had taken an interest in the little girl. Then Khrelyn remembered Tawtanya was from the Capital City team, and Ananaya was probably just proud of the team. 'Maybe,' Khrelyn thought to himself, 'it was Myana the Chief Scientist was pointing towards.'

Intrigued, Khrelyn watched as one of the Chief Scientist's Capital City guards scrambled down from the seating and went in the direction Myana and Tawtanya headed. On impulse, Khrelyn followed the man.

Moving discretely in the crowd, Khrelyn continued to shadow the man who was secretly following the girls. Khrelyn was more than interested at this point. It was one thing for Ananaya to be proud of his team, but another to have one of his Capital City guards follow the girls. As the crowd diminished in size and the spectators returned to their homes, Khrelyn found it more difficult to be discreet as he followed the guard. Twice the guard turned, and Khrelyn wasn't sure if he was spotted.

Slipping into a doorway, Khrelyn stayed awhile to make sure the guard thought he was no longer being followed. When Khrelyn stepped back out into the street, he saw no sign of the guard or Myana and Tawtanya. Racing down the street where he last saw the trio, Khrelyn realized he was now lost, and his escapade was for nothing. The guard, Tawtanya, and Myana were gone. Into which of many streets or alleys they may have turned, were too numerous to continue the search? All Khrelyn could do at this point was to backtrack until he saw something familiar and hope he would be able to connect with his coach or his host family. Walking back, he thought of scenarios why the girls would capture the attention of the most powerful man on Surtees.

CHAPTER THIRTEEN

Ananaya stopped at Kaycee'na's lab station to tell her about Tawtanya's performance at the Zrymyr competition. Barely looking up from her work, Kaycee'na feigned little interest. Her heart swelled with pride as she listened to Ananaya talk about Tawtanya, but fear crept in as Ananaya spoke as if Tawtanya was nothing more than a lab rat.

"I can't decide if physical exercise is an attribute or not. Tawtanya was quite masterful up on the masts of the ship for such a little child. She was the youngest contestant. Of course, she is our offspring, so I would expect excellence, but I was not expecting to even see her compete since she is so young and then for her to excel. I would really like to see her brain under a microscope," Ananaya said more to himself than to his wife.

"Just because she has some excellent physical prowess does not mean that she is a superb specimen in any other capacity. We are looking for perfection. Doesn't that mean both mentally and physically?" Kaycee'na said, trying hard not to sound meek and afraid.

"Yes, my dear, you are right," Ananaya said, surprising Kaycee'na with his odd agreeability. "I have heard from my sources that Tawtanya also excels at her studies. Maybe, we should allow Yyemara more time outdoors to develop her body. It would be interesting to see if her brain capacity increases with motor development."

Without another word, Ananaya left the lab. Kaycee'na couldn't help but worry when her husband mention dissecting the twins' brain to inspect them under a microscope. Surely, he was just speculating, and he would never actually kill his children just to satisfy his curiosity.

Kaycee'na stopped momentarily and looked at Yyemara, who was deep in thought over a problem Fyyenen posed to her. Kaycee'na tried to suppress a shudder as she looked upon her daughter. The young girl was growing into a capable scientist. It would be a pity to end her life. Even keeping an arm's length from the girl, Kaycee'na felt stirrings in her heart at her sight. Yyemara was quite beautiful. Her dark lashes and large green eyes were full of curiosity and purpose. She was tall for her age, so it was hard to think of her as only twelve. 'Or is she eleven?' Kaycee'na asked herself, realizing as a mother she should know for sure what her daughter's age might be.

'Is this what love feels like?' Kaycee'na questioned. 'Would I put my own life in danger to save her?' Shaking her head to clear the thoughts Ananaya's conversation forced upon her mind, Kaycee'na tried to return to her work. Dark thoughts kept Kaycee'na from being productive. 'Did the other twin look like Yyemara? Is she in danger from Ananaya? Is Yyemara?'

Yyemara, sitting back for a moment to ponder the problem set before her, noticed Kaycee'na looking at her. Thinking it meant that Kaycee'na thought she was not applying herself vigorously to the solution, Yyemara forced herself back to work.

CHAPTER FOURTEEN

Giddy with the experience of her first competition, Tawtanya chattered nonstop to her mother and aunt. "It was incredible. I couldn't believe it when my coach said I needed to fill in for Tyessa. He said she was afraid of the rolling deck and the heights and couldn't maintain her balance. I wasn't a bit afraid up on the topmast even though I was forty rods above the deck."

Syonne exclaimed, "You were how many rods off the deck?"

"I just concentrated on what I needed to do, and I did it! A boy from another team even came and congratulated me on how well I did. He said I should be on the team and not just an alternate. He was really good, so that meant a lot to me. If he had a bad routine, I wouldn't have even listened to him, but he was really good, Mother."

Syonne beamed as she listened to Tawtanya's recounting of the day. It warmed her heart to hear the girl call her, Mother. Syonne wasn't sure which made her the proudest. The fact that all Tawtanya's hard work was starting to pay off or the fact that Tawtanya was completely happy in her care.

"One odd thing did happen after the competition," Tawtanya said, startling Syonne out of her reverie. "Myana noticed one of the Capital City guards was following us. She could not figure out why he would do that."

"Was she sure it was a Capital City guard?" Syonne said, alarmed.

"Yes, she was sure. The man wore the uniform, and Myana said that not only was he a Capital City guard, but he was one of the special guards who accompanied the Chief Scientist," Tawtanya answered. "Myana would know. Her father is a scientist at the center. Myana has been to her father's work many times before."

Becoming increasingly unsettled, Syonne tried to become calm, so Tawtanya would not pick up on her anxiety. "Probably Myana's father asked the guard to make sure his daughter was safe in an unfamiliar city. Don't you think that might be the case?"

"Mother! Why would the Chief Scientist be bothered to send one of his own guards to do the bidding of one of his underlings? I doubt he even knows Myana's father," Tawtanya said, sounding very adult.

Laughing at how silly her mother was, Tawtanya skipped off to her bedroom, taking the steps two at a time. "I will call you when dinner is ready," Syonne called after the girl, glad that Tawtanya was not troubled by the man following them.

Turning to her sister, Syonne quietly said, "This is not good. I really thought Ananaya had no interest in Tawtanya when he let me take her away from the science center. I am afraid that he might want her back. What am I going to do? I can't let that monster have my little girl!"

Syonne's sister came and hugged her. "There is no place that you can hide. Ananaya has eyes and ears everywhere. If he wants Tawtanya for any reason, he will have her. I don't say that to be mean. I just want you to be prepared for whatever might happen."

Tawtanya, found herself looking out of her window. 'I wonder if I will see the boy from the Astro Science Center team at the next competition. He was cute. I sure hope I get to see him again.' Without closing her window, Tawtanya twirled around and around in her room. She was too excited to sit down and do her studies. Maybe later in the evening, she could concentrate long enough to catch up on what she missed by going to the Zrymyr games. Maybe....

The next morning found Tawtanya prepared for the day. She managed to settle down long enough to get her studies completed, and after school, the team would be preparing for the next game. Tawtanya wondered what the Agriculture Research Center Zrymyr games would be like. It was obvious that the Marine Science Center would include a ship, but what might the Agriculture Research Center throw at them?

"Windmills!" Tawtanya said out loud.

Not noticing Myana, who came up behind her, Tawtanya startled at her question. "Windmills, what?"

"Hi Myana," Tawtanya said happily at seeing her mentor. "I was trying to figure out what the game plan would be for the farming community. Are we going to need to be on windmills or traversing silos and barns...or what?

"All the above, little one," Myana said with a wicked smile. "It never is easy."

Tawtanya found that Myana's words were true. However, the time between competitions became routine. Not so for Khrelyn.

The head Astroscientist, Hoygazor, did notice Khrelyn at the Zrymyr competition just as Khrelyn hoped. He was immediately accepted into the special school for Spaceprobes with the promise that his pilot training would commence within the month as well. That left no time for training for the Zrymyr games. His coach, sadly, accepted his resignation from the team. There were no other options.

At the next competition, Tawtanya found she would sit and cheer on the team. No one asked to be eliminated from the Zrymyr games being held at the Agriculture Research Center. With more time free, Tawtanya was allowed to explore before and after her team competed. Tawtanya waited to watch for the boy who congratulated her after her first appearance, but he was not competing for the Astro Science team. With feelings of disappointment at not seeing the boy again, Tawtanya wandered into the vendor's stalls.

Being a child, no one paid any attention to her, as Tawtanya stood, eating a treat she purchased. The whispered conversations from three huddled adults fascinated the child.

"I don't think I can last another season," one farmer said, looking drained of any physical stamina he may have once had.

"I know what you mean. My last crop was the worst. Remember the abundance when we grew our heritage crops?" the other farmer said a bit louder than he should have.

"Quiet, Wylmer! You never know if one of the Head Scientist's spies are around," warned a third farmer. "Remember what happened to Noryan?" Snapping his finger, he continued. "Just like that, he was gone after he openly complained about the genetically altered seeds we are forced to use. We need to disband now. I see an Enforcer's head above the crowd."

The men moved on in different directions, leaving Tawtanya puzzled. The men looked so unhappy. She looked at the large Enforcer moving in her direction and shivered at his appearance. Everyone moved aside when one of the Head Scientist's guards came into view. It was easy to see why. Not only were they exceptionally large, hideous in features, but they smelled bad, too.

Before Tawtanya could leave, the Enforcer blocked her way. "Little girl, who were those men who were standing here a moment ago?" the Enforcer said on a gruff voice.

"I don't know, Syr," Tawtanya answered. "I am from the Capital City Zrymyr Team and not from this community."

"Did you hear what they were talking about in their grouping?" the Enforcer pushed for an answer.

"I wasn't listening to them," Tawtanya lied. "I was just eating my treat and thinking that I should get back to my team. The coach will be looking for me soon."

"Get going then," the Enforcer said with a shove to Tawtanya's back as the crowd parted to let him continue his movement forward.

A whispered voice said in her ear, "Thank you, girl, for not saying anything about what we were talking about."

Tawtanya looked into the tired eyes of one of the farmers who was talking about his heritage crops. "If the Enforcer ever finds out who we are, we will be taken to the Internment Camp where we will either be killed or enslaved. Neither is a good option." Patting Tawtanya's shoulder gently, he turned and left.

Returning home, Tawtanya couldn't hardly wait until she was inside the door to tell Syonne what happened. "What did the farmers mean, Mother? They were so afraid for their lives. Do you know why?"

"Come with me, and we can sit down and talk," Syonne said as she led Tawtanya to the small, quiet sitting area.

The interior room was small and furnished sparsely with four chairs and one small table. The light source was kept dim, so even if there were pictures on the walls, they would not be easily seen. There were no additional trade-chips for such luxuries.

"Tawtanya lives matter. Unfortunately, the Chief Scientist has not learned that yet. He cares little for people. What he cares for are the results. The results he is looking for is the longevity of life for himself." Syonne said carefully.

"How do you know this, Mother?"

"I used to work in the Central Science Center as a nurse. I learned many things that I should not tell anyone, including you. The farmers have good reason to be afraid to talk in public. Anything I tell you cannot be repeated for any reason. Do you understand? If you should tell anyone what I am telling you now, both of us could disappear without a trace. You do understand, don't you?" Syonne impressed on her daughter.

"Why are you telling me now? Am I in danger?" Tawtanya said with fear creeping into her words.

"Have you seen anyone following you again as before when you thought a guard was following Myana to keep her safe?" Syonne asked directly.

"I am not sure. From time to time, I have a strange feeling someone is watching me, but when I turn around, I don't see anyone in particular. Why would I be in danger? I am just a member of the Zrymyr team and nothing else."

"You are more than that, my darling. I have much to tell you, but I don't know where to start. For now, just know that you are being followed, and you could be in danger. Go straight to your practices and school and then come home. Do that for me, so I won't need to worry about you so much. In time, I will explain more."

Tawtanya started to protest, but the look on Syonne's face scared her. Tawtanya wasn't sure she wanted to know more.

CHAPTER FIFTEEN

Khrelyn couldn't understand why his mother was not happier for him when he came home with the news that he would be starting the Spaceprobe program immediately. Josyah beamed at his brother's news.

"Are you going to get to fly? You have wanted this for so long. I am happy for you. Will you take me up in your skyplane when you learn how to be a pilot?" Josyah asked, almost dancing a jig in delight.

"Of course, I will. I will fly you to one of our moons and back if you would like," Khrelyn said giddily.

"Can I pick the moon?" Josyah said, continuing, knowing it was just a game.

"Enough, boys," Merlynn said abruptly. "I am sure Khrelyn has studies to do if he wants to stay in the program. Josyah, I know you have a project due for school tomorrow, so both of you go to your room and study quietly."

Merlynn retired to the small room that she shared with her sister. She buried her face in her hands and cried. The mixed emotions she was feeling overwhelmed her. She wished she did not promise her husband that she would support Khrelyn's desire to be a pilot. More than that, she missed Noryan deeply. Raising his sons without his help was difficult, even with her sister to help carry the burden of the expenses. Where was her husband? Was he dead or enslaved? Would she ever know? It was so many seasons now since Noryan sent them away to her sister's house. What did he know that she did not know at that time?

Remembering her husband's warning not to tell anyone, not even her best friend, what they talked about at night when the boys were asleep, came back to haunt her. Had her best friend betrayed Noryan? Did Noryan know that someone would come for him, and that is why he made sure his family went away using the back roads?

Merlynn's life had become a nightmare since that day. Afraid all the time that someone would come for her and her boys, she kept the doors locked, and shades pulled even in the daytime.

Upstairs, Merlynn heard laughing as the boys continued to share the excitement of Khrelyn's news. Wanting to rejoice for her now oldest son, she found herself instead of thinking of her son that disappeared with more dread filling her mind.

"What about the Zrymyr games, Khrelyn?" Josyah asked.

"I had to quit the team. Two-thirds of my days will be spent in studies, so my instructors said I must quit. The coach said he knew from the start when he accepted me on the team that I would be quitting. My coach reminded me that he allowed me on the team as a favor to one of the instructors who felt the physical training would benefit me and help me to get into the pilot's training program. I sort of forgot that." Khrelyn answered.

"I liked bragging about how good you were at the game at the Marine Science Center. Even though I didn't get to watch you, I could almost imagine you up high on the topmast. Won't you miss the games? Josyah asked again.

"I will definitely miss the games," Khrelyn said and wondered why the image of that little girl popped into his head when he answered his brother.

Becoming serious, the two boys settled down to their studies. They had only a little time before their mother would insist that their light source was turned off, and they went to bed.

"Khrelyn," Josyah whispered once he heard his mother's footsteps receding down the stairs, "I am proud of you."

"Thank you, Josyah," Khrelyn whispered back. It felt good to have his brother's admiration since his father was not there to share his dream come true.

Studies filled the months ahead, and Khrelyn was not given a moment off. He wanted to watch the Zrymyr games but did not get an opportunity to do so. He followed the games as best as he could from his ex-teammates when he ran into them on the streets. He always asked how the little girl on the Capital City Team was doing and was rewarded with a description of her latest feat. It seemed after sitting out for two competitions, her coach realized she was an asset as the team scores were starting to diminish without her help. Next season she would be a team member and not an alternate. In the meantime, the coach made sure she replaced one member at each remaining competition. With her scores added in, her team managed to take the first-place trophy for the season.

Khrelyn burst with pride when he heard about the girl, whose name he learned was Tawtanya. He longed for the day that his studies would be completed so he could go and watch the games as a spectator. He wanted to cheer her on to victory.

"Why are you so fascinated with Tawtanya, Khrelyn?" his ex-teammates would regularly ask when he would enquire about the girl. "I do believe you have a crush on her," the teasing would continue.

Khrelyn couldn't answer them. He didn't know himself why he was so fascinated with the girl. He had only seen her that one time. She was good, but that didn't explain his feelings. Myana was good, too, and he didn't think about her at all. Shaking his head to clear his mind, Khrelyn tried to dismiss his friends' teasing and go back to his studies.

The studies were difficult. Khrelyn applied himself and was receiving praise from his instructors. He didn't understand why he was in the Spaceprobe program when all he wanted to do was fly. His instructors said he would find out in a few seasons what Hoygazor had in mind for him and his fellow students in the Spaceprobe program. When asked about flying, the instructor said to wait. The instructor reminded Khrelyn the starprobe program would allow him to learn all about the intricacies of the universe.

The day of waiting came to an end. His instructor told him that it was time to put his studies into practical use. Khrelyn was to report to the Astroport for his first flight instruction. Finally, all his classroom work would be tested, and Khrelyn felt a churning in his stomach. What if he failed? He couldn't let the negative thought enter his mind. This was the culmination of seasons of dreams and hard work. He was going to get to fly a skyplane.

Disappointment set in when he was seated into the right seat of the skyplane, and a pilot slipped in behind the controls. "You didn't actually think you were going to get to fly without me by your side, did you?" the pilot asked when he saw the glum look on the student's face. Laughing at his student's naïveté, the pilot continued to clarify what would happen next.

"You will watch me closely. I will take us up, and I will land. You will take the controls once we are air born. Eventually, I will allow you to land once I believe you are ready. You will do exactly as I say or I will ground you. Do you understand?" the pilot said sternly.

"Yes, Syr!" Khrelyn said with his attitude brightened by the fact he would be able to take the controls once in the air.

Taking off and climbing to the stratosphere in a skyplane was everything Khrelyn hoped it would be. His joy was evident as a smile spread from cheek to cheek. Looking behind, he noted the vapor trail his skyplane was leaving across the sky. Everyone on the ground would look up and see the trail and know a pilot was on the plane. Today, he was that pilot! If only his father could see him. Just maybe his father was down below somewhere and was looking up at the vapor trail right now. Would he be proud of his boy? Khrelyn knew he would be, and that fact made him happier than he had been in seasons.

CHAPTER SIXTEEN

Looking up at the vapor trails in the sky, Tawtanya felt total disgust. She talked with many of the common people and knew that the vapor trails contained chemicals that were polluting the air they breathe. Mothers complained that their small children were increasingly ill with diseases of the lungs. Fathers complained that their eyes itched and stung when they worked outside all day long. Why couldn't the scientists see what the common person could see? Our air is becoming poisoned.

"Tawtanya, come inside. You need to finish your studies before you go to practice. Zrymyr games are not the only important thing in your life. Your education is equally important. Remember, you can only compete for a short time when you are young, but someday, the games will end for you, and you will need to make a living at something else," Syonne said, bursting into Tawtanya's thoughts about the future of their planet.

"Mother, aren't you concerned about what the scientists are doing to Surtees. When I am in different cities to compete, I hear the problems of the people. The people complain about breathing problems, the water is polluted, the crops failing, and the UberBugs destroying everything except the weeds they were invented to destroy. All the cities complain about boys missing—just vanishing into thin air. What is going on?" Tawtanya asked earnestly.

Syonne looked anxiously up and down the street and motioned for Tawtanya to go inside. Once the door was shut, Syonne ushered Tawtanya to the windowless room in the center of their small house.

"Tawtanya, you must not talk about such things in the street. You might be heard by one of the Chief Scientist's spies. The Enforcers would come for you, and your involvement in the Zrymyr games would be over forever. It is not safe to talk about such things," Syonne said, looking straight into Tawtanya's eyes.

"But why would the scientists want to destroy Surtees?" Tawtanya continued to push for answers.

"The scientists don't want to ruin Surtees, …but they need to do as they are told. Ananaya is driven to find an answer to aging. He pushes the scientists to explore all avenues to discover the answer he seeks," Syonne said, hoping her answer would be sufficient to stop the questions.

"They know they are destroying Surtees, but you are saying they are so afraid of Ananaya that they continue anyway?"

When Syonne did not answer the last question, Tawtanya took a closer look at her mother. She was quaking and nervous. Her eyes kept flickering towards the door, and Tawtanya knew she was just as afraid as the scientists.

"Mother, if everyone would band together against Ananaya, they could overcome him. Why don't they?"

"Tawtanya, don't talk like that. I told you that Ananaya has spies everywhere. The reason people don't band together is that if they do, they disappear. Everyone is afraid of the Enforcers and what will happen to them if the Enforcers come for them in the night. People disappear, and no one ever sees them again. Don't you understand? It isn't safe to say the things you are saying. You must stop!

When Syonne started crying, Tawtanya felt horrible. She never saw her mother cry before. "Don't cry, Mother. I will stop. I promise."

Syonne's sobs started to lessen, but her tears continued to stream down her cheeks. "Thank you, Tawtanya. I don't know what I would do if something happened to you. Now go to your room and study before you need to leave for your practice with the team."

Leaving the room, Tawtanya took a backward glance at her mother and saw that she buried her face in her hands. She was still crying. Tawtanya couldn't understand why Syonne was so afraid. Tawtanya felt she needed to know the answer.

CHAPTER SEVENTEEN

Ananaya was in a rage. Finding out that the last experiment on the young boys failed once again, caused him great exasperation. Instead of the boys becoming stronger, they were dying. That was not in his plan.

"Kaycee'na!" Ananaya yelled as he entered the lab of his wife. "Explain why this experimental group of boys is dying. You administered the doses as I directed, didn't you?"

Kaycee'na's face drained of all color. Visibly shaken, she stuttered an answer, "Yuh yuh yes, Ananaya. I...I did exactly as you wrote in your plans. I don't know what went wrong. I did exactly as you directed."

"Well, something went wrong! Which one or more of your technicians injected the boys?" Ananaya said in a threatening voice.

Knowing that whatever names she gave to her husband would mean the re-education camp for the men, Kaycee'na hesitated with a reply.

"I am waiting, and I should never be kept waiting—even by my wife. The names, Kaycee'na!

Quietly, Kaycee'na said, "It was Jystyce, Henryyn, and Rystyn."

Without another word, Ananaya turned on his heels and exited the lab. Yyemara watched as the Chief Scientist left the room and glanced at Kaycee'na, who continued to quake in her shoes.

Fyyenen went to her side and talked quietly to Kaycee'na. Yyemara heard her mother's response. "It is not their fault. Ananaya expects miracles. It is not possible. It just is not possible."

As Fyyenen led Kaycee'na to a small connecting room, Yyemara thought how Kaycee'na must be to blame. Ananaya was brilliant. She vowed she would always follow the Chief Scientist's directives to the letter.

In the hallway, Ananaya told his personal guard to summon the Enforcers. He wanted the three technicians to be taken away in full view of their fellow employees. 'It will teach all of them a lesson,' was Ananaya's thoughts.

"My directives must be followed exactly as I dictate. There can be no failures under my rule. I believe it is time that I make the rounds to each science center. I am the only one who will be able to see whether my underlings are following orders," Ananaya said. "Arrange for my transportation. I want my visits to be a complete surprise. It is the only way that I will be able to cull out the inept."

Without expression, the guard clicked his heels. Ananaya knew this was one man who would die for him. His orders would be followed exactly as directed. That is what Ananaya wanted from all the people on the planet. Obedience, complete obedience was the only way for his plan to work.

CHAPTER EIGHTEEN

Khrelyn was flying high, figuratively, and literally. He was excelling with the Spaceprobe project, and Hoygazor recommended him to the Chief Scientist for the ultimate position in the Astro Science Starfreighter and Starcruiser classes.

As busy as life had become for the young pilot, Khrelyn took every chance available to follow the athletic Zrymyr competition. Tawtanya was becoming the crowd favorite even when competing against the opposing science center's team. Tall, athletic, and outspoken, Tawtanya never missed a chance to incite the crowd to excitement and anger with chants against the failures of the scientists.

Staying within the crowd for fear of anyone recognizing him as a former Zrymyr athlete, Khrelyn wished Tawtanya would be more careful. Noting the Enforcers on the edge of the crowd, Khrelyn wondered that Tawtanya remained safe. Anyone else would have been ryked away never to be seen again.

As the coach came forward and assisted Tawtanya from her podium, where she received accumulated points towards the Champion of Surtees, the crowd noticeably scattered, knowing they were not immune to the Enforcers' punishment. Khrelyn took his leave as everyone else darted in different directions. He wondered whether Hoygazor would come for him if he were arrested, but Khrelyn didn't want to put Hoygazor to that test.

Feeling drawn towards direction Tawtanya and her coach retreated, Khrelyn caught a glimpse of the doorway from which the two vanished. Without knocking, Khrelyn slipped inside the doorway and found himself in the team's dressing rooms. Seeing the coach leave by an opened door across the room from where Khrelyn stood, Khrelyn found himself heading straight to the now-closed door. Quietly, Khrelyn opened the door and slipped inside. Tawtanya looked up in surprise.

"Oh, it is you. I wondered if I would ever see you again," Tawtanya said with a sweet smile. "Why are you here?"

"I had to let you know that I have been following your career in the Zrymyr games ever since the first time you set foot on that ship as an alternate. You are incredible!" Khrelyn blurted out.

"Thank you…I have pondered for seasons why you just disappeared from the games. You were so good. Why did you quit?" Tawtanya asked.

Proudly Khrelyn answered, "I got accepted in the Astro Science Spaceprobe and pilot's program."

Tawtanya's smile vanished. "So, you are the one polluting our air?"

She turned her back on Khrelyn and continued to get out of her team's uniform. "You do realize that you are part of the reason Surtees is dying, don't you?"

Stunned, Khrelyn just stood with his mouth wide open. No one had ever told him that he was responsible for poisoning the air. In fact, he was told by instructors that he would be the savior of Surtees.

"I don't believe I am poisoning the air. I am helping science to better our planet—not to destroy it," Khrelyn said without conviction and wondered why he was feeling so sheepish.

"Do you really think those vapor trails are harmless? Maybe you should spend more time amongst the regular people and see what is happening to the children and the people who must work outside to make a living for their families. People are dying from the poisoned air. Children can't even play outside for any length of time anymore. Haven't you noticed the lack of children playing outside?"

"I can't say that I have. I am inside studying most of the day when I am not flying missions," Khrelyn said suddenly aware that he lost contact with normal citizens.

"What is exactly so important to the Chief Scientist that he needs you and the others to be flying so much? Ananaya is very much aware of the pollution you are causing. Don't doubt that for a moment!" Tawtanya said with fire in her eyes as she turned her gaze directly into Khrelyn.

Feeling disappointed with the encounter and feeling confused as well, Khrelyn backed to the door and excused himself, saying once again that he was impressed with her performance. With those quickly spoken words, he disappeared out the door he entered.

Tawtanya's intense gaze did not shift from the door opening for several more seconds. Irritated as well as feeling saddened by the encounter with the young pilot, Tawtanya returned to pack her satchel with her team colors.

Khrelyn found himself running back the way he had come. He decided it might be best if he never came to another Zrymyr game again. There were better things to do with his time than to be scolded by a fanatic like Tawtanya.

As he retraced his way towards his transport, Khrelyn pondered how a girl like Tawtanya could become such a fanatic. She was going to be the Champion of Surtees someday—maybe even this season. Why would she waste so much time spouting out anger which would only get herself and others in trouble? While still in that thought process, Khrelyn noted several Enforcers pushing men and women in front of them…to what end? Why were these people being herded away from their homes? Was Tawtanya correct about Ananaya? The Enforcers were doing his work, weren't they?

Finding himself at his transporter, Khrelyn entered. He tried to dismiss the disturbing thoughts from his mind. Once into the air, Khrelyn let all thoughts leave his mind except for the pure joy of flying. The planet looked small below. The sleek skyplane disappeared into the clouds, leaving a visible vapor trail high above.

CHAPTER NINETEEN

"Sir, the crowd seems larger than ever when the young female athlete from the Capital City is competing in the Zrymyr games. She seems to rouse the crowds to a frenzy. Would you like for her to disappear?" an Enforcer asked without intonation.

Irritated with the interruption, Ananaya didn't even look up from his work. "No! I said she was to be untouched. Now leave!"

The Enforcer turned abruptly and left. Even with the angry rejection, the Enforcer felt no rebuff. His eyes didn't narrow, his jaws didn't harden, his breathing did not quicken. His stiff stance remained straight forward as he left the room.

Guyzar stood behind Ananaya, silent and watchful. "And I suppose you agree with that foul-smelling Enforcer?" Ananaya asked.

"No, Syr! I never question your motives. I know that you always think twenty steps ahead. If you are allowing Tawtanya to speak openly against you, I know you have your reasons," Guyzar replied without moving from his position.

"Make a note. Find out why the Enforcers smell so bad," Ananaya said to his personal bodyguard. "I can no longer tolerate their presence. From now on, any Enforcer who wishes to speak with me must go through you."

"Yes, Syr," Guyzar replied.

"Actually, I would like you to request my wife's attendance here. She should be able to come up with a genetic solution to de-foul these creatures. Send for her immediately."

Guyzar did not reply but turned and left the room. Within seconds he was back at his position behind Ananaya. The Chief Scientist knew his request or command would be carried out efficiently. Guyzar never failed him.

Almost instantly Kaycee'na flushed and breathing rapidly, meekly entered the lab where Ananaya spent his days. She waited quietly until her husband was ready to speak to her.

"What took you so long?" snapped Ananaya.

"I came immediately," his wife answered quietly.

"Hmm, not fast enough. Oh well, that isn't the point. I am not testing your speed. I want to know why you can't do something, so the Enforcer's don't smell so foul," Ananaya said as he turned to intimidate his wife.

Ananaya's intense gaze always caused Kaycee'na to stammer. "Ah, um, I am not sure what I can do." Hesitating to reveal the truth to her spouse, Kaycee'na stood frozen.

"There is something you aren't telling me. What is it?" Ananaya's eyes pierced even more deeply into Kaycee'na's eyes.

Kaycee'na felt the daggers stabbing into her heart. She remembered once when she loved this man. Now she was terrorized at being near him. She stayed day and every night in her lab to avoid being around him.

"Well…?" Ananaya pressed.

Under the pressure of his demanding gaze, Kaycee'na could not think fast enough to come up with a reasonable lie. Instead, she blurted out the truth.

"The Enforcers are dying. The smell is from their decay. I am so sorry that I can't figure out how to create Enforcers that last. The boys' bodies seem to reject the transformation, and the tissues eventually break down," Kaycee'na's voice trembled as she revealed her long-kept secret.

"Do something about it. Now leave my sight," Ananaya said harshly as he turned back to his work.

Kaycee'na scrambled to the door and left without a single word of farewell. Outside, in the hall, Kaycee'na's body broke into a sweat, and her limbs trembled uncontrollably. She had no idea how she was going to create Enforcers, who did not decay. All she knew is that she must try.

"I have no idea why I married that dolt," Ananaya said to Guyzar. "She used to be pretty and fairly talented. Now she seems to be inferior and an imbecile. I may need to get rid of her yet."

Smiling, Ananaya allowed himself a moment to daydream. Often new ideas came to him in these rare times. His imagination was released, and even the most outrageous thoughts often would guide his plans for the future. One such thought materialized in his head.

CHAPTER TWENTY

The wind whirled through Tawtanya's hair as she flew across the tops of the buildings. Adding points by achieving a high level of difficulty as she somersaulted from one building to another. The dizzying view of the streets below no longer bothered her as she learned to use a point of reference as she tumbled head-over-heels in midair just to land decidedly on her feet in mid-stride. With no hesitation, Tawtanya cruised across the rooftop rim of the next building doing walk-overs on the narrow rim to the amazement of the on-lookers.

Spectator seating was placed on the rooftops of the buildings used for the games. They applauded and cheered as their favorite contestant amazed them with feats no normal person could achieve. Sitting in the grandstands were the heads of many science departments. Kaycee'na, Ananaya, and Yyemara sat side-by-side, viewing the girl's athletic prowess. Stoic and expressionless, Kaycee'na watched her estranged daughter in amazement at how much she had grown, with pride that she dared not show.

"I've heard so much about her for several seasons now. She is quite splendid in person, isn't she?" Yyemara said to her mother, seated by her side.

Ananaya looked at his daughter with warning disapproval in his voice. "She does not have your magnificent brain. Would you trade places with her?"

"Of course not, Father," Yyemara said as she returned her eyes to the next contestant to start the course. Yyemara determined to stay in her father's good graces knew silence was the best action. Already, the Chief Scientist was talking about a path he had chosen for his daughter.

Reliving the conversation, Yyemara beamed with pride. Remembering Ananaya quietly walking into the lab, where Yyemara was working diligently on a project. She recalled verbatim what her father said. "I have a special project lined up for you. Within the next season, you will be leaving this planet to do very important work for me on a planet in another galaxy. This is between you and me and no one else at this time. Do you understand?"

Yyemara vividly recalled how fervently she nodded her head at the question. Ananaya continued with these words. "I will be working closely with you this season. You will move from your mother's lab to my own. This will be a very intense season for you. I know that you are ready."

'I know that you are ready,' kept ringing in Yyemara's head. Smiling, she allowed her eyes to focus on the competition. Four other contestants participated while Yyemara remembered that fateful day. Yyemara chastised herself for not paying better attention. Now she unaware if any of the other contestants had a chance to surpass Tawtanya for the coveted points necessary to be crowned the Champion of Surtees.

Ananaya whispered to his bodyguard, and within seconds, the Enforcers cleared a path through the crowd for the Chief Scientist and his family to retire from the games. Ananaya always left the games before the end when he knew Tawtanya would get on her soapbox and start her speech. One never knew when the crowd might become too unruly. The Enforcers were a deterrent, but Ananaya was not about to put himself in danger. This time

Ananaya made it clear that he wanted the most fanatical people to be silenced...leaving a strong message. He also wanted to make sure the Enforcers arrested several boys as well. His plans were too important for any delays.

The other scientists took their cue from the departure of Ananaya. They also sensed the unrest in the crowd. The young champion, Tawtanya, always caused a disturbance. Many of the other scientists wondered why Ananaya tolerated her outrageous behavior. A few suspected it was intentional.

Tawtanya watched as the scientist left the rooftop. The Chief Scientist had a Spaceplane waiting, and Tawtanya could see in horror that it was the young pilot that she rebuked for his part in polluting the world. Their eyes met momentarily as the young pilot opened the door to allow the Chief Scientist to enter. Was it regret that Tawtanya saw in his eyes?

Tawtanya's coach laid a hand on her shoulder. He observed Tawtanya's body stiffening at the sight of the Chief Scientist and knew from previous games that his star athlete was about to step forward and fling insults at the departing scientists. The coach also knew from past experiences that many of the people in the crowd would be punished by the Enforcers if they joined in with Tawtanya's rants. If he could protect the people from the Enforcers by stopping Tawtanya today, he would certainly try.

"The scientists are gone, and you will only hurt the people you say that you love. Don't start harping against science today, please," he pleaded.

Relief filled the coach as he could feel her muscles relax. Maybe today could just be about the Zrymyr games and nothing else. To his horror, the crowd started to chant, "No more Science...No more Scientist!"

Lured on by the chant, Tawtanya broke from the contestants and stood alone, leading the crowd in the chant that had become the rallying cry for the common people. Enforcers pushed through the crowd, hitting many with batons as they attempted to drive the people away.

Chaos erupted as many of the young men fought back against the Enforcers. Chilling screams filled the air as the Enforcers stood shoulder-to-shoulder and used their bodies to push many of the young men over the rim of the buildings to their deaths.

People panicked, scattered, and raced for the stairwells that might allow them to escape. Pushing and shoving caused many to fall on the stairs, cascading down the flight of steps while others continued to step over them to run for their lives.

The coach grabbed Tawtanya and yelled, "See what you have done? You need to leave now!"

Tawtanya, torn between wanting to stand and fight and her desire to escape the terrible scene, chose to flee. Gathering speed, Tawtanya leaped from one building to another until she was far away. Gathering one last burst of energy, Tawtanya free-fell to a smaller building many feet below. With tears in her eyes, she bellowed one last defying scream of rage and ran down the stairs to the street.

Entering her home, Tawtanya fled straight to her room, locked the door, and refused to answer when her adopted mother knocked frantically to see what was wrong. "Go away! I am nothing but trouble to you and everyone else. Just go away and leave me alone for your own protection!"

Syonne leaned against the door and slowly allowed her body to slide down to a sitting position. She was determined to sit outside Tawtanya's door until she opened it to find out what disaster might have befallen her daughter. Shortly, Syonne heard the click of the door as it unlocked. Syonne got to her feet and slowly opened the door.

"Can I come in?" she asked quietly.

Tawtanya only nodded, indicating that her mother could enter.

"What happened?" Syonne asked as she sat and cradled her near grown daughter. Smoothing Tawtanya's dark hair, as she had done many times in the past, Syonne noted how puffy her daughter's eyes were from crying. Tawtanya sat like a limp doll in her arms. As time went past, Syonne didn't press but waited to hear what her daughter had to say. As Tawtanya relayed to Syonne the events of the day, horror was seen in her mother's enlarged eyes. She could all but picture the muddled and shocking scene on the rooftop.

"We need to leave!" Syonne said as she jumped up from the bed and hurriedly started to pull clothes out of the closet to pack.

"There is no place to go, Mother. Ananaya has spies everywhere. They are probably watching the house right now. If he wants to imprison me, he will. There is nothing we can do to stop it."

Syonne knew Tawtanya was right, and her shoulders sagged under that realization. She marveled that Ananaya allowed Tawtanya to rant against him for this long. Even knowing that Ananaya was Tawtanya's father, Syonne questioned his tolerance. There was something else happening other than fatherly love for an offspring. No, Ananaya had something else in mind for Tawtanya, and that scared Syonne more than finding themselves in a rehabilitation camp.

CHAPTER TWENTY-ONE

Days later, Tawtanya finally got up enough nerve to venture out on the streets. She headed towards the team's training grounds and was greeted with a jeer from V'zeyuk.

"You won't be the Champion of Surtees ever again!" V'zeyuk called after Tawtanya as she passed by him and his gang of envious losers.

The words jarred against Tawtanya's brain. 'What did they know that she did not,' she wondered. Moments later, Tawtanya found out.

The coach didn't brighten upon seeing her enter the training facilities as he usually did. Instead, he cast his eyes to the floor and set his jaw in a manner Tawtanya had only seen when the coach was about to reprimand one of the team members. This time, his jaws were set against her.

Not speaking, Tawtanya walked to the coach and stood before him. She knew it was going to be difficult for the coach to say what he was about to say, and Tawtanya was not going to make it more problematic for him.

"I don't like having to tell you this, Tawtanya, but I have cut you from the team."

Myana, the newly appointed assistant coach, walking into the facility, heard what the head coach was saying to her friend. "What?

You can't be serious. I won the Champion of Surtees four seasons ago under your coaching. Tawtanya won the Champion of Surtees the next two seasons; now this season she is your only hope of keeping the trophy and getting all the glory that goes with the Champion of Surtees honor. Why would you drop her now when we only have one more competition in front of us?"

"This is not a decision I made lightly. After the horrible events hosting the last competition in our own district, I have been under incredible pressure by the leading citizens to cut Tawtanya. Many lives were lost…."

Interrupting the coach, Myana shouted passionately with spittle flying into his face. "That was not Tawtanya's fault! It was the fault of the Enforcers. They did not need to push the young men off the roofs. They could have allowed the unrest to dissipate on its own. It always has in the past, and it would have done so this time as well. The Enforcers made it an issue, not Tawtanya!".

"The crowds show up for Tawtanya," the coach intervened. "They don't show up for the competition any longer. Tawtanya is their champion, whether she is in the competition or not. I would rather that the Zrymyr Games remain pure. I don't want the games ruined by political unrest."

"It doesn't matter that Tawtanya is right?" Myana continued to shout above her coach's voice. "The scientists are ruining Surtees. Haven't you noticed what is happening around us? Are you wearing blinders? Gosh, man, wake up before it is too late."

Calming herself, Myana quietly said, "If you cut Tawtanya, I will quit. I refuse to remain in a sport that only cares for its image. We owe more to the people than to put on a show. We owe it to the people to point out injustices and to stand by their sides in protest…and even a revolution, if it comes to that."

"I am sorry to hear you say that. You have been an asset to the coaching team. I guess you and Tawtanya both should leave," the coach said as he turned and walked away.

"Myana, please don't quit because of me," Tawtanya pleaded. "The coach is right; you are an asset. The team won't be near as good as it is today if you leave."

"I don't care about the team, Tawtanya. There are so many more important things than games. Our planet is dying. You are the one who opened my eyes to the facts. We need to do something before our world is beyond repair. Right now, we can reverse the wrongs. In a few more seasons, it will be too late. Come on. We have plans to make."

Myana guided Tawtanya out the door and into the hazy sunlight. Noting the pollution, Myana pointed to the skies. "We don't have much time before it is too late. You are right about people dying. The few young men who died on the rooftops can't compare to the many who are dying each day from their lungs being poisoned."

Tawtanya allowed her eyes to look skyward. While doing so, a rock hit her square in the head. Screaming in pain, and finding blood trickling down her cheek, Tawtanya was distracted from watching Myana giving V'zeyuk the beating he deserved.

Returning to Tawtanya's side and handing her a clean cloth to stop the bleeding, Myana gave V'zeyuk one last kick in the rump as she passed the boy as he remained on the ground in a fetal position. "I never liked that kid in the first place," Myana said under her breath.

Syonne wasn't home, working late as usual when Myana and Tawtanya came into the small house. Myana helped Tawtanya to wash and bandage the wound.

"It isn't too bad. I doubt that it will leave much of a scar," Myana said while placing the bandage in place. You can pull your hair over your forehead, and Syonne won't even notice it."

A smile crossed Tawtanya's face. "I wish I was watching better when you took on V'zeyuk. He has been a pain in my side since day one. I don't know why he hated me at first sight, but I can't say I am sorry that you gave him his up-and-comings. He really is a spoiled brat."

Myana looked at her swollen knuckles. "Yes, I have always disliked him. It felt good to land a couple solid punches. He sure did buckle quickly. He is the typical bully who can dish it out, but he can't take it. I had to laugh when his friends ran off the moment, he threw that rock. I guess they aren't as stupid as I thought they were."

Both girls chuckled. It was fun to relax in each other's company. Seriousness settled back in quickly. "Now what?" Tawtanya asked.

"You are going to run for governor of our district. I am going to manage your campaign," Myana said casually as if this was not a new idea that just popped into her head.

CHAPTER TWENTY-TWO

Working side-by-side with her father, Yyemara realized that Ananaya was even more brilliant than she imagined. Her own understanding of genetics was now beyond anything she learned from Kaycee'na' or Fyyenen. 'It was just sad that Ananaya could not clone himself and be the head of each scientific project,' Yyemara thought to herself. 'Just imagine the potential of this planet with his total domination.' Another thought popped into her head. This thought was spoken aloud before she had time to check herself.

"Father, I heard a rumor that the dismissed athlete from the Zrymyr games is running for governor of her district. How can she since she is not from the ruling class?" Yyemara asked without raising her head from her work.

Ananaya kept his head down, concentrating on his project. "She is an experiment of mine. You have heard the old saying from the common people the 'cream always floats to the top,' haven't you? Well, it is proving true in this case."

Puzzled, Yyemara wanted to ask another question but knew she should not. She already stepped over boundaries that any other technician would have been fired for doing so.

"Yyemara, you will be leaving this planet soon. I want you to read this profile of a planet to which I intend to send you. You have an important job to do for me." When Yyemara looked as if she was about to ask another question, Ananaya cut her off with one last remark. "Read and study it first before you open your mouth another time."

Accepting the reading device, Yyemara said, not another word. She knew all the answers that she would need would be inside the volume. Any other questions she might have would be incidental or not questions she needed answered. Her job was to do as she was told and nothing else. That was something she came to understand while in her father's company.

"You may leave now to study. You will be leaving quite soon. I have sent items to your room that you will need. Be prepared to leave at a moment's notice."

As Yyemara stood to leave, Ananaya made one more comment without looking up from his work. "I am counting on you to do exactly what I have laid out in my plan. Don't disappoint me."

Yyemara squared her shoulders and lifted her head up high. "I will not disappoint you, Father." With these final words, the young lady walked out of the door with obvious pride that the Chief Scientist trusted her to do something important.

CHAPTER TWENTY-THREE

Khrelyn's intense studies had paid off. He was now commanding his own Starcruiser, the SSC Emissary. His trips through space were exhilarating. Thoughts of his family never entered his mind while piloting the crew through the expanse of outer space. The only person who ever entered his mind was the beautiful young athlete, Tawtanya. Khrelyn thought of her every day and wondered how he could be near her again.

Trying hard not to be distracted from his new position, Khrelyn found himself reliving a recent memory. "You will be on a special mission soon." His commanding officer's voice rang in his head.

Khrelyn poured over the star maps and studied the coordinates carefully. This trip would take months to complete. All the supplies were being carefully stored in the hold of the ship at this very moment.

The destination was known. Khrelyn's new orders directed him to command the piloting of a very important person to an inhabited planet. Nothing else was necessary for him to know, or so his commanding officer said when Khrelyn raised some questions.

"Just make sure you get to your destination on the appointed date and make sure your passenger is in good health. That means mentally as well as physically. She is your responsibility, so make sure she has every comfort imaginable. If she does not arrive at the scheduled time and place, you may as well not return. Do you fully understand the importance of this mission?"

Khrelyn answered with a sharp salute and "Yes, Syr," but he did not understand. How could he understand when he was not given all the information about the mission, nor was he allowed to ask the Mission Superior a single question. Shrugging his shoulders, he smiled. At least, he would be flying through space. That was all that really mattered.

Khrelyn reveled that he, a son of a common farmer, could actually be in the position he was in. It was amazing. It was beyond belief. The fact that his father mysteriously disappeared and his mother and brother seemed to live in fear did not completely register with Khrelyn. Why his brother stayed in the shadows behind his mother was just odd. Why didn't he prove his worth and try to excel in school?

Josyah was bright, but all he wanted in life was to run the family farm, which no longer existed. Allowing his mind to take a brief side trip, which was very unusual for Khrelyn anymore, the young pilot briefly wondered what happened to his father. His mother, Merlynn, said in a hushed voice over their quiet dinners, when Khrelyn still lived at home, that neither of her boys should ever ask what happened to their father or try to find out for any reason. All was a mystery that didn't really matter anymore.

Shaking the memory from his head, Khrelyn decided that he had some free time. He heard that the new candidate for governor was in town. Now was the only time he would have available to listen to her speech since he would be gone for quite some time. Even if he was not close enough to hear her words, he could see her.

His chest felt suddenly tight at the thought of seeing Tawtanya. He wanted to talk with her again, but the memory of the last rebuking he received from her made his strength wilt. His standings in life hadn't changed. He was still the young man polluting the skies in her eyes. Nothing changed, so there was no way she would see him. Khrelyn knew, for now, he needed to be content just to view her from afar.

CHAPTER TWENTY-FOUR

"You look beautiful," Myana said with pride in her eyes. "No one will be able to take their eyes off of you."

"It isn't their eyes that I want but their ears," Tawtanya said as she brushed past Myana. "Our planet is being destroyed. Why won't people wake up and do something about it?"

"You don't have to convince me, Tawtanya. One reason that I decided to be your campaign manager is that I believe in you. I know you will be the one who wakes up the people of this planet. Already, you have a large following, not only in this district but in every single one on this planet. Even if you are not the Zrymyr champion, you are still Surtees's Champion."

Myana circled Tawtanya to make sure everything was perfect. Her short hair gleamed in the light of the room. Myana knew from experience that her hair would shine brilliantly in the sunlight, almost looking like a halo around the young woman's head. The outfit picked out for today's speech was utilitarian but softened with a looser cut and lighter material. Myana wanted Tawtanya to look strong but also approachable. People of Surtees could not see her as another hand-picked candidate of Ananaya's.

Myana stepped back and said with approval. "Beautiful is not the right word. You look spectacular!"

Settling her nerves, Tawtanya hardly listened to the compliment. Searching her mind for words that would strike chords in the heart of the people was the only thing she was thinking at the moment. Tawtanya knew she said everything a thousand times. People were hearing, but they were afraid. How could she get past their fears and ignite the revolution that was needed? Saying the same old things about children disappearing, food, water, and the skies being contaminated was not falling on deaf ears, but it was not rousing the people to action.

"Why do I bother?" Tawtanya said loudly, startling Myana.

Looking at the young woman, Myana knew she must act quickly to settle Tawtanya's nerves. "You bother because you love this planet. You love the people of Surtees. You love your mother and me, right?"

"Yes, all that is true. I do love everything about Surtees except the villainous scientists who are ruining our planet," Tawtanya said with less heat.

"Not all the scientists are bad, you know," Myana reflected. "Most of them are just as afraid of Ananaya and the Enforcers as the rest of the people of Surtees. It is really just Ananaya that deserves your hatred. He is the real reason this planet is dying. We all know that he only cares about himself. His endless search for longevity and power has created a monster. It is up to you to push these thoughts home to the people of Surtees. Maybe even the other scientists will realize that doing Ananaya's bidding is destroying the world they live upon."

"I don't understand why Ananaya has not imprisoned me. He is aware that I speak out against him all the time. Anyone else who speaks out against him is taken away by the Enforcers, never to be seen again. Why haven't I been taken away?" Tawtanya asked in earnest.

"I think Ananaya knows that you are the one public person that everyone would miss. If he did imprison you, there would be an uprising. I think he is smart enough to know that the people are afraid, and they won't react, so why give them a catalyst? It is easier for Ananaya to let you speak out and let the Enforcers ryke away a few in the crowd to keep the people afraid. Who knows what he does with the ones he rykes away? He may feel you are doing him a service by identifying and giving him a reason to cull out the dissenters."

"You aren't helping, Myana. Now I feel responsible for the people that are being taken from my rallies. Maybe I should not speak out against him. I am putting peoples' lives at risk," Tawtanya said in horror.

"Peoples' lives are at risk every day, whether you speak or not. We both know that boys are disappearing every single day. People are dragged from their homes for no reason. It isn't you causing this injustice. It is Ananaya. You must speak out! If you don't, the planet is doomed."

Myana slumped into a chair and watched Tawtanya under heavy eyelids. She knew she could not let her champion falter in any way. Time is our opponent. Passivity is the adversary. People must be moved to action. Now!

CHAPTER TWENTY-FIVE

"This is going to really hurt." was the last words Yyemara heard before flashing lights, and searing pain slammed into her head. Screams of pain rang out, and suddenly the world went black.

Coming slowly to consciousness, Yyemara heard Ananaya say, "This was necessary."

Trying to sit up, Ananaya put a restraining arm on Yyemara's shoulder. "Stay resting til mid-day. You have work before you, so get your strength." Taking his hand from her body, Ananaya continued. "I altered your DNA. You will notice a few small changes to your appearance. It was necessary for your new identity on the planet you will be inhabiting. I trust you have studied the plan carefully that I extended to you?"

Yyemara nodded carefully, still feeling the dull thud in the back of her skull. Not wanting to talk due to her pain, nodding was the easiest way to communicate her understanding of what she was required to do.

"You will be leaving today. All arrangements have been made. The transporter will take you to the Starcruiser SSC Emissary before long. The commander of the starcruiser will see to your every need. I will leave you to prepare yourself for the journey."

Without any sign of fatherly affection, Ananaya left. Yyemara knew she would not be seeing him again before she left for the

Spaceport. Slowly rising to a sitting position, Yyemara felt for the mirror that was left by her bedside. Ananaya mentioned a few small changes to her appearance, and Yyemara wanted to see what they might be.

Staring into the mirror, Yyemara recognized herself by her long flowing black hair. Looking more closely, Yyemara noticed that her nose was longer, her ears smaller, and her eye color was changed to blue; otherwise, she still looked similar to her old reflection. Maybe her cheekbones were a bit less prominent, but Yyemara was not entirely sure. She spent very little time in front of a mirror. Most days, she only looked to see if she had any strands of her long black hair hanging loose from her tightly twisted bun. Professionalism was valued and not vanity by the Chief Scientist. Yyemara did her best to appear efficient. She never blackened the lids around her eyes as some young women did to make their eyes appear larger.

Putting the mirror back on the stand, Yyemara looked around her room to see two cases packed and ready for placement on the starcruiser. A knock at the door announced the arrival of the servants who would take the items to her transport. Noting that she was already dressed in a utilitarian style outfit, Yyemara realized she was ready to leave the planet Surtees.

CHAPTER TWENTY-SIX

The walk around and preflight of the starcruiser was completed to Khrelyn's satisfaction. All systems appeared ready for the long flight through outer space. The charts to the planet Earth had been studied so often since Khrelyn received his assignment that he knew every star, wormhole, and dark matter in the galaxies he would be navigating.

All his work with the Spaceprobe program must have paid off. Programing space probes had become Khrelyn's work for many seasons. However, he was never privileged to find out the results. When the probes returned, the scientists alone were allowed into the hanger to retrieve the valuable information. Khrelyn's curiosity remained unsatisfied even today. Not knowing the results of all his hard work made the same work unfulfilling.

"Commander, we have received word that our passenger is enroute. Her cabin has been prepared to the specifications given to us by the Chief Scientist. Is there anything else that is required of me at the moment?" asked the young officer, standing tall and erect before Khrelyn.

"Thank you for your commendable work in preparing for our guest. I will call for you if anything else is required. You are dismissed." Khrelyn said to the young man, who was most likely seasons older than Khrelyn himself.

The cargo was loaded and stored. Khrelyn was puzzled that his guest was traveling so light. There were only a few crates loaded for the passenger. Most of the freight loaded were supplies for the crew and additional comprobes that would be placed along the way in space for superluminal communication back to Surtees and the Chief Scientist.

Khrelyn could not help but reflect on his good fortune. As a commoner, Khrelyn remembered traveling from his farm to the city by ryke pulled by beasts of burden. Now, he was one of the few Surtarians who was able to fly through outer space. How drab and colorless his world would have been if his father was still alive, and he was being raised to be a farmer.

Walking the narrow passageways of the starcruiser, Khrelyn stifled a chuckle. He had thought the words drab and colorless to describe what his life as a farmer would have been, but inspecting the inside of his starcruiser, Khrelyn realized anyone, but himself would describe the starcruiser as drab and colorless.

Starcruiser s by nature were serviceable, built for hyperluminal speeds, without frills. The internal structure was built using lightweight and strong girders and beams that support the craft and internal electrical and ventilation systems. The flooring and walls were made from the same composite material and were very cold and austere. By design, there were no windows, not even in the control center at the nose of the craft.

The control center normally allowed for visual navigation by large full width and height monitors at the front and sides of the craft. Their intergalactic hyperluminal speed of travel never allowed the crew more than a blur to be displayed on the monitors when traveling at such infinite relative velocities. Once Commander Khrelyn inputted the preset waypoints, the navigation system took over complete control, creating dark energy pathways through the universe to their destination.

A voice from one crew member blared into Khrelyn's earpiece, informing the commander that their guest arrived, and she was being escorted onto the starcruiser at that very moment. Khrelyn sprinted towards the door that would allow the passenger to enter his ship. While it might be imperative, it is also a military practice that he, as the commander, be at the door to meet this special passenger to show his respect.

Arriving just in time to meet the passenger at the doorway, Khrelyn was surprised to see such a young woman standing just outside of the starcruiser entrance. Knowing this guest was important, Khrelyn stood with shoulders back and head high.

"We hope that your stay on our craft will be a pleasant one, Mam. I am Commander Khrelyn. I will show you to your cabin. If there is anything that I can do to make your time aboard Starcruiser SSC Emissary more comfortable, please let me know," Khrelyn said, trying hard to sound pleasant yet official.

"Thank you, Commander. I will be spending most of my time in my cabin as I have much research to do. I will let you know if I have any needs. Thank you very much for your kindness," the guest replied. "Please show me directly to my cabin."

Leading the way to the cabin, Khrelyn attempted small talk several times but with few results. The most information he received was the woman's name—Yyemara. He was curious why she was being sent to Earth, but her answer was evasive. Khrelyn started to believe that she did not know why she was being sent to another planet by her stammering short answers.

"This is your cabin. It is small, but we set aside another cabin for you to use as a study. If the two rooms are not sufficient, I can try to find more space for you to use. It just won't be as private," Khrelyn said as he pushed the door open to allow Yyemara to enter.

"I have several crates. Do you know where they are? I will need access to them from time to time," Yyemara said as she entered the cabin.

"I can have anything brought to you that you might need from your crates if you wish," was Khrelyn's reply.

"No, I will retrieve what I might need myself. Make sure that my crates are marked with my name and placed where I can get to them easily," Yyemara said succinctly. "If you don't mind, I would like to get settled into my cabin now."

"Would you like your food brought to your cabin, or will you be joining myself and the crew for meals?" Khrelyn asked quickly before the door was closed on his face.

"Oh, meals. I think I would prefer to eat in my cabin, thank you. Just have someone place my food at the door and knock," Yyemara said, not looking at the commander as she closed the door.

Shaking his head, Khrelyn found himself a bit insulted. Thinking to himself that Yyemara was rather aloof and rude, he remembered she was a scientist and shrugged his shoulders. Under his breath, Khrelyn mumbled, "They are an odd bunch, those scientists."

Once the door was safely closed, Yyemara sat on her bed. Looking around the small cabin, she was glad she had so much work to do. Being on the starcruiser would be unbearable if not for the fact that she needed to find out why she was going to Earth. Ananaya told her she would learn everything she needed to know on the trip. His final words not to disappoint him rang in her mind. She would probably need every waking moment of the journey to learn all that she would need to know. She was not about to disappoint her father. Bringing out a large bound notebook Ananaya had personally written for her, Yyemara decided to start immediately.

CHAPTER TWENTY-SEVEN

Ananaya watched from his balcony as the Starcruiser SSC Emissary lifted off from the Spaceport. Even from a distance, the starcruiser looked impressive as it left a trail in the sky exiting Surtees' gravitational pull. A smile crossed his face. His plan was playing out on schedule. He knew his daughter would do exactly as he directed.

The Spaceprobes were indispensable to his work. The information gleaned from the probes made the decision as to which planets to investigate further for relocation. Surtees was no longer hospitable to Ananaya's needs and desires. Nothing went according to his plans on this planet. Ananaya knew the problem. Most of the scientists were underqualified or not competent enough to fulfill his expectations. The handful that was competent would be relocated with him to the next planet.

Smiling, Ananaya thought about Kaycee'na. He had plans for her, as well. Even the incompetent had value.

Turning to leave the balcony, Ananaya, leaning on Guyzar, walked slowly back into his lab. There was still much work to do.

"Guyzar, how is the work on the tunnels progressing?" Ananaya asked as he lowered himself carefully into a chair.

"We have a large contingent of men from the rehabilitation camp working endlessly on the tunnels. I estimate the tunnels are halfway completed. The work is slow since you instructed only picks and shovels and no explosives," Guyzar replied.

"That is fine. We are on schedule. You understand that explosives would signal to the populace that something was amiss, don't you?" Ananaya said, looking directly into his personal body guard's eyes.

"Syr, I was not questioning your orders. I was just assuring you that explosives were not being used as you ordered," Guyzar said without expression.

Without another word, Ananaya returned to his studies. As long as Guyzar said the work was progressing, Ananaya could dismiss that project from his mind. There was so much more he needed to be thinking and planning for. Ananaya felt confident that Yyemara would be successful on Earth. It was too early yet to set in motion his plans for Kaycee'na and the other planet that would be instrumental soon. There was so much to be done.

Ananaya sighed. 'If only I had more competent people around me. Maybe I would not have to leave Surtees, but failures abound, and very little had gone as I planned. What my rabble-rousing athletic offspring is spouting is all true. The scientists are destroying Surtees. If they had not deviated from my guidelines, all would be as it should be. Even Kaycee'na, my supposed devoted wife, is the most incompetent. The creation of the Enforcers was her job, and she furtively tried to keep the truth of their imminent decay from me, even now. How stupid she must think I am, but she is wrong. There is nothing that happens on Surtees that I do not know', Ananaya thought. 'The incompetent will pay dearly for their disloyalty.'

A smile crossed Ananaya's lips as he studied the results from the starprobe of the planet Aztara. 'This time, all my plans will work exactly as I demand. Aztara will be the perfect planet. I just need to make a few adjustments to the local inhabitants,' Ananaya's devious mind thought happily.

CHAPTER TWENTY-EIGHT

It seemed a long time since Noryan thought about his family's wellbeing. He dreadfully guessed, they were either alive, or they were not. There was nothing that he could do anyway from this retched rehabilitation camp. Days and nights ran into each other. He had no way of knowing how long he was there. Each day was like the one before—nothing but drudgery.

"Get up, lazy dirt farmer!" a loud voice rang into his ear as a kick in the ribs was added for accent. The strong unpleasant odor alone made it clear that an Enforcer entered the dingy cabin where he and several other men were housed when they were not forced into labor. As the Enforcer went to the next straw mat to kick the man lying beside Noryan, Noryan rolled to a sitting position, rubbing his ribs.

All the men got up without a word. Only low moaning could be heard from two men who did not rise from their mats on the dirt floor. "Get up, or the Enforcers will be back!" hissed one of the men who was pulling on torn, filthy trousers. "If they come back, you won't be the only one punished. We all will be."

Moving to pull the men to their feet, Noryan steadied the one older man who was clearly suffering from some ailment. "You should be allowed to rest, old man. I am so sorry the Enforcers are without compassion. I wonder where those monsters come from anyway. They sure aren't Surtarians."

The old man did not comment. He was in the rehabilitation camp long enough to know the truth. He never spoke to anyone about what he knew. He was determined to go to his grave with the horrible knowledge of who the Enforcers really were.

"Come on, or you will miss the meager crumbs they call breakfast. As if we ever do anything but fast. I don't know how we can break our fast when our meals are nothing but crumbs and dirty water," Noryan said in disgust.

As they moved into the common yard where other men gathered, waiting to be herded into the large hall they joking referred to as the dining hall, Noryan noted that the sun was just starting to peek above the mountain tops.

Besides the Enforcers, the forest and craggy hills to the north and snow-peaked mountains to the west walled off the internment camp, lovingly called the rehabilitation camp, while the ocean with its rogue waves blocked their means of escape to the east and south side. Without large boats, that route of escape was impossible.

Several men tried to escape in the past. Most died trying while others were dragged back in chains. None of those that returned survived the harsh disciplinary action taken for their efforts at freedom.

Eating took no time since there was little food to be had. Noryan yearned for the days where he could farm his own crops, raise winged creatures, and quadrupeds for his family's table. Those days were gone the moment his wife, Merlynn, confided in her best friend Lyrica about the crazy scientists, their diseased beasts, UberBugs, and the crops that sickened her family. Noryan knew the moment he found out that Merlynn complained, out loud, to her friend that his days were numbered. Sending his wife and two remaining sons away was his only solution to keep them alive and safe.

"What are you thinking about?" asked the old man who was seated on the ground next to Noryan. "You have that faraway look in your eyes."

"Stupid of me, I know, but I was thinking about my wife and two sons. I was also wondering what happened to my oldest son. He just disappeared, you know," Noryan whispered.

"Yes, you have told me your story before. It does you no good to keep pondering on the past. It will only break your spirit more," the old man said.

"On the contrary, thinking of the past gives me some hope that the good old days may return. Don't you ever think about what may happen in the future?" Noryan asked.

"I have no doubts that I will die here. There is no future for me. If it keeps you alive to think that you have a future, then good for you. Keep your spirits up. It serves the Chief Scientist just fine," the old man said with cynicism ringing in this hushed voice.

Noryan stopped talking to the old man. He didn't need his negativity. It was hard enough to concentrate on anything positive as they were herded down into the tunnel to continue the arduous day of digging. Noryan looked towards the early morning sky. This would be his only glimpse at the sky for the rest of the day.

On cue, the Enforcers roused the group of men to their feet. "Get moving! Work won't get done with you sitting around all day!" One Enforcer said as he raised his crop above his head to spur on the men not rising fast enough.

Teeth clenched between blows of the whip; the last few men got as quickly to their feet as they were physically able with little food to nourish their tired and underweight bodies. Most of the men had little strength to carry the shovels and pickaxes, let alone lift them in continued use to excavate the grudging mountain of its innards.

The walk into the forest to the site of the tunnel was relatively short. It was a moment Noryan found refreshing. The smell of the trees and the sounds of the birds in the branches gave him a moment respite from what he would encounter next.

Entering the tunnel, each man knew what was expected of him until the daylight was diminishing from the skies. Backbreaking work was all that they knew. From time to time, one of the laborers would fall over in death, with no one stopping their work. An Enforcer would haul the dead body out of the tunnel, never to be seen again. Noryan supposed the body was buried in the dirt that was exhumed from their diggings. No words would be said over the body. It would just be buried out of sight, and that would be that. It was the end most of the men expected.

Noryan didn't want to think about his end. He still had hope…burning in his soul. He tried to picture his son, Khrelyn, living his dream. He hoped Merlynn encouraged their son to apply for flight school.

Josyah, the youngest son, was who Noryan felt the most compassion towards as he knew his son was a farmer at heart. With the farm being confiscated, Noryan knew there was little chance that Josyah would ever be able to feel the rich soil in his hands or watch his crops sprout up through the ground. Noryan knew there was no place to plant anything in the city. He could almost feel Josyah's despair.

If he ever escaped, would he find his family? Would they be alive, or did the Enforcers hunt them down when they took him as a prisoner? These thoughts occupied Noryan's mind as he did the tedious work in the tunnel. His mind had plenty of time to think about anything, but the next shovelful of dirt or clearing rocks and boulders buried deep within the belly of the mountain. Some days, Noryan was so numb, he thought of nothing. His mind was just blank, and he worked by rote.

Thoughts in his head blurred together. Frantically, Noryan tried to picture his wife and sons' face, and what they might look like now. He was even unaware of how long he was away from them. Letting his imagination play out, he fanaticized what their reunion may look like. He pictured his wife's shocked expression as he walked through the door of her small apartment. He visualized her shocked look, melting into sudden joy at recognizing her husband and then, running into his arms. He knew he would not be able to lift his youngest son high into the air as he would be as old or older than his brother Khrelyn was when they were forced to part. Shaking his hand and embracing him in a tight hug would mean more than anything to both of them.

Khrelyn was harder to imagine. If he were living his dream, he would probably not be home. He would be pressed into the service of the Astro Science department. Noryan tried to picture his son in a uniform. Depression set in as he thought about his son being brainwashed by the establishment. Josyah, no…but Khrelyn, might be susceptible, just for the privilege to fly.

A whip sliced into his back, not only bringing blood to his filthy shirt, but it also brought his mind back to the reality of his present situation.

CHAPTER TWENTY-NINE

Tawtanya rubbed elbows with the people of Surtees daily. She heard the horror stories they told her of life on Surtees. Young Boys missing, minimal harvests, or even no harvests due to the modified seeds and the UberBugs. The children were not thriving as they should, and the elderly were dying earlier than in the past. Dissenters were dragged from their homes, never to be seen again. It was heart-breaking.

Myana sat at a table with Tawtanya as she talked with some of the locals in the eating establishment. Her face was drained of color as she listened to the woes of her eating companions.

"Together, we will make changes, but we need to work together. It is the only way," Tawtanya said. "If we don't band together and watch out for one another, things will continue as they are."

"Just how do we do that?" one man asked. "The Enforcers are stronger than we are. It would take a crowd just to bring down one of them, and they always travel in pairs."

"Then I suggest that you travel in crowds...I know that is not always possible as you go about your business, but if your neighbors will not stand up for you and you won't stand up for your neighbors, then we are lost. We need to work together. Maybe we need to form a city militia."

"We are barely able to make a living for our families as it is. Are we to quit our jobs and become an army? Who will feed my family if I do that?" the man asked in all seriousness.

Myana broke into the conversation. "When Tawtanya is the governor, she will be able to allocate trade-chips to be used for a militia. In the meantime, you all need to watch out for each other."

"Right," the man said without enthusiasm, "you know the Chief Scientist will not give you trade-chips for a militia."

"The governorship has resources that are not dependent upon the Chief Scientist," Myana spoke back.

"We all know traditionally, there are trade-chips set aside for health issues and helping people when their crops fail completely. There is still barely enough for that purpose. How will we survive if even part of those trade chips is set aside for a militia?" Despair filled the man's voice.

"It may be difficult in the very beginning, but if we don't take steps to improve our lot in life, we will all die anyway," Myana countered.

The man and his friends got up slowly from the table. Shaking his head, he left the room with his friends in tow.

"That didn't go well, did it?" Tawtanya said sadly.

"They just need to think about it," Myana said as she patted Tawtanya's hand.

Pulling her hand free to rake her fingers through her short-cropped hair, Tawtanya continued her discussion with Myana. "There is no good solution. However, we need to find a way to upset the balance of power. Ananaya and his scientists have ruled Surtees long enough. They have not fulfilled even one of their promises. It is clearly time for the people to revolt."

"I agree," Myana said, "but first, we need to get them to see it is totally up to them. Do they want to slowly watch their children starve to death or die from lung diseases? At present, we do have a following. We just need to continue to push our point," Myana hesitated for a moment before continuing.

"I know this is disheartening for you, Tawtanya. Once we overthrow Ananaya, we can undo the damages he and his scientists did to Surtees. I know some farmers have secreted away Heritage seeds that we can plant after the revolt. Some changes will take longer than others. It will take time for our air to be clean and our water source to be free of the chemicals the scientists keep pumping into it. We need to start somewhere. First things first, we must rouse the people to revolt."

Tawtanya looked over her shoulder to see if anyone was within earshot of the conversation. "Myana, keep your voice down. The last thing I need is for you to be arrested. I could not do this without you. Please be more careful about when you make statements like that."

"I am not at risk. You are," Myana said. "It is you that is on the podium making speeches. We are both aware that Ananaya knows what you are saying in public. Why he has not tried to stop you is beyond me, but as long as he is not stopping you, we have to continue to try to make the people understand how dire the situation is on Surtees. I will risk being arrested if it stirs even one community to rise up."

Seeing that her words were not calming Tawtanya, she spoke softly. "You have a speech to give tomorrow. We should go back to our sleeping quarters and let you relax. I can see that you are becoming stressed."

"It isn't for myself that I am feeling stressed. It is for you, Myana. For some reason, Ananaya is leaving me alone, but that does not mean that he won't send Enforcers for you if you become too vocal.

Please, let me be the spokesperson. I need you by my side to give me encouragement. I couldn't do this if you were taken away. You must, for my sake, be quiet. Can you do that? Please…." Tawtanya pleaded.

"For you, I will do anything. If you want my lips sealed, you have got it. I will be as quiet as that fly on the wall," Myana said, pointing to the speck of black on the far wall.

"That isn't a fly, Myana. That is a spider," Tawtanya laughed, releasing some of the tension she was holding in her shoulders.

"I know what we should do," Myana said cheerfully. "Let's take to the rooftops. A good workout would do wonders for both of us."

"That sounds perfect to me. I would love to bound head over heels across the rooftops like we used to do when we both competed in the Zrymyr Games. I have to admit that I miss the competitions, but we can still get our exercise. Come on. I will race you!" Tawtanya said as she sprinted from the room.

Tawtanya and Myana laughed gleefully as they navigated the roofs of the buildings, scaling from one to another with the wind whipping Myana's longer locks. Myana reached for a band to bind her hair away from her face as she continued to run full-out to spring into a flip landing gracefully on the next rooftop. Tawtanya stayed close to her side, doing her own routine of flips, twists, and somersaults as she landed next to her friend. Out of breath but exhilarated, Tawtanya and Myana collapsed to the rooftop and laughed giddily.

"This was such a good suggestion. I feel so much better," Tawtanya said just before they heard the loud applause. Neither was aware of the crowd that gathered on a neighboring rooftop across the roadway. Cheers continued as the two former champions of the Zrymyr Games stood and took a bow.

Leaving the rooftops, the crowd began a cheer, "Tawtanya, Tawtanya, Tawtanya…No More Science, No More Scientists…." As the door to the stairway descending back to the streets closed, only a muffled chant could be heard.

"It is beginning, Tawtanya. The people of Surtees will follow you," Myana said as she gave Tawtanya a big hug. " Time for you to rest. You have a big day ahead of you tomorrow.

CHAPTER THIRTY

Yyemara was scarcely seen aboard the starcruiser. She made a rare appearance from time-to-time to retrieve items from her crates in the cargo hold. Khrelyn came upon her on one of these infrequent trips outside her cabin.

"Do you have everything that you need?" Khrelyn said, startling Yyemara as she crouched over the crate to take the items she required.

"Oh! Commander, you surprised me," Yyemara said as she stood to her full height.

Khrelyn noted that she was tall for a female. There were many similarities to Tawtanya, he noted. Mentally, he compared the two women and decided that they were cut from a similar mold except, of course, that Tawtanya was much stronger and healthier looking.

His thoughts betrayed him as Yyemara noted a sadness that came over his face.

"You must be missing your wife and family," Yyemara said in a moment of compassion.

"Oh, no. I am not married," Khrelyn replied quickly.

"I'm sorry. I didn't mean to intrude. It is just that you looked so sad for a moment. I just assumed you were missing your family. Well, excuse me. I have more work to do."

"Can I carry that for you? That looks to be a very heavy stack," Khrelyn asked.

"It is rather heavy. Thank you. I would appreciate the assistance," Yyemara said with a brief smile crossing her pretty face.

Once again, a tinge of recognition forced itself into Khrelyn's mind. "I'm sorry about staring. You remind me so much of another woman on Surtees."

When Yyemara did not respond, Khrelyn dropped the subject. "You must be lonely for your family. You have been gone from Surtees for quite some time now."

"On the contrary, I am not lonely at all. I am doing very important work. Besides, I enjoy working alone. Most of my research has been done in a lab with only one or two other people in the room. Labs are very quiet places since each person has their own important work to do," Yyemara offered.

"What are you working on, if you don't mind me asking?" Khrelyn asked, emboldened by the conversation.

"I have much to study. I am learning several languages from the planet Earth so that I may communicate when I arrive. I also have things that I am doing that I am not at liberty to discuss with you. I know you understand since you are in a similar position as the commander of this starcruiser," Yyemara said in reply.

Khrelyn knew that was his cue to stop asking questions. As they arrived at the entrance to her cabin, Khrelyn asked if she would like him to carry the stack of notebooks into the cabin.

"No, I can carry them from here. Thank you for your help," Yyemara said as she took the stack from Khrelyn's arms.

"Would you like a break from all your work? You could have dinner with me if you would. We will be serving the evening meal at the normal time. That would give you a short break from your work," Khrelyn offered.

Looking unsure, Yyemara looked down at the stack she now held in her arms. "I don't know. I have an awful lot of material to digest," she said with concern in her voice.

"A break will do you good. It will allow your brain to digest what you have learned thus far. It will benefit you, I am sure," Khrelyn said with a smile.

"Okay, I will join you for a meal…but then I must excuse myself and get back to learning this material. I don't want to be unprepared when I reach Earth."

Khrelyn was about to ask her more about why she was going to Earth but thought better of asking. He knew Yyemara would be offended and then refuse the dinner invitation. Instead, he said, "It will be nice to have your company at dinner. I will see you then."

Khrelyn walked back to his quarters. He thought seriously about changing into a fresher uniform for dinner. He was about to do so when he received a summons from the control deck. Rushing to the deck, Khrelyn found the first lieutenant duty officer looking worried.

"What is wrong, Lieutenant Jystyn?" Khrelyn asked as he came closer to the monitor Jystyn was studying.

"Sir, I fear we are deviating from the planned course," the officer said. "Look!"

Jystyn was pointing at a series of dots and another series of dashes blinking on the monitor. Khrelyn stared at the monitor.

"We are alright. The flashing dashes are indicating that we will enter an alternate dark energy pathway, sooner than expected. The system will re-engage the transluminal drive unit, accelerating us to our targeted hyperluminal speed. The dotted lights indicate the trytanium magnetic crystal shield will deploy into the pathway protecting us from potential asteroid obstructions and radiation hazards. Just follow my flight plan. I apologize for not explicitly informing you of the change. I discovered a short-cut pathway, on my last trip to earth, that will save us a lot of time." Laughing, Khrelyn added, "You won't mind getting home earlier than planned on the return flight, will you?"

First Officer Jystyn, still a bit rattled from the unexpected change in plans, relaxed when he heard his commander laughing. "No, Syr, I would love to get back to my sweetheart sooner. We plan to marry when I return."

"That is great news. Myllye is a charming girl. I hope I will be invited to the festivities. I suspect you would not have been alarmed by the monitor if you were daydreaming less of Myllye while on duty and studying the flight charts." Khrelyn added.

Smiling as he left the control deck, Khrelyn thought, 'Nothing works better than a kiss followed by a slap to motivate.' Noting he no longer had time to return to his quarters to change into a fresh uniform, Khrelyn went directly to the dining hall. Yyemara was already seated and being served the first course as he entered.

"Please forgive me for not being here to greet you when you arrived. The control deck summoned me," Khrelyn added as he took his seat across from the scientist.

"Is there something wrong?" Yyemara asked as she placed her cloth napkin on her lap.

"On the contrary, everything is fine. We will be entering a dark energy pathway that will shorten your trip," Khrelyn explained, knowing Yyemara would be delighted.

"Oh, gosh! You mean I have less time to learn everything I need to know?" Yyemara said with fear showing in her blue eyes.

"I thought you would be glad to arrive early," Khrelyn said, puzzled by Yyemara's response.

Settling herself, Yyemara said quietly, "I guess I should be. The sooner I arrive on Earth, the sooner I can put Ananaya's plan into action. It is just that there is so much I must absorb before you place me on Earth. I have new languages to learn and a persona that I must execute flawlessly. My duties will be extensive, and I have a timetable on top of everything else. It is rather daunting, to say the least."

"Exactly what are you required to do on Earth for the Chief Scientist?" Khrelyn asked foolishly without thinking.

Yyemara pushed her chair back suddenly. "As I have already told you, I am not at liberty to share any of my assignments with you or anyone else. If you are going to ask me questions beyond your need to know, I will be eating my meal in my quarters."

Khrelyn quickly apologized and looked to see if the main course was being brought, hoping its arrival would calm the lady, and the meal could proceed politely. Seeing a tray of food being carried into the room, Khrelyn nodded his head towards the man carrying it.

"I promise not to ask another question. Once again, I apologize for my rudeness. Please stay and eat your meal…with me," Khrelyn pleaded.

Yyemara lifted her body and brought the chair back to the table. "You can tell me about yourself. That should be a safe topic," she suggested.

As the plates were placed on the table, Khrelyn broke the silence and began. "Well, I was born on a farm."

Immediately, Yyemara interrupted the sentence. "A farm? An actual farm? I have never seen a farm. What was it like to live on a farm?"

Khrelyn was about to ask why she had never seen a farm when he thought better of it. Instead, he began to answer her question.

"It was actually fun to be brought up on a farm…most of the time. Chores were physically hard, but the freedom of living in the country was exciting. My brother and I would play endlessly in the outbuildings or run in the fields. In fact, the time spent playing in the rafters of the outbuildings is what got me in shape to participate in the Zrymyr games," Khrelyn paused for a breath.

"You were in the Zrymyr Games?" Yyemara asked, trying to hide her excitement at the prospect.

"Not for long, really. I was accepted into the aerospace program, and I had to quit the games," Khrelyn said with a note of sadness in his voice.

"I watched the Zrymyr Games once," Yyemara added. "It was exciting. It must have taken hard work to be able to do the stunts needed to compete."

"Definitely! It took copious time each day of grueling exercises and practice to be able to do even the simplest routine. It was wonderful but not near as wonderful as flying," Khrelyn said with enthusiasm.

Adding, Khrelyn ventured a bit further by asking, "You said you went once to the games. Only once? You didn't enjoy it?"

"On the contrary, I thoroughly enjoyed the competition. It is just that I have so much work that I need to do. I am not allowed much free time. Only recently, did Ananaya suggest that I take more walks outdoors."

"You mean you did not play outside as a child?" Khrelyn pushed boldly ahead with this question.

Yyemara did not seem to mind the question and answered it without a furrowed forehead or any other physical sign of objection. "From little on, I was educated by my tutors to develop my mind for the scientific work I would be doing for the Chief Scientist. It has culminated in this rather important assignment."

Realizing she had opened the door for further questions into official matters, Yyemara quickly shut down the topic. "But of course, that line of questioning is off-limits."

"Do you have any siblings?" Khrelyn asked, feeling the topic was safe.

"No, I don't. I was raised alone," Yyemara said. "You said you have a brother; what was it like to have a sibling?"

"I actually have two brothers," Khrelyn said sadly. "One disappeared, and we never found out what happened to him. He just disappeared without a trace. My parents never fully recovered from the loss."

"I can't begin to act as if I understand what your family went through. I am sorry, though, for your family's loss," Yyemara said, extending herself beyond her normal comfort zone.

Khrelyn, not sensing how difficult it was for Yyemara to try to be empathetic, continued his conversation. "That and the fact that the crops stopped flourishing made life for my father very difficult. Even the beasts that my father raised was no longer lucrative. Farming just became so difficult. Then one day, for reasons I was never told, my father packed up my mother, my brother, and myself and sent us to live with my aunt in the Astro Science city. Mother never would speak of the reason. To this day, I have never seen my father again. I have no idea what happened to him, and my mother said I should never speak of it to anyone…but here I am telling you."

Yyemara reached out her hand and placed it on top of Khrelyn's hand that rested on the table. "If it is a family secret, you have my promise that I will never speak of it either. Thank you for confiding in me. No one has ever done that before."

No words were spoken for the last few bites of the meal. Eyes met, and words were not needed. Khrelyn felt as though he had a new friend aboard the craft.

CHAPTER THIRTY-ONE

The sun was peeking through the blinds that covered the window of the small, modest room where Tawtanya lay in a small bed pushed against the adjacent wall. She slowly allowed herself to wake and watched the beams of light that filtered through the small opening of the window blind. The beams of light seemed to be dancing on the wall as she rubbed her eyes to wake herself from the deep sleep she had previously been in.

Tawtanya could hear her foster mother moving around outside of her room. She smiled, knowing she was very lucky to have Syonne in her life. She wished, however, that Syonne would not be so evasive when she asked questions about her childhood. What she did know was that for some reason, the Chief Scientist seemed to have an odd interest in her. It was both a positive and a negative. At this point, the positive was that Tawtanya seemed to be protected from the Enforcers when she spoke at rallies. The negative was that she never knew when the positive would end.

Today Myana was to come and pick her up so that they could mingle in the common square with people from the center. There was no rally planned, but Myana felt it was good to be in the public eye as much as possible before the election for governor.

Tawtanya didn't mind. She enjoyed talking with the people to find out how she could make their lives better if she became the governor. On cue, Syonne opened the door.

"Time to get up, lazy girl," Syonne said with a warm smile. "Myana will be here shortly. Of course, I could tell her that you aren't feeling well today, and you need to stay in bed."

"Now, why would you do that?" Tawtanya asked.

A frown appeared where the smile had once been on Syonne's face. "I fear for you, Tawtanya. I never know if you will return from your outings. I wish that you would give up your bid for the governorship. It just isn't safe to attack the Chief Scientist."

"Mother, what kind of person would I be if I gave up because of my own personal safety. You know what is at stake…." Tawtanya said as she got up and stood to face her mother, eye-to-eye.

"I know that nothing I will say will change your mind," Syonne said, "but know that I love you, and I always tried my best to keep you safe. You can't blame me for continuing to try."

Tawtanya stepped forward and hugged her mother, fiercely. "I love you more than you will ever know. I want to change Surtees so you will never have to fear again. I love you that much."

"You should dress quickly now. I have a small breakfast for you and Myana to eat before you leave. I guess that is the only thing I can offer to my grown-up girl," Syonne said as she closed the door behind her to allow Tawtanya time to dress.

Myana arrived on time, and after shoveling down a quick breakfast, the two left the small home with Syonne busying herself so as not to cry in their presence. Both girls were so focused on their day that neither noticed the tears welling up in Syonne's eyes.

"We don't exactly have a game plan for today," Myana admitted. "I thought we would just mingle at the market place and talk to people as they go about their normal routines."

The square was buzzing with life as people set up their wares to sell. Good-natured joking soared between stalls as neighbors who had known each other for their lifetimes, threw insults about each person's wares in jest.

"My infant son could make a better pot than that out of modeling clay," laughed a burly man from the safety of his stall.

"Oh yeah? Well, my granny wouldn't need help to set up your stall. How come a big burly man like you need two sons to do the work my frail old granny could do alone. You are getting feeble in your old age?" his sparring partner bantered in return.

Myana laughed loudly when she heard the two joking. "That sounds like my family reunions."

Tawtanya's smile evaporated. She thought how nice it would be to be part of a large family. Her thoughts were interrupted as some of the crowd recognized her.

"Tawtanya!" yelled one person, "when is the next rally. I want to be there to support you."

"Thank you," Tawtanya said with her smile returning. "You will need to ask Myana. She is the one who is heading my campaign. I am sure she will give you advanced notice."

A crowd gathered around the two young women, and questions flowed freely until a look-out noticed two Enforcers heading down the narrow street. Most started to disperse back to their stalls, but the burly man stood his ground and continued to talk openly with Myana and Tawtanya.

One of the Enforcers reached out to grab the burly man, who now looked small in comparison. "You are coming with us. Trouble makers are not allowed in the square."

Grabbing the man tightly by the arm, the Enforcer nearly jerked the man off his feet. Outraged, Tawtanya stepped forward and pushed the Enforcer, barely causing the being to take a step back.

"You leave this man alone. He was not doing anything wrong. Unhand him right this moment!" Tawtanya yelled fiercely.

As the Enforcer raised his hand to strike Tawtanya, the other Enforcer quickly stepped between his comrade and Tawtanya. "Don't you recognize this woman?" was all the other Enforcer needed to say.

Without emotion registering in his face, the raised arm dropped back to his side, but he did not release the burly man. Tawtanya realized she had the upper hand at the moment.

"Release my friend now or suffer the consequences!" Tawtanya said defiantly.

Releasing his grip on the man, the Enforcers turned and continued their march down the street. Cheers broke out from the other merchants, but Myana quickly signaled that they should stop.

"You don't want the Enforcers returning when we aren't here. It is best not to provoke them. However, I am proud that you are showing spirit. It will take all of you as a group to stop the Enforcers. I suggest that you talk together to decide how you will combat the Enforcers in the future when they return. You outnumber them, but you need to have a plan of action…and weapons, if you want to live a safe and secure life from this day on," Myana said.

As Myana and Tawtanya walked down the path in the direction the two Enforcers had taken, Tawtanya said to Myana, "I think the wrong person is running for governor. You would make a better politician than me. You were amazing back there. You told the people exactly what they needed to hear."

"I've had plenty of time to think about what is happening on Surtees. Being a governor is not something I would want to do. The people need a champion, and that is you, not me. I will be right beside you all the way," Myana said contentedly. "Together, we will make Surtees a good place to live again."

Tawtanya didn't respond. She continued to watch the two Enforcers in front of them as they pushed and bullied people as they moved through the crowds. Her thoughts turned to what the Enforcers might be and how they were created. They were big, burly, and had distorted features. If they were ever Surtarians, it would be impossible to recognize who they might have once been.

"Myana, do you remember exactly when the first Enforcers appeared on the planet?" Tawtanya queried.

Myana didn't answer immediately. She stopped and stood, puzzled for a moment. "You know, it was just a few seasons ago. It seems like they have been here much longer, doesn't it?"

"A really awful thought has pushed its way to the front of my brain," Tawtanya said quietly. "You know how so many boys disappeared, and no one knows what happened to them? What if the boys were turned into Enforcers?"

"It is a theory. The timing of the boys going missing and the sudden appearance of the Enforcers, cannot be a coincidence. However, many more boys disappeared than we have Enforcers. What do you suppose happened to the rest of the boys?" Myana asked, continuing Tawtanya's chain of thought.

"I guess that they didn't make it. Whatever horrible method the scientists used to create the Enforcers may not work on every single boy. Of course, this is just a theory. I have no proof, and I don't know how to get it. Who would know where the scientists would do such horrible experiments? It would need to be an isolated place away from prying eyes. I have only been to the centers when we compete at the games. We aren't free to go just anywhere. The scientists could have laboratories tucked away in many places on this planet doing who knows what kind of awful experiments," Tawtanya said with horror emanating from her whispered voice.

"Parents who lost boys are very distressed. I don't think we dare share this thought with them. We are asking them to rebel against the Enforcers. If they suspect the Enforcers are their lost boys, what do you think they would do?" Myana asked.

"I suspect some would drop their weapons and would be slaughtered by the Enforcers. Others would probably try to kill the Enforcers to put their sons out of their misery. I doubt any of the parents would think it possible to change the Enforcers back to the boys. I suspect that is impossible," Tawtanya said. "It does explain why they only took boys. Most girls, except for maybe, you and me, wouldn't be strong enough to be turned into Enforcers. Isn't that a chilling thought? If the Chief Scientist thought we were becoming too much of a threat, that he would capture us and turn us into Enforcers...."

Stopping and standing still in the street, the two young women watched as the Enforcers in front of them slowly diminished in size as they continued to stomp further down the street. Soon the masses that parted to let them through merged back into the streets concealing the Enforcers from sight altogether.

CHAPTER THIRTY-TWO

Khrelyn felt disappointed when Yyemara sent word that she would not be joining him for the evening meal. The scientist locked herself away in her cabin for most of the time. She told Khrelyn at the previous dinner that she had much to cram into her head before she was placed on the planet Earth. Occasionally, Yyemara would practice her new language skills on Khrelyn. He found the sounds odd in most cases, but occasionally Yyemara would speak a language that sounded beautiful.

"What language are you speaking now?" Khrelyn recalled from the last meal they ate together.

Yyemara laughed with giddy delight. "They call that language French. You like how it sounds, don't you?"

Khrelyn admitted that it flowed nicely off her tongue. He was surprised when he asked how many languages she learned onboard the ship, and her reply was ten languages at present. Khrelyn marveled at her capacity to retain so much, and then he remembered that she was not really Surtarian.

The scientists lived on the planet Surtees for so long that most people had no recollection of them never being there. In fact, Ananaya's parents immigrated to Surtees with their parents from another planet when they were just infants. No living Surtarian knew from whence they came or how long ago for sure that they arrived. The present generation only knew from their grandparents that the scientists brought many advanced technologies that made life easier for the Surtarians at first. Like a jolt, Khrelyn heard Tawtanya's rants about how the scientists were destroying Surtees in his mind. 'No more science! No more Scientists...."

'What if Tawtanya was correct? What if this trip is just an expedition to find a new planet for the scientists to escape to once they destroy the planet Surtees...his home?' flooded thoughts into the young commander's head. Troubled by the thoughts, Khrelyn pushed his plate away and got up from the table. He hoped Tawtanya was safe back home on the planet. His fear for her life clouded his mind as he walked from the dining hall.

Returning to his duties helped to take the disquieting thoughts from his mind. There was much to do to make sure the cargo and his passenger arrived safely. Drop off was scheduled soon, and everything needed to be timed perfectly. Settling in front of his monitor, Khrelyn concentrated on the task at hand, and all thoughts of Tawtanya evaporated, like soft clouds dispersing as the gentle winds whisked them from the sky.

Yyemara nibbled absent-mindedly on her meal. The last crate, she needed to assume her new personality sat on the floor unpacked. She had already crammed more information into her head than she thought possible, but the fear of disappointing her father kept her working determinedly. Only her brief respite with Khrelyn kept her from serious meltdowns. Yyemara wished she could take a break and enjoyed the comradery with her new friend. She found his company pleasant when he wasn't asking veiled questions about her destination and her father's plans.

It would be hard for Khrelyn to understand why she followed Ananaya's plan without question, Yyemara thought to herself. Laughing softly, she knew that was a lie since Khrelyn was doing the same. He obviously had no idea why he was piloting the spacecraft towards this particular galaxy and planet once again. He had orders, and he was following them as blindly as Yyemara was herself. No, they were the same. They blindly followed their directives without knowledge of the greater plan. The difference between herself and Khrelyn was that Yyemara knew her father was a genius, and she would follow his directives without question because he was infallible. Khrelyn only did as he was told because he was trained to do so, and he loved space travel.

Feeling relief that her father was in charge, Yyemara opened the last crate and studied the contents. Everything that she would need to start her new life on Earth was lying before her.

CHAPTER THIRTY-THREE

Noryan rubbed his eyes. Coming out of the tunnel was always painful until his eyes adjusted to the light of day, even when it was now approaching dusk. The extremely long days of working below ground were crushing the spirits of even the youngest, hardiest men. The only reason that Noryan did not find himself totally despondent was the realization that the Enforcers seemed to be failing in health right along with the men who were doing all the labor.

Whispering to the man next to him, Noryan risked punishment by not remaining silent. "Have you noticed that one brut over there seems to be about to drop to his knees?"

The man next to him barely raised his eyes to glance at the Enforcer that Noryan was making reference to. He let his eyes drop quickly back to the man's head before him. He did not comment. He just kept putting one foot in front of the other, hoping to get back to their barracks to sleep until the break of the next day.

Sighing, Noryan felt sorry for his companion. It was obvious that he had lost all hope. Noryan knew he would not last much longer working in the tunnels. Without hope, the spirit died sooner than the body, but the body would follow rapidly thereafter. Noryan knew from experience that the man beside him would not be working much longer.

Noryan couldn't help but wonder where the man had come from. Did he have a family? No one talked about their previous lives. Once confined, it was as if their old selves no longer existed. Each man was just a vessel without identity. Noryan refused to become nothing. He felt his resolve to fight against despondency. Somehow, he would return to his family.

Barely, having closed his eyes, the alarm indicating that he must rise and begin another day of work, caused Noryan to wince. His mind, even in sleep, was working out a plan for escape. Stumbling to his feet, he noticed that the man he whispered to the evening before, seemed rigid, and Noryan knew he was dead before even going to his side.

A sharp crack of a whip on his back and harsh words to leave the scum, drove Noryan to the door to march to the hall for a small bit of food before he started his day's labor. Looking back, Noryan saw the man's body being dragged out the door by an Enforcer.

Barely having a chance to swallow some water to force the dry bread down his throat, Noryan was being herded out the door to form a line to trudge to their day's work. Noryan deliberately stayed at the back of the line. He didn't know why, but something deep down inside of him told him to be watchful this day.

As the line moved slowly towards the tunnel, Noryan noted how many Enforcers were assigned to guard duty that day. Scanning the group of distorted figures, Noryan noted that the one weak Enforcer that he spotted the previous day was lagging behind and bringing up the tail. Noryan deliberately slowed his pace to allow the three other men who were behind him to overtake him. He casually lagged behind, maintaining the same slow pace of the frail Enforcer.

The Enforcer didn't seem to notice that Noryan was no longer on the heels of the last laborer, but was several footfalls behind.

Coughing loudly, the Enforcer doubled over and dropped to his knees.

Noryan instinctively knew this was his only chance. He needed to find cover before one of the other Enforcers noted that the ill Enforcer was down. Sprinting to the cover of trees, Noryan glanced back to see if his departure was noted by anyone and was relieved to see that he was in the clear.

There was no sense delaying even for a moment, so Noryan continued to run deeper into the woods in the direction where the sun would set later that day. His sparse breakfast would not sustain him at a fast run for long, but Noryan knew he needed to get as far away as possible before slowing his pace. Finally, heaving with exhaustion and doubling over with a stitch in his side, Noryan sank to the ground behind a large boulder to recuperate and to think.

He knew basically, by the setting and rising sun, where he was in reference to his farm, but the choices for his escape were minimal. He either would need to climb and cross a mountain range or travel south for days until he would reach civilization. Knowing the Enforcers would assume he would take the easier route, Noryan decided the climb would be the most difficult but the most sensible route to take to avoid being recaptured.

If he were recaptured, he would be killed. There would be no mercy. The Enforcers were not programmed to be merciful. Noryan wondered whether the dying Enforcer noticed his escape and whether he would remain alive long enough to tell the other Enforcers if he even noticed. Not knowing one way of the other, only made Noryan more desperate to keep moving.

Without food or water, Noryan was most likely going to die on the mountain tops anyway, was his thoughts as he pulled himself back to his feet, taking note of the terrain and the direction he must head. Taking a deep breath, Noryan started his trek towards the mountains easily seen above the dense woods.

As he moved through the forest, Noryan kept his eyes open for anything edible. Wild berries or nuts from certain trees would help to sustain him. It would be possible to find dew in the early morning on leaves, and he would take in as much moisture as possible from the succulent plants on the forest floor. Living off the land as a farmer all his life was definitely in his favor at this moment.

Noryan moved quickly with stops only when he found a few precious berries. He savored the juice as it trickled down his throat, not quite quenching his thirst but giving him hope. Finding a small amount of water that settled into a small dip in a boulder was a life send. Lapping every ounce of liquid-like an animal, Noryan realized that he had become no different than a wild creature at the hands of the Enforcers.

Setting his eyes on the path he needed to continue, Noryan settled into a comfortable pace. He no longer felt the intense fear that settled over him as he skirted away from his prison. He knew that Enforcers could be on his trail, but he felt certain he was a half-day ahead of them if they were tracking him. However, a half-day was not much of a buffer from certain death, and Noryan knew his diminished strength would not sustain him for long.

How long he had been a prisoner was fuzzy. He knew it was a very long time. He was always strong with excellent stamina, from working hard as a farmer, but his frame was now skeletal from lack of nutrients. Hard labor kept his muscles taut within his thin frame, but stamina was hard to sustain. The only reason he was able to get up each morning was the thought that someday he would escape.

That same determination stirred Noryan onward even when his muscles were cramping from lack of water and essential minerals.

Dropping to the ground often to rub out a severe cramp now seemed to be part of his normal routine as he pushed himself on towards the base of the mountain.

The land seemed to gradually rise as he pushed himself forward. Finding shelter to sleep for a short time was another item he continually searched for as much as for food and water. Finding a plant with seeds, Noryan gathered as many as he could carry.

Continuing his trek, Noryan discovered two boulders at the end of the woods before the edge of the mountain. He discovered he could push himself into a natural opening between them for a short rest. Dropping to his knees, he crawled as far back into the opening as possible and sat picking the seeds with his fingers. Chewing each mouthful of seeds until they became mush, Noryan tried to get every bit of nutrients from the plants. When the last little seed was licked from his fingers, Noryan allowed himself to sleep.

A disgusting smell filled his nose. Noryan dreamed the Enforcers were prodding him towards the tunnel. He felt the sting of the whip on his back and winced in pain. Suddenly startled awake, Noryan hit his head on the boulder as he sat up erect.

The smell lingered from his dream. Rubbing his head, Noryan lay back down on the ground in his shelter. Sniffing quietly, Noryan realized he was not dreaming. The odor was real, and he knew the smell. There was at least one Enforcer near. Noryan would never forget the stench of the foul creatures who tormented his every waking moment ever since he was captured and imprisoned.

Fearing to move a finger, Noryan listened intently. The odor was not as strong as it was when he first awakened. Did that mean the Enforcers moved on away from his hiding place? Not feeling brave enough to leave his shelter to find out, Noryan remained still, thinking about what he should do next.

The need to relieve himself is what finally drove Noryan out of his protected small cave. Crawling out between the boulders took time, but finally, Noryan was back into the edge of the woods. The mountain stood before him. The Enforcers would spot him quickly once he started his ascent. That was the choice he made when he was sure the Enforcers would assume he would take the longer, easier route through the woods to escape. Now Noryan wondered if he made the wrong choice.

Taking care of his personal needs, Noryan kept to the trees until the ground started to slowly rise to meet the base of the mountain. Continuing to sniff the air without catching the scent of the Enforcer emboldened Noryan as he moved quickly forward to reach his goal. Leaving the trees, Noryan started his ascent up the mountain, knowing that he could be now in full view of the Enforcers.

Scrambling up the jagged and craggy ledges with small rocks being dislodged by his feet, made the climb difficult and noisy. Often the rocks cascading down under his feet caused Noryan to slip and slide back down nearly a rod in distance before being able to catch himself on a ledge. Frustrated by the loss in the gain to reach the top, and the pain he felt in his arms and legs, Noryan almost decided to descend and try another route when the wind picked up the awful odor of the Enforcers.

Noryan dared not look down to see if they were standing at the base of the mountain looking up at him. His fear drove him forward with renewed unbounded energy. He knew what would be his fate if the Enforcers caught him.

Reaching another ledge, Noryan looked down to see his pursuer was a single Enforcer. He was climbing after him. The Enforcer seemed to be struggling with the climb as much as Noryan had himself. Noryan turned his gaze upward to study the mountain to find the best route from where he was.

Seeing a possible route, Noryan started his climb with even greater determination. Grabbing handholds and searching for places to secure his feet, Noryan continued to climb without looking down. He would know when the Enforcer was closing in on him by the stronger stench offending his nostrils.

Onward and upward was the goal. Noryan continued to make slow progress with every muscle in his body, screaming out in pain. Reaching another small ledge just in time as a muscle cramp tore into Noryan's calf. Trying desperately to rub the muscle to relax it so he could continue his climb, Noryan was aware that the Enforcer was making gains on him.

Looking down, Noryan could easily make out the gross, distorted features of his tormentor. After seasons of living with these creatures, he was able to tell one brute from another. This particular Enforcer was even more vicious than most. He knew he could not let this foul being catch him.

Noryan reached for large rocks and hurtled them down upon the Enforcer, missing him more often than not. Realizing he had no other weapon available, Noryan got to his feet and reached for his next handhold and continued his climb carelessly.

As the Enforcer reached the ledge that Noryan just vacated, he knew it was just a matter of moments before the Enforcer would grab his leg and send him crashing down the mountainside to his sure death. Peddling his feet against the mountain to find a small foothold, released a cascade of gravel from under his feet.

The small rocks tumbled down upon the Enforcer's head, causing growls of anger to erupt from the monster. As he scowled his displeasure and grunted a threat towards his prey, Noryan doubled his efforts, kicking even more loose rocks down to hit the Enforcer.

Finally, finding a foothold, Noryan heaved himself up to the next landing, where a large boulder rested in front of a fissure. Noryan wedged behind the boulder, leaned back against the wall of the crevice, curling his body while placing his legs against the boulder to push with all his might. Straining with intense effort, he felt the boulder move slightly. Renewed energy again swept through him with this small success, and he put all his efforts into pushing as hard as he could.

The Enforcer was heard growling another threat as his hand found the same hold Noryan used just moments ago. Seeing the Enforcer's hand and knowing the rest of the creature would soon be standing over him, Noryan gritted his teeth and allowed a primal scream to rush from his lungs as he exerted all his strength into one last push.

The boulder moved to the edge of the crag just as the Enforcer's face appeared over the ledge. A look of horror crossed the Enforcer's face as he realized his predicament. The boulder crashed into his face and carried the Enforcer back down the mountain, where he landed with the stone bouncing off his body as it continued to roll down into the trees below.

Noryan dared to peek over the ledge, and his mind was flooded with relief as he saw the body of the Enforcer lying shattered on the ground far below. No pity was felt by the farmer, only a sense of liberation, as he allowed himself to sit and rest. Noryan would continue his climb once his strength returned.

Unfortunately, his strength didn't return as quickly as he hoped. His body was fatigued, and his lack of food didn't help matters. If the ledge were broader, Noryan might have stayed longer, but a need for food and water drove him to his feet. Looking up, Noryan noted birds flittering on the next ledge. Hoping beyond hope that the birds may have a nest with eggs, gave Noryan the boost he needed to continue on.

As he approached the next ledge, the birds frantically dove down upon Noryan with sharp little beaks tweaking his skin and causing bleeding. Irritating more than painful, Noryan did not let go of his handhold to swat the little creatures away. Hoping the next attack would not be aimed at his eyes, he climbed faster to avoid that consequence. As he finally pulled himself up on the ledge, Noryan saw the nest was filled with small baby birds. His hopes for an egg breakfast were dashed at the sight of the small birds.

The parents continued their attack with fury. Desperation to save their offspring made the birds emboldened in their attack. Noryan covered his face with his hands and tried to shoo the angry birds away with the flailing of arms. Deciding quickly that he needed to abandon his breakfast, Noryan stood and made his way to the top of the mountain, leaving the birds to settle back into their nests with their hatchlings.

Reaching the peak of the mountain exhilarated Noryan. He stood and looked down on the farmlands below through the ghastly orange haze that hovered over the land. He knew his own farm was within the patchwork of colors that lay beneath the haze. Breathing in the fresh, thin air on the mountain top, Noryan stood only for a short time before he started the descent and long trek around the bay.

CHAPTER THIRTY-FOUR

"You will be speaking to the farmers soon," Myana said to Tawtanya. "I need to remind you that this group of people see the Enforcers less often than the city dwellers. Chances are that they may not be receptive to your speech. You should talk more about the UberBugs and the loss of their heritage crops to stir them to action. It is also possible that some of these farmers have lost their sons. That could also trigger a response."

"I know the farmers are suspicious of outsiders. I will just be another outsider," Tawtanya responded, not feeling sure of herself.

"You aren't just an outsider. We are both champions. Farmers love champions as much as anyone else. Remember, you are the celebrated one everywhere on Surtees. It won't be any different here," Myana said to boost Tawtanya's failing confidence.

"I hope you are right. We need to stir the farming communities into action, as well. They tend to be suspicious of city dwellers, and I am a city dweller first and a champion secondly."

"I don't agree with you, Tawtanya. You are a champion first and a city dweller secondly. Now, come on and stop the negative talk. You will be great. The farmers will love you," Myana said as she turned Tawtanya towards the podium.

Tawtanya took the stage and looked upon the faces of the common folk. She saw hopelessness in their eyes. Seasons of crops failing, animals withering when they should be thriving, and the normal hardships of farming showed in their worn faces. Even the children looked serious and showed no joy. Tawtanya felt sorrow for these people.

"People, are you tired of working crops that fail?" Tawtanya started her speech almost in a whisper. "Do you barely have enough food for your family with little left to sell? Do you remember the days of plenty when your heritage crops filled the market places across the planet? Do you remember the words of the scientists that the UberBugs would kill the weeds, and you would have greater success with crops than ever? Do you remember the other lies the scientists told you as they took away your strongest animals for their experiments, leaving you with the scrawny, weak animals for your breeding stock? Of course, you remember all that because you are living lives of desperation now due to the lies. You need to stand together to make the good days return before it is too late!" Tawtanya said as her voice rose louder and louder from the quiet start.

Murmurs of agreement started slowly and softly in the crowd. Tawtanya felt she was making headway with the farming community when suddenly, a man walked in from the fields close to the village. The startled reaction made it clear that this man was known by the villagers.

What amazed Tawtanya and Myana the most was the fear in the eyes of the villagers as the man walked closer. Quickly, the women grabbed their children by their hands and raced for their homes or to the rykes by which they came to the town. The men huddled together as a mass to confront the lone man.

"You are going to bring the Enforcers down on us! Get out of this village now!" one man yelled with the others supporting his command.

"I just came through to get my belongings so I can go and find my wife and family. You can't fault me for that," the lone man said in rebuttal.

"You need to go now and never come back. The way it is, the Enforcers will be knocking on each of our doors looking for you. Chances are, we will pay for your actions. Just leave now and quickly!" another man in the crowd said vehemently.

As the crowd dispersed rapidly to their own homes and farms, the man stood looking completely dejected. Myana nudged Tawtanya forward to talk to the man.

"Where have you come from, Syr?" asked Tawtanya as nicely as possible, feeling sorry for the man by the greeting he just received at the hands of his neighbors and supposed friends.

The kind words were not lost on the man. "I escaped the internment camp. I suppose my neighbors are correct. I probably have set the Enforcers upon this village. I didn't mean to cause them any harm. I just need some valuables that I hid away at my farm to sell along the way in my search to find my family."

"You can travel with us," Myana broke into the conversation. "We can take you to your farm in our ryke and then on to your destination.

Noryan cast his eyes down to the ground. He was more than appreciative to have people being nice to him after all these seasons. "I am grateful to you beyond words, but I can't put you in danger. You heard the men from my village. The Enforcers will be after me, and they will hurt you if you help me. Thank you, but I need to go on alone."

Tawtanya looked carefully at the man before her. She was saddened to see how skeletal he was under his ragged clothing. His eyes were hollowed and looked almost defeated except for a tiny glint of hope that she could see when she looked directly into those deep dark-circled eyes. Letting her eyes check out his upper body, Tawtanya could see multiple scars on his arms where his clothing was ripped away from whiplashing, she assumed.

"You are exhausted," Tawtanya said forcefully. "We will risk the Enforcers. You will come with us."

Noryan started to protest. Myana casually came beside him and linked her arm into Noryan's. "Come on…. I have you. It isn't very far to our ryke. Now, which way is your farm?"

Reluctantly Noryan walked the many steps to the waiting ryke. He could feel the eyes of the many villagers peering through their covered windows. He knew their fear would be his undoing.

As the three jostled around in the ryke, the two women asked many questions. Noryan answered as best as he could with the fact that time had almost come to a standstill at the prison. One day was exactly as the day before, with the exception as to who died on certain days.

"How is it that you were taken?" Myana asked bluntly.

Noryan rubbed his head as if he was trying to pry out the memory with his bare hands. "It is all one big nightmare now. Let me see if I can backtrack in my brain to the beginning."

Noryan seemed to be reliving his life in reverse as he closed his eyes and winced many times. "It was such a long time ago that I felt happy. My farm was thriving, and my three little boys were the joy of my existence. Everything seemed to change when the scientist took an interest in farming. At first, it was subtle changes that were supposed to benefit us. However, season after season found us in worse situations with bad crops and weak animals. When my oldest son disappeared, I couldn't stand it any longer. I ranted to my wife to let off steam, but I told her repeatedly that she was never to repeat anything that I said at home. I guess the stress was too much, and she told her best friend…and her friend told someone else...and once I found out my wife betrayed my trust, I knew it was only a matter of time before the Enforcers would come for me...as they eventually did. However, knowing the inevitable, I was able to send my family to safety, or at least, I hope they are safe...."

"Why is it that we are going to your farm now. Won't it be in the hands of strangers?" Tawtanya asked.

"We aren't actually going to need to go to the farmhouse. I buried valuables in the woods nearby. I am hoping no one found my hiding place. I deliberately hid the items where farming would be impractical. I believe I can retrieve the items without being observed. I hope that I can sell the valuables so I can continue my journey to find my wife and two remaining boys," Noryan explained.

Remaining quiet for the rest of the short trip to the farmland allowed all three to process what Noryan just told them. Myana broke the silence. "Where is the internment camp from here, and how many people are being held as prisoners?"

"Wow! I can only give you a vague count on the prisoners. I was in one dorm, and there were many more. However, I didn't mingle with any of the other prisoners—just the ones in my dorm. We were assigned the task of digging a tunnel. I can only assume, the other dorms had similar tasks. Why we were digging a tunnel is something that I was not privy to the answer. We were hardly allowed to speak, let alone ask questions," Noryan said, and then he continued. "As to where the camp is, I can point in the direction, but I can't possibly tell you how far it is from here. It is over that mountain and through a forest. I lost track of how long I traveled, but I think it is only a few days from here."

"What would it take to free the other prisoners?" Tawtanya asked.

"An army!" Noryan said flatly. "Do you have one?"

"Not yet," Myana answered. "We are working on it."

Noryan sat puzzled. "You mean there is a resistance movement on Surtees? How is that possible?"

Myana beamed. "You are looking at it. It was your lucky day when you stumbled into the village while we were there."

A cloud passed over Noryan's face. "The two of you are the only hope for Surtees? Excuse me if I don't get too excited."

Myana laughed. "The movement is happening as we speak. Tawtanya, here, is the Champion of Surtees. People listen to her. In the cities, we are seeing many people roused to action. Some are banding together to take down Enforcers. You might be surprised what many can do when stirred to action."

"What I saw of the villagers, I can't get too excited. It didn't seem like they were being stirred into action to me," Noryan said with sarcasm.

"Before you came, the villagers were actually starting to see reason. They were murmuring their discontent in the group. I believe if they really stop and think about how their lives have changed, and not for good, that they will band together and become a force."

"They are too isolated and afraid. Believe me, I know what I am talking about. Remember, I lived amongst those people. They are scared all the time. They won't help defeat the Enforcers."

Myana said almost menacingly, "They will when they realize the sons stolen become Enforcers. Wouldn't you fight to keep another son from being made into one of those hideous monsters?"

Gasping audibly, Noryan could only stare at Myana. The thought was too awful to even think. Finally, a hoarse, choked sentence was emitted from Noryan. "That can't be possible."

"We can't prove it yet, but that is what we believe. How else can one explain the disappearance of the boys and the sudden appearance of Enforcers?" Myana asked.

"That is too horrible to believe, let alone think. If you are correct, one of those monsters that beat me and goaded me could have been my eldest son." Noryan covered his eyes and wept. "I can't accept that, and neither will the farmers."

Tawtanya patted Noryan on his back. "You don't want to lose another son to the scientists, do you? I am sure once the horror sinks into the heads of the other farmers, they, too, will be willing to fight. It isn't just the loss of crops and livelihood now."

"You will need proof. I told you the farmers are timid and not easily stirred to action," Noryan spoke.

"You sound as if you believe us," Myana said. "We will find out where the boys are being turned. We will stop it!"

As they approached the site in the woods, Noryan remembered his hiding spot. The ryke pulled to a stop. "I will go with you and help as best as I can," Myana said as she hopped down off the ryke. "We carry tools as well as supplies in the back of the ryke. Come on. Show me the way.".

Tawtanya barely allowed herself to relax when the two returned with a bag that took the two of them to carry. Tawtanya, noting the bag was not that large, realized just how weak Noryan was from his journey. Stowing the bag in the back with the tools, Myana and Noryan jumped onto the seat beside Tawtanya.

"Now, where are we going?" Tawtanya asked.

"There is a small village just southwest of the capital city of Surtees, where I hope to find my wife and sons. Unfortunately, the most direct route is through the Capital City Science Center. We could take the dirt roads, but it would take three to four times longer, and I am sure you ladies have other obligations than ryking me around."

"It will be more dangerous to go through the capital since more Enforcers patrol the city. However, we seem to have a certain amount of immunity from the Enforcers. If you aren't visible, we should be able to pass through the city unmolested. Before we reach the outskirts, we will make a hiding place for you in the ryke. I think that will get us through safely," Myana said almost cheerfully.

"Why would you have protection from the Enforcers since you are rabble-rousers?" Noryan asked.

"To tell you the truth, we don't know. What we do know is that the Enforcers seem to be afraid to touch Tawtanya. As long as she is with us, we are most likely safe," Myana answered.

"How completely rude we have been, Myana," Tawtanya said exasperatedly. "Noryan is starving, and we haven't even thought to give him food or drink. I can't believe we have been that thoughtless."

"You are completely right, Tawtanya. I will crawl into the back of the ryke while you drive, and I will find food for our guest."

Noryan accepted the provisions from Myana's hand along with a jug of a clear liquid that was not water. Wolfing down the food at first, Noryan realized he would soon be sick if he did not slow down.

"You can't begin to imagine how good this taste. I haven't eaten much more than moldy bread or a thin gruel since I became a prisoner. I watched many Surtarians die of starvation or dehydration in the camp," Noryan said sadly.

Tears escaped Tawtanya's eyes as she stared straight forward at the road ahead. Resolving to end the tyranny, Tawtanya's resolution was strengthened, and she jutted her jaw forward and clenched her teeth.

CHAPTER THIRTY-FIVE

Everything was ready for Yyemara to be teleported on the planet Earth. The items needed were piled on the platform, ready to be dropped at the exact coordinates indicated by the Chief Scientist. Khrelyn stood ready to do his part in the relocation of the young scientist. Khrelyn knew he was going to miss Yyemara's company on the return trip.

As Yyemara made her appearance on the platform, Khrelyn could hardly recognize the scientist. The clothing she wore seemed oddly exotic compared to the utilitarian dress of Surtees. Yyemara stood just a fraction taller in shoes that seemed outrageously uncomfortable and ill-equipped for any type of terrain. Yyemara's hair, always styled in a practical bun, was now loose on her shoulders, and her eyes were heavily accented with color on her lids and outlining the shape of her eyes.

Khrelyn said nothing since his post on the spaceship required professionality, but his shocked look on his face could not hide the fact from Yyemara that she no longer looked like herself in his eyes. She admitted that she didn't recognize herself either when she looked in the mirror. Yyemara followed her directives perfectly, and she would continue to do so. She was no longer Yyemara while on Earth, she was Ava Padden. From here on, everyone will call her by that foreign-sounding name.

Ava Padden was Yyemara's new identity. Ananaya went to extreme trouble to find the exact right person and history for the new persona that Yyemara would become. The village, as well as all the people who would know Ava was no longer an issue. Two major earthquakes caused an avalanche to cover the small Swiss Alps village, killing the townsfolk. No one was left to identify the real Ava Padden.

Ava would start her career as a professor at a university in Switzerland that was renowned for its work in genetics. Everything was carefully planned out, and all that Ava would require was now being sent ahead for her future use.

The only thing necessary was to teleport Ava onto the ground near the university. The timetable was established before leaving Surtees as to when Ava would build her empire based on genetics. The currency was placed in accounts around the planet for Ava's use to buy companies to continue Ananaya's ultimate goal.

Settling herself, she walked towards Khrelyn. "I am in your hands," Yyemara/Ava said with a smile. "I depend on you to place me exactly at the coordinates and time that my father prescribed. I know it will be some time before we see each other again, but I want you to know that I have enjoyed meeting you and getting to know you as a person. I will look forward to the next time you will make this same flight to bring me supplies. If you would be so kind, would you mind bringing one favorite item that I forgot when you return?"

Khrelyn wrinkled his forehead in puzzlement. "And what might that be, Yyemara?"

"Please, from now on, you must refer to me as Ava. That item can be found in the science center. My mother, Kaycee'na, will be able to retrieve it for you. It is my only childhood toy that I kept. I don't know why it is so important to me, but I would really like to have it," Ava said, feeling suddenly foolish.

"What shall I ask for when I see your mother?" Khrelyn asked once more.

"It is a small soft doll that was made to resemble me when I was a toddler," Ava said. "It will help me to stay rooted in Surtees while I'm still breathing the air of Earth. Oh, and if you would, please bring me a bag of my favorite delicacies as well, I would appreciate it. There is a dried fruit that grows on Surtees that has such a delicious taste. I know this fruit does not grow anywhere on Earth. Please!" Ava said, revealing Yyemara inside of the new body Ava occupied.

"I promise I will bring both items on my return," Khrelyn said as he held out his hand to bind the promise.

"It is time if you are ready. We only have a small window of opportunity to place you exactly where you need to go," Khrelyn said softly.

Ava took her position on the platform and stood quietly with a forced smile. She had never experienced teleportation and was visibly nervous. Trying to put on a brave front with her forced smile was the best that she could manage.

"When I return, I will bring your requested items in person," Khrelyn said, giving Yyemara the reassurance that teleportation was so safe that Khrelyn would even make the trip himself. "Ready?"

With a slight nod of Ava's head, Khrelyn gave the technician a sign to begin. With a shimmering light, Ava disappeared.

Khrelyn turned to his staff. "Time to return to Surtees."

CHAPTER THIRTY-SIX

"The trip in the ryke being pulled by a beast of burden was slow. Noryan sat in the seat with the two athletes until getting closer to the science center. Myana commented that Noryan looked seasons younger after only a few days with some food in his stomach and rest that he so desperately needed.

"It won't be long now until we need to hide you. Soon, we will start to meet more traffic on this road, and that could mean Enforcers, as well. Are you ready to curl up into a ball until we pass through the capital?" Myana asked of their guest and traveling companion.

"I surely have been in worse situations. Until we made the tunnel large enough to stand, we had to work on our bellies to cut through the rock. There were more times than I like to recount, where workers were crushed to death when the rock roof or walls gave way," Noryan said with little expression.

"I can't even imagine the atrocities that you saw and experienced," Tawtanya said. "It makes me all the more determined to put a stop to what the evil scientists are doing!"

Noryan did not comment. His mind was lost in remembrance, and the horror showed on his face. Myana changed the subject jolting Noryan from his memories.

"I think we should stop here. It might be advisable for us to take a break, relieve ourselves, and get some lunch before pushing through the city."

"You have a point. We could use a break," Tawtanya agreed. "While you two stretch your legs, I will pull out some food for us to nibble on. One thing the scientists were not able to ruin is the fruit trees. I guess even they knew the fruit was at its best and would not get any better with genetic prodding."

"I did have a nice orchard on the farm. You are right. The scientists never insisted on taking a cutting from our trees to graft to other trees. Odd, they did not think of that," Noryan mused.

It wasn't a long stop. Before long, Noryan found himself without a view and being bumped around with the supplies in the back of the ryke. The two women softened his hiding place with as much cushioning as possible, but other than their change of clothing, not much else was soft. Noryan was content since he was accustomed to sleeping on the floor with hardly a blanket to keep him warm.

As they drew closer to the city, Noryan could occasionally catch snatches of muted conversation as people walked past the ryke. He knew he needed to be very quiet so as not to be discovered.

As Tawtanya was recognized, crowds started to gather, and it was more difficult to keep the trydox moving forward. Voices erupted in unison, "No more science! No more scientists!"

Desperate to keep the ryke moving out of the city to get Noryan to safety, Tawtanya smiled and kept clicking with her tongue to the trydox team to hasten their pace. Myana waved unconcernedly to the people gathering.

"People of Surtees, Tawtanya will be back soon. At the moment, we have an engagement elsewhere. Continue to stand together, and we will be back to lend you our support and encouragement. Keep the faith! Keep Surtees safe!" Myana yelled, with cheers erupting throughout the streets.

Noryan cringed when he smelled the Enforcers. They were pushing their way through the crowd, and for the first time, the people were not dispersing as they usually did. Noryan couldn't see the crowd from his hiding place in the ryke, but he could hear the defiance in the people's voices as they jeered the Enforcers who were now pushing and lifting their arms to strike individuals.

"You there in the ryke—troublemakers. Get down from your seat now!" One of the Enforcers yelled in anger. He was sure if he took the two women into custody, the crowd would leave.

When Myana and Tawtanya didn't move, the Enforcer's face grew even more distorted with rage. Marching to the ryke, he reached up and grabbed Myana from her seat, pulling her roughly to the ground.

The crowd's reaction was instantaneous. Screaming insults at the Enforcer, people started to throw anything within their reach at the creature.

The second Enforcer quickly stepped to his partner's side. "Stop! Leave the women. Don't you recognize the one still in the cart?"

Releasing Myana's arm, the first Enforcer stared hard at Tawtanya. Without another word, he and his partner turned to leave but deliberately struck several people in the crowd as they did so.

The crowd continued cheered wildly while picking up their fallen patriots. "Tawtanya! Tawtanya! Tawtanya!

As the odor dissipated, Noryan allowed his held breath to escape his lips. Just a whiff of the foul creatures caused his mind to shrivel in fear as memories flooded back from the seasons being tortured by the Enforcers. Finally, talking himself into a more relaxed state, Noryan listened to Tawtanya's reaction to the crowd.

"People of Surtees, you just won your first battle. You stood up to the Chief Scientist by standing your ground against his Enforcers. It is a message Ananaya will receive loud and clear. You can no longer tolerate Ananaya destroying your planet. If you accept what he has done, then you will surely die or find yourself in servitude for the rest of your lives. You WILL take your planet back and live free and happy lives without interference from the scientists. Go now and spread the word. We will fight for Surtees. Raise your voices to the community. Let them hear you as you leave this street. WE WILL FIGHT FOR SURTEES!"

The crowd answered back with unified voices. 'WE WILL FIGHT FOR SURTEES!"

As the crowd marched the streets of the capital city, more people joined, and the chants could be heard for k-rods as Tawtanya and Myana moved the trydox forward, hoping to get through the rest of the city without any further incidence. Once back in the countryside and with the outline of the city far out of sight, Tawtanya pulled the ryke to a stop.

"You can come out now, Noryan. We are far from any peering eyes," Tawtanya said happily.

As packages moved and slipped from side to side, Noryan's hand was the first sign of life. Finally, his head and body followed as he struggled to get to his feet out from under all the supplies.

"That was too close for comfort back there. When I smelled the Enforcers, I almost lost it. How is it that the Enforcers gave you clearance?" Noryan asked curiously with astonishment ringing in his voice.

Myana answered. "We don't know. All we know is that the Enforcers leave us alone. We don't know if Ananaya has given them a command to leave us be. We are as astounded as you to their response each and every time we encounter them."

Tawtanya added, "Let us count our blessings and hope this good fortune never ends. I will dread being put into the internment camps if they are as horrible as you describe."

"They are more horrible than I described. Words can't define what I have seen and lived through," Noryan said sadly, and the two young women let it alone without further comment.

"Time for food. I can only imagine how hungry you must be. It has been quite some time since you have eaten, and I know you need as much food as you can consume to put some weight back on your body," Myana said cheerfully, trying to leave the last conversation for another time and place.

Pulling sacks of supplies from out of the ryke, the two women set up an area under a tree where the three of them could eat peacefully and recuperate from the ordeal of the capital city. A blanket was spread, and food and drink were passed to Noryan, who waited until the two women had food before them as well.

Taking a piece of fruit, Noryan took a bite, and the juices ran down his chin. "I don't know how long it has been since I tasted anything as good as this pyke fruit. We never got anything other than watered-down gruel or moldy bread. I feel like a human again, just eating this fruit."

"You never lost your humanity otherwise; you would be dead right now. Your driving source or soul is what makes you human. That is what got you out of that camp," Myana said as she, too, bit into the pyke fruit.

"If you want something that makes you feel human again, wait until you see what we have as dessert!" Tawtanya said with a twinkle in her eye.

Myana laughed. "I don't know how this girl stays so slim with her appetite for sweets. She is right, though, you are going to enjoy the dessert."

"Nothing could be better than this pyke fruit," Noryan said as he took another bite to savor.

"Just you wait," Tawtanya said.

When the break was over, nothing remained in the site under the trees. The trydox was fed and watered as they ate their dessert. Noryan commented that the savory pastry was perfect and better than Tawtanya teased. Once they were all packed and settled into the ryke, they continued the journey.

"The village where your wife and sons may be living is not too far from here. Will you recognize your sister-in-law's dwelling once we arrive?" Tawtanya asked.

"It is a small village, very near the Astro Science factories. We only made the trip once together as a family, but I will remember how to get to her door," Noryan replied.

Noryan sat puzzled. He didn't remember a wall surrounding the small village where he and his family visited his sister-in-law many seasons ago. Scratching his head in bewilderment, he spoke out loud to his traveling companions.

"I don't remember a gated wall, at all. Has my brain become mush from seasons of hard work?" Noryan queried.

"No, your brain is fine. Many of the smaller villages have built walls around themselves since Enforcers began roaming Surtees. I guess it makes them feel safer, but what they don't realize is that it is the fear itself that imprisons them. Some of the common folk are so afraid that they will inform on their neighbors just to gain favor with the scientists. It really is a shame," Myana answered. "I guess you know that from experience since it was your wife's best friend that turned you in."

As they moved into the village, curiosity roused children first from their games to see who entered their commune. Adults left their chores to peer out windows or their gardens to see as well. No one spoke to the trio as they made their way through narrow streets.

"This is the place; I am sure," Noryan said as Tawtanya pulled the trydox to a stop in front of a small dwelling. Getting off the seat, Noryan tapped quietly on the door, feeling somehow nervous when he told himself that he should be excited.

The door opened slowly and cautiously. Merlynn's jaw dropped in surprise, and then horror crept over her face. She hissed, "Why are you here? Go away! You will bring the Enforcers down on us! Go away now!" Her eyes darted fearfully back and forth down the streets hoping no one was watching.

Myana jumped from the seat angrily. "This man just walked k-rods through the mountains to get to you. Why are you treating him badly? What is wrong with you? Look at him...I said, look at him!" Myana continued with vehemence. "This man is a walking skeleton. He has endured more tragedy to be with you and his sons than you can ever imagine!"

Merlynn said with a quivering voice, "If he loves his sons, he will go away. Does he want them to endure what he has endured? No, Noryan, you must go away and leave us in peace. The Enforcers will come for you, but they will take our sons as well. Please, for our sake, leave now before anyone knows who you are...." Stepping back inside, Merlynn closed the door, and the lock could be heard clicking in place.

Noryan stood frozen. He could not digest what just happened to him. His whole reason to live was just taken from him.

Myana stood next to him. "Come with us, Noryan. You have work to do." Turning the man physically by the shoulders, she gently guided him back to the ryke. Tears streamed down his face as he climbed up on the seat next to the two gallant women.

As the ryke rumbled along the rutted road, Noryan sat silent. The two women glanced at each other and felt enormous sympathy for the man.

Almost in a whisper, the women heard Noryan's next words. "I want to join the rebellion. I can't start a new life until the scientists are overthrown, and the Enforcers are all gone...forever. I want to free the people in the internment camps first. Can you help me?"

CHAPTER THIRTY-SEVEN

The countryside where Yyemara landed was not unfamiliar. The Spaceprobes sent by Khrelyn many seasons earlier, and his previous flights returned with information, including images of the planet Earth. Yyemara studied every aspect of the probes while in flight to the planet. Her crates were stashed in hiding places to be retrieved as needed, but now, she must appear at her new assignment with as little suspicion as possible. She knew Ananaya planned every detail for her success, including the automobile simulator required to maneuver around in her new country.

Finding the ground transport on earth easy to maneuver, Yyemara drove the few miles to the university where she would function as a staff member for a while. Ananaya said the posting would be for a very short time, just long enough to become known as a specialist in genetics on the planet Earth. Afterward, Yyemara would follow Ananaya's directives as to which companies to purchase, and her work would truly begin. The time at the university could be considered a small break from her real work, but Yyemara knew Ananaya expected her to be working hard even while at the university.

As Yyemara approached the stately buildings of the university, she marveled that Earth humans were more advanced than she supposed. Yes, she had seen images from the probes, but being on Earth was more spectacular than she imagined. The air was fresh, and the buildings were impressive, with each one being built from stones many generations ago. The craftsmanship was obvious. How else could the buildings still be standing for the many seasons since they were built? Yyemara learned they were constructed by many men working with their hands.

Ananaya built a capital city with a skyway transportation system unequaled to any place on this planet. On Surtees, only the elite scientists had this unique transportation. All others traveled by trydox and ryke. Here on Earth, everyone enjoyed driving ground vehicles of their choice.

Looking around, Yyemara saw a place to park her vehicle. Taking only a briefcase supplied by her father, Yyemara walked up the stairs for the first time, to the entrance of the administrative offices to meet the Dean of the university to introduce herself.

Stopping at the desk where the secretary greeted her, Yyemara was gratified that her father simulated this event for her perfectly. Yyemara noted that her own clothing seemed to be appropriate, judging by the attire of the lady standing before her. A smile crossed the mature face of the secretary as she extended her hand in greeting.

"You must be Ava Padden. We have been looking forward to your arrival. Dean Wilhelm will be right with you. May I offer you a cup of coffee?" Jolene asked.

"Merci, I would love a cup," Yyemara said, using some French to make known the fact that she could converse in either language.

Smiling, Jolene left to retrieve the cup of coffee. Before she could return, Dean Wilhelm walked out of his office, shaking a tall man's hand. "Welcome to our staff. Go and get settled into your office."

As the tall man left, he gave Yyemara an appreciative look from her toes to her head and smiled. Yyemara coldly stared back. No man ever looked at her like that on Surtees. If they had, her father would have sent them to the rehabilitation camp. Yyemara told herself that this may well be something she will need to get used to.

"Ms. Padden, I presume. Will you come into my office?" Dean Wilhelm said as he stepped back to hold the door open. Jolene followed behind Yyemara with the coffee on a tray.

Indicating a chair in front of his enormous desk, Yyemara sat gracefully. The cup of coffee was placed on the desk before her.

"First off, I am Dean Wilhelm, but everyone just calls me Lukas. May I call you Ava?"

Without a smile, Yyemara indicated that the familiarity was unwelcome but agreed with reservations. Dean Wilhelm immediately picked up on her reserve.

"Ms. Padden, then, you will have an office in the genetic studies building. Your students will expect you on Monday, where you will be teaching. I see from your resume that you are qualified to teach the more advanced classes. I trust that you have found your residence before coming to this office. If you have not, I will have Jolene provide directions after you complete some of the necessary paperwork for our human resource department. I am sure you would like to get that behind you quickly, right?" Dean Wilhelm said, trying to lighten the mood.

Yyemara realized that she was supposed to smile at the man's attempt at a joke. In doing so, Dean Wilhelm continued more relaxed. He talked for ten minutes about her duties, who she would report to, and other miscellaneous official matters. Finally, feeling relieved that he had come to the end of his material, he opened the door for Yyemara to exit.

"Jolene, will you please take Ms. Padden to the Human Resource Department to sign the paperwork. Also, would you make sure that someone in the department shows Ms. Padden to her residence?" Giving Jolene a look of sympathy for needing to accompany the humorless woman, Dean Wilhelm stepped back into his office and closed the door. Seeing that Yyemara had not touched the coffee, Dean Wilhelm took the cup and swallowed the tepid liquid in two gulps.

"Boy, we've got a live one there," Lukas said sarcastically under his breath to no one but himself. "I feel sorry for her students."

Yyemara took her suitcase from the vehicle and went to the residence where she would sleep. Looking around at the rooms, Yyemara decided it was more than satisfactory. On Surtees, she was in her room only to sleep. She had a bed and nothing else except a small desk. Here on Earth, her residence had a large bed for her solitary sleep and four other rooms for sitting, cooking, dining, and bathing. The sitting room was sunny with a large window allowing her to look down upon the common grounds of the university. She watched students walking and laughing together as friends. A moment of sadness entered her heart as she thought about not seeing Khrelyn, her one, and only friend, for nearly half a season.

Yyemara knew the return trip home to Surtees would be just as long as the trip had been to get her to Earth. Once Khrelyn was back on Surtees, she knew her father would have other assignments for him before Ananaya would plan Khrelyn's next trip to Earth. Yyemara was no stranger to loneliness. She had grown up alone in a sterile world where her only focus was on her career. The time spent with Khrelyn was a refreshing break, but now, she needed to return to work. Pleasing Ananaya was her driving force and succeed she would.

CHAPTER THIRTY-EIGHT

Hoygazor was startled when an out of breath, redheaded, freckled-faced junior scientist raced in to announce that a skyplane carrying Ananaya had just landed. Hoygazor saw the fear in his underlings' eyes and quickly dismissed him for his own sake.

'I can't have my staff on edge just because of the Chief Scientist's arrival. We have too much to accomplish without them wetting themselves', he thought to himself. Turning from his thoughts, he looked around his lab to see what was out of place before Ananaya made his appearance. There were things he was working on that he did not wish to share with the chief scientist.

Quickly placing items into drawers and locking them, Hoygazor felt relatively secure as Ananaya made his appearance. "Hoygazor, how good to see you, my friend."

Hoygazor remembered more than one of his fellow scientists being called Ananaya's friend before they were terminated permanently. A shiver crept down his spine at that thought.

"Ananaya, welcome. What an honor to have you come personally to my department. What can I do for you?" Hoygazor said, trying hard to sound friendly and sincere.

"There is nothing you can do for me at this moment," Ananaya said with a smile that never reached his eyes. "I just want to commend you on a fine job. Because of your seasons of work with the Spaceprobe program, my daughter has successfully been established on the planet Earth. Her identity is secure thanks to the earth-based modifications your Spaceprobes have done in the many past seasons--way too many seasons for me to count, in fact. Yyemara is now Ava Padden with a rich recorded history that no one will be able to question. You did a magnificent job right down to the smallest detail, like substituting her likeness into their school yearbooks under every photograph of the real Ava Padden. I laud you again!" Ananaya said as he slapped Hoygazor on his back.

Hoygazor looked embarrassed at the praise. He never knew if Ananaya was sincere or if he was using flattery for some evil purpose.

As Ananaya walked to the expanse of windows that looked down on the Spaceport, he puffed with pride. "This Astro Science Department is one of my greatest achievements."

Hoygazor stiffened at the remark. He hated the fact that Ananaya took credit for anything good. He never took any blame when things went wrong.

Turning, Ananaya noted the stiffened demeanor of Hoygazor. "Relax. You deserve a break. I want you and your lovely wife to join me and Kaycee'na for dinner tomorrow night. I want to make a toast to you and the success that we share. I will see you tomorrow."

Walking out of Hoygazor's lab, the Astroscientist could see two large Enforcers standing at the door. They immediately fell in behind Ananaya as he left the building.

Hoygazor walked to his chair and slumped down. There was no need for Ananaya to come all this way just to extend an invitation to dinner. Ananaya could have sent any subordinates to do his bidding. Why did he come himself?

Glancing towards his locked drawer, Hoygazor got up and pulled out his plans for his skyfyters and starkarry'er. At that moment, he only had two paths. One path would be to turn over the plans to Ananaya when the Chief Scientist would need them, or the other path would be to keep the plans for himself when Surtees needed them. Hoygazor would know when the moment was right and which path he should take.

CHAPTER THIRTY-NINE

"Stop! Wait for me, Father," came a voice from behind the ryke. Noryan turned and couldn't believe his eyes. It had to be Josyah. He was no longer a small boy.

"Stop the ryke, stop the ryke, Tawtanya. It is my son!" Noryan yelled as he sprung from the seat and raced back to meet his boy.

"Father, I am coming with you," Josyah panted.

Noryan hugged his son fiercely. "Josyah, is that really you? You have grown so much since I was taken."

Josyah laughed. "And you have grown so…thin. Father, I can't believe that you are alive. How did you escape?"

Myana walked back to join Josyah and his father. Not wanting to interrupt the reunion, Myana kept a short distance away. Finally, she said, "Did your mother change her mind?"

Josyah looked at Myana. Noryan knew this was the moment he should make introductions. "Josyah, these women are my friends. Myana, this is my youngest son. Tawtanya is the one sitting on the seat holding the reins."

"Tawtanya? Are you talking about the Champion of Surtees?" Josyah said excitedly.

"I guess people call her that. You know about Tawtanya?" Noryan asked.

"Of course, I do. I know all about Tawtanya and how she started as an athlete in the Zrymyr Games and how now she is the Champion of Surtees. I know everything about her and how she is causing changes on our planet to better the lives of the citizens," Josyah said beaming. "Mother tries to keep me protected like a young child, but I know everything. I know how the scientists are killing our planet, and I know Tawtanya is going to right the wrongs."

Leaving his father and Myana in the dust, Josyah stopped short of jumping into the ryke to grab Tawtanya's hand. "I am your biggest fan. I can't believe you are here…and you are my father's friend. Did you rescue him?"

Before Tawtanya could answer, Myana interjected, "No, your father escaped on his own just to be with you and your mother."

"Forget mother. She is too scared to be her own person. She isn't going to change her mind anytime soon. I told her that I was going to be with my father and she didn't try to stop me. I think she knows that it is just a matter of time before Enforcers would come for me anyway. I am coming with you."

Tawtanya looked to Noryan. "It is fine with us if it is fine with you. Josyah, you are in luck, Myana was also the Champion of Surtees."

Blushing, Josyah looked at Myana, embarrassed that he had not recognized her. With a twinkle in his eyes, he smiled boldly at the beautiful woman. Hearing his father's voice, Josyah listened intently.

"Josyah, will your mother be alright without you? I hate to leave her alone." Concern lingered heavily on the last words from Noryan.

"Mother will be in less danger with me gone. I barely escaped the last culling of boys when the Enforcers made their rounds. If I had not been fishing far from the village, I would have been taken. Our mother might have been killed if she tried to protect me. With me gone, she is safer."

"Okay, then climb aboard. I am not exactly sure where we are heading. I will leave our fate in the hands of these two charming ladies," Noryan said as he joined his son in the back of the ryke.

"I can tell you exactly where we are going, Tawtanya said with a wink. "I hope you don't get seasick."

"Seasick? Not me. Nothing much bothers me after what I have been through. If I can take the beatings, I can surely handle a few waves. Where are we going? I am really eager to see what is next in your plans."

"Between here and the Agricultural Research Center is a very small port. We have friends there who will keep you safe until we can plan our attack against the scientists. You will be on the ground floor of this revolution. *All Hands-on Deck*, so to say," Tawtanya continued.

"Me, too?" asked Josyah.

"Wherever I go, you go," Noryan said, giving his son a hearty squeeze.

The small band continued their trek, using the less used back roads to the port. Upon arrival, a large man came out of the small shack near the pier and greeted Myana and Tawtanya as if they were family.

"Ladies, what good fortune I must have to bring you to my humble abode," the large man said.

"Toybyn, it is our good fortune to be with you again," Myana blurted back, good-naturedly.

"Come inside, and I will give you food and drink while you tell me your newest tale," Toybyn said, "but first, who is this skinny man and the fresh young lad?"

Noryan stepped forward and extended his hand in greeting. "I am Noryan, and I fear I am the reason we are here. This is my son, Josyah. We are a packaged deal."

Lifting a bushy eyebrow to showing his interest, Toybyn took Noryan's hand in a firm grip. Pulling Noryan slightly towards him, he used his other hand to guide Noryan to the small shack, well-seasoned by both wind and salty sea. The rest followed behind.

The smells of fish filled the room as Toybyn pan-fried fish for his guests. Heavy bread was served with the meal as well as a strong drink that Noryan took from his son.

"Ah, Father, can't I have some, too?" Josyah asked with hope gleaming in his eyes.

"You may as well let him have some. That is about all they serve where you will be going," Toybyn laughed cheerfully.

"I think water will be sufficient for Josyah," Noryan said fatherly.

"The water is tainted. Your boy is going to need to learn how to survive on this liquid or not at all," Toybyn said seriously as he leaned forward, putting his elbows on the table.

"It isn't that strong, Noryan. Let the boy drink. Toybyn knows what he is saying is true," Myana added to comfort the unsure father.

"Where are we going?" Noryan asked, feeling a bit suspicious.

"Tonight, I will signal one of our ships to come close to shore but far enough away to be safe. When they sail closer to shore, I will row you out to put you aboard. We have ships all along the coastline full of men and boys that we have stashed away from villages all over Surtees to keep them out of the hands of the Enforcers. Someday, these men and boys will need to fight for Surtees. You might call these military training ships," Toybyn explained.

"I wish I knew there was another option before the Enforcers came for me seasons ago," Noryan said sadly.

"Sorry, fella. This training facility just started a season ago when our fearless leaders thought of it," Toybyn said as he gave Tawtanya and Myana a grateful smile.

"You two thought this out?" Noryan asked in surprise.

"When Tawtanya and I put our heads together, it is amazing what we can come up with. Why do you look so surprised?

"You are so young," Noryan said, continuing to look at them in awe.

The conversations continued until it was dark. Toybyn excused himself and took a lantern outside.

Josyah became visibly shaken when he realized that his life was going to change forever.

"It isn't too late for you to return to your mother," Noryan said quietly.

"And just wait until the Enforcers come for me?" Josyah said, straightening his back and squaring his shoulders. "No, this is the right choice. Besides, I missed too many seasons of being with my father. I want to get to know you again."

Noryan beamed with pride. "You have grown into a fine young man. Tell me, what has become of your brother?"

"You will be happy to learn he is the commander of starfreighter and starcruisers. He actually was an athlete in the Zrymyr Games before he was accepted into the flight academy," Josyah beamed with pride. "Mother didn't stop him from achieving his dreams, even though she wanted him to stop."

"Your mother is a good woman. I see what a wonderful job she did with both of my sons. I will be grateful to her forever for that," Noryan said quietly.

Tawtanya's ears perked at the mention of a former Zrymyr athlete that is now a starcruiser pilot. "Is your brother's name…."

Before Tawtanya could finish her question, the door burst open. Toybyn stood in the opening, filling it with his great bulk. "You need to come now. I sense Enforcers are nearby. Hurry! Ladies, I think you might want to leave now as well. Your trydox is hitched to the ryke and ready for your departure. Use the path behind the large boulders to the northwest. The ground is hard, and the beasts' prints will not show. Go now!" Toybyn directed.

All four got to their feet and grabbed what few belongings they had brought with them into the shack. Hasty good-byes were said, and everyone parted quickly. As Tawtanya gave a command for the trydox to move forward, Myana looked behind her to watch Noryan and Josyah enter the small boat to make their journey to the waiting ship.

"May luck be on your side, and may God protect you," Myana said softly.

CHAPTER FORTY

Khrelyn made a list of all the things he wanted to do on his return to Surtees. Of course, retrieving the soft doll for Yyemara was second on the list right behind seeing Tawtanya again. Khrelyn knew she was only a few seasons younger than himself, but it seemed like Tawtanya had grown up faster than she should have. He watched for seasons as she developed from a strong athlete to the champion of the people. He still wondered at her passion and where it came from. Remembering the look of disgust on her face when she found out that Khrelyn flew for Ananaya made his heart heavy.

'Why did she hate the scientists so much?' Khrelyn wondered. His own life was a dream because of science. All his life, he wanted nothing more than to fly. Because of the scientists, he was living that dream. All Tawtanya saw was skyplanes polluting the air. 'Did the skyplanes really cause the people below to become sick?'

Interrupted from further thoughts about Surtees and Tawtanya was a knock at his quarters. "Sir, we will be landing very soon. Do you want to be in the control center?"

Khrelyn nodded an affirmation. "I will be there momentarily. Thank you for keeping me posted. Return to your duty."

As Khrelyn straightened his uniform, he gave a glance around his quarters. 'It will be nice to sleep in a bed, eat with my family, and travel in a skyplane instead of being cooped up in this starcruiser.'

A second home is what the starcruiser was not. It had too many limitations. Khrelyn was the commander, and once Yyemara left, the return trip was lonely. He was hungering for companionship that did not need to salute him or hold him at arm's length. He could never be just one of the crew and enjoy the merriment they enjoyed when off duty. The leave was exactly what he needed to rejuvenate himself. Seeing his mother and brother was going to be such a treat. Walking up to the control center, Khrelyn watched as Surtees came into view on the front screen.

Shortly after landing, briefings took place as the spacecraft was being repaired, upgraded, and refitted for its next journey. All the crew was already on leave, and Khrelyn thought that having a command had its drawbacks. It would be nice to be off the grounds of the spaceport and actually doing what he wanted to do…free of responsibility.

Finally, Khrelyn was about to leave when his superior told him that he must remain awhile longer. It seems Ananaya wanted to discuss the recent mission to Earth.

Khrelyn sat waiting until his name was called to enter the borrowed office Ananaya was occupying. "Commander, you may enter now," said the voice of the assistant, who seemed unsettled and afraid to have the Chief Scientist at her worksite.

"Good Afternoon, Commander Khrelyn. I have heard good things about you from your superiors. Please sit. This won't take long," the Chief Scientist said as a way of greeting.

Khrelyn took a seat but remained at attention in his demeanor. Eyes forward and shoulders squared, Khrelyn looked the obedient professional that he was.

"How did my daughter seem to you on the trip?" was Ananaya's first question.

"Sir, she seemed quite dedicated to her mission," Khrelyn replied without hesitation.

"Of course, she would…I mean, did she seem relaxed or nervous?" Ananaya questioned further.

Khrelyn hesitated before answering. "Both Syr. At times she was very relaxed, and at other times, she seemed a bit nervous."

Under his breath, Ananaya said, "I thought I trained her better." Louder, he said, "How did she seem nervous. Exactly when did this nervousness present itself?"

"I would say she seemed nervous about the teleport system and whether it was programmed appropriately so that she would be placed at the exact coordinance prescribed by yourself."

Laughing gleefully, Ananaya said, "That makes perfect sense. She was not nervous about the mission; she was only nervous about human error. Thank you, Commander, you may leave."

Khrelyn felt relief when he was excused. There was no way that he wanted to discuss his personal relationship with the Chief Scientist's daughter. A smile crossed Khrelyn's lips when he remembered the robotized matron who arrived with not a speck of personality and the Yyemara that he finally got to know…the beautiful, intelligent woman with a keen wit. This woman, he was proud to call a friend.

Khrelyn quickly left the building to acquire his skyplane. It was getting late, and he wanted to get to his aunt's and mother's home before it was dark. Stopping first at the supply building, Khrelyn purchased various items that might please his mother and brother as well as enough food to make his visit less of a strain on their budget.

Landing in a field close to the village, Khrelyn was surprised to see a wall was built around the small village. Walking to the gate, he called out for admission to the compound. When the gatekeeper saw that it was a man from the village, he allowed him to enter.

Reaching the home of his later seasons of childhood, he knocked. "Khrelyn, how good to see you. It has been so long. You look well. Come in and tell us all about your travels," his mother said while embracing him fiercely.

Giving his aunt a hug, Khrelyn relinquished the bags of supplies to her and allowed his mother to drag him to the tiny living room. Sitting, where his mother indicated, the honored chair in the room, Khrelyn was given a mug of liquid by his aunt.

"Where is Josyah? Is he off with some cute girl from the village?" Khrelyn asked in a joking manner.

When his mother and aunt did not smile but sat looking quite nervous, Khrelyn grew fearful. "Did the Enforcers come for him?"

"No, he left before they could do that. He was almost culled less than a season ago, but he was gone fishing, and the Enforcers did not want to spend time trying to find him," Merlynn answered.

"Is he hiding, then? And where?" Khrelyn pushed for clarification.

"Yes, he is hiding, but we don't have any idea where. We shouldn't know in case the Enforcers would return."

Khrelyn could tell that he was not going to get any further answers from his mother. He let the subject drop and talked about his time in space.

"It is getting late, and I am tired. May I stay the night in Josyah's room?" Khrelyn asked and then excused himself to retire.

Looking around Josyah's room, Khrelyn saw hardly anything missing. It was as if Josyah left without making any plans to be gone. Khrelyn felt the hair on the back of his neck rise. Suspicion was pushing its way into his mind. Why would Josyah leave in such a big hurry that he wouldn't even take a change of clothing? Finding Josyah's most valued personal object still tucked away in his brother's favorite hiding place, Khrelyn became fearful that his little brother was no longer alive and that his mother lied to him.

The next morning, Khrelyn ate a quiet breakfast with his mother and aunt. "I will be leaving right after breakfast. I have limited time before my next assignment. Could you tell me which direction Josyah headed when he left here? Exactly how long ago did he leave?"

Pushing away from the table, Khrelyn walked out the front door with her eldest son. She pointed down the road heading southwest. "He went that way three nights ago," Merlynn pointed towards the narrow ryke path heading out of town, as she answered.

"Was he on foot and alone?" Khrelyn asked.

"No, he was in a ryke, and there were three other people with him," Merlynn stated vaguely.

"Who were the other people that he was with?" Khrelyn continued to prod his mother for answers.

As Merlynn's eyes flicked to the side, she lied, "I don't know who they were. Josyah left in such a hurry I did not have a chance to meet them."

Khrelyn was about to challenge his mother, knowing she was lying. He decided against it. It was obvious that his mother was afraid, and she needed this untruth for her own justifications.

"I am not sure when I will be back to see you again. I left some trade chips for you on Josyah's bed to help you and Aunt Teryess with future needs. I love you, Mother." With these words, Khrelyn walked back through the gate and headed for his skyplane.

"Next on my list is to fly southwest to see if I can see my little brother," Khrelyn said out loud to himself. Getting into his skyplane Khrelyn flew low to the ground, startling beasts in the fields as he flew over. Khrelyn was disappointed not to see a single ryke on any of the dirt roads as he flew back and forth across the countryside, trying to find any movement besides farmers in their fields or animals scurrying in fright.

Realizing he was wasting his time, he headed towards the Neuro-Chemical Research Center, where he hoped to find Kaycee'na to retrieve the doll that Yyemara requested. Permission to land was given, and Khrelyn took ground transport to the genetic studies building. Being guided into the laboratory, which Kaycee'na supervised, Khrelyn waited to speak with the scientist and mother of Yyemara.

"How can I help you, Commander?" Kaycee'na asked formally.

"I am here at the request of your daughter. She asked if I might retrieve one personal item for her. She told me to find you and ask that you give me her soft doll from her childhood," Khrelyn said, hoping he had given all the information needed to make this a quick trip. Khrelyn still hoped to be able to find Tawtanya before needing to report back to duty.

"Odd that she would want that silly old toy. However, if it is something she really feels she needs, then I will have Gyddyn retrieve it for you. You may wait in the lobby until his return," Kaycee'na said and returned to her station without a dismissing farewell.

When Gyddyn arrived in the lobby with the soft doll, Khrelyn tucked it into his pilot's tunic without a glance. He could check off another thing from his list of things to do while on leave. Racing back to his skyplane, he wondered where he might find Tawtanya. Sitting in the skyplane without knowing where to head next left him in a quandary. Tawtanya could be anywhere. How was he going to narrow his search?

Realizing it would be impossible to fly to each community in search of Tawtanya, Khrelyn gave up and headed back to the Astro Science Research Center. His leave was limited, and he needed some rest. At the center, he would be able to flop in one of the dorms for the pilots and crews. There was still time to go to the market and try to find the delicacies Yyemara requested, even though the next trip to Earth was not for some time.

Khrelyn headed his spaceplane in that direction and landed. He found the supply officer, who also gave him permission to stay in the dorms. Tucking a few belongings into a locked container, Khrelyn headed out to the marketplace.

It felt good to be on land. Even though he loved flying above all else, from time to time, Khrelyn relished a walk outdoors. It seemed like a lifetime ago that he participated in the games. He stayed in shape physically because it was required, but the sheer joy of leaping from rooftop to rooftop was no longer something he did. He looked to the rooftop and wondered if he could still make the leap. Feeling relaxed and foolhardy, Khrelyn decided to test himself and give it a try. Moments later, he was on the rooftop, calculating the amount of thrust he would need in his jump to make it to the next roof when he noticed a large gathering of people in the center of the marketplace. Straining to hear the sound of the crowd in the distance, he thought he heard 'Tawtanya...Tawtanya...Tawtanya'. Khrelyn's heart pounded in his chest.

Looking for the quickest way down from the rooftop, Khrelyn decided to shorten the trip by leaping from rooftop to rooftop until he was within a manageable distance to the gathered crowd. Stopping just above the crowd, Khrelyn looked down and saw Tawtanya's eyes staring up into his own. An amused smile crossed her lips.

Making his way down to the ground as quickly as he could, Khrelyn elbowed his way through the crowd to get closer to the staging area. He stood mesmerized by the young woman that captured his heart seasons ago when she was just a girl. What she was saying was incidental. He was just happy to see her and watch her animated face as she roused each and every person gathered to action.

As the crowd grew louder and louder, Khrelyn knew it was just a matter of time before the Enforcers would come to disperse them. He was not surprised then when the Enforcers pushed their way into the crowd, violently striking those who did not give ground soon enough.

Tawtanya stood her ground on the make-shift podium and yelled insults at the Enforcers. Soon, she descended onto the ground and rushed towards the nearest Enforcer yelling for him to stop and leave immediately.

The Enforcer stopped beating the people nearest him on her command and stood rigid. "If you care for these people, tell them to leave now. We have orders to stop an assembly larger than five people. This crowd is becoming a mob. We cannot tolerate such behavior. I would get great pleasure arresting you; however, I was directed to leave you alone".

"Who told you not to arrest me, and why?" Tawtanya yelled at the retreating Enforcer, who continued to move people away from the podium.

Frustrated, Tawtanya turned to leave. Standing before her was Khrelyn.

"It's been a long time," Tawtanya said, the smile was long gone. "What have you been doing with yourself? I see you are still practicing for the Zrymyr games." Tawtanya's eyes looked up to the rooftops.

"Oh, that. It was just an impulsive moment. I wanted to see if I could still make the leaps," Khrelyn said, feeling sheepish at being caught in such frivolity.

Tawtanya looked down the streets to watch the last of the crowd being moved along by Enforcers. She was relieved to see that the Enforcers were no longer using brute strength to control the crowd.

"Do you have time to sit with me and talk. I would love to buy you some food and drink while we do so," Khrelyn asked awkwardly.

Myana came forward, and Tawtanya told her that she would join her shortly. Myana gave Khrelyn an appreciative glance and turned to leave, grinning from ear to ear.

"I know a quiet eatery within a short walk from here. It is down an alley. I doubt we will run into any Enforcers," Khrelyn said as he guided Tawtanya in the general direction he wanted to go.

After ordering, the two sat in a quiet corner of the establishment. The place was decorated modestly, but murals painted on the walls depicted past days on Surtees with lush emerald green and golden fields with sparkling blue rivers and streams.

"This is what I want for the people," Tawtanya said, waving her hands in a circular motion indicating the expanse of murals. "Surtees was a beautiful planet before the scientists arrived and decided to destroy it. Do you remember better days, Khrelyn?"

Khrelyn said nothing at first. He was searching for his past memories and allowing his mind to focus on the mental pictures of his boyhood days. "I do remember a time when my father worked hard in the fields, but we had plenty to eat and even more to share with others. I can still see my dad loading the ryke full of the harvest to take to the marketplace. He was a happier man then."

"And now…?" Tawtanya invading Khrelyn's memories.

"And now, my father is probably dead. No one has heard from him since he sent my mother, brother, and me away to stay with my aunt. I guess he knew the Enforcers would come for him," Khrelyn said sadly.

"Why would the Enforcers come for him?" Tawtanya asked curiously.

"My father became discontent with what was happening. Our crops were no longer thriving, the UberBugs were eating more than the pests that they were supposed to eat, and our livestock was no longer breeding true," Khrelyn replied. "I guess my father was starting to talk out loud, and the Enforcers took him away before he could cause others to be discontent as well."

"Your father was a brave man," Tawtanya said. "I wish I could have met him."

Touching Khrelyn's arm from across the small table, Tawtanya added softly. "Do you understand why I get so angry when I hear you are still flying the skyplanes? You do realize the skyplanes are polluting our planet, don't you?"

Khrelyn hesitated before replying, "I guess I didn't really think about it. I love flying so much that I just couldn't allow myself to believe something that wonderful could really be so bad."

"You never thought about what chemicals were in those vapor trails you and the other pilots leave in the skies?" Tawtanya questioned further.

"When one is up in the sky, one doesn't see what is behind the skyplane," Khrelyn said wistfully. "I know that ignorance is not a good excuse."

"What I would like from you is a promise that you will not fly unless it is absolutely necessary and that you go one step further and convince the other pilots not to fly just for fun. If we can diminish the chemicals in the air, we can save lives. I think these small compromises are worth saving lives, don't you?"

Looking into Tawtanya's eyes, Khrelyn saw steel resolve. She was talking softly, but Khrelyn knew she would not accept anything but his promise to stop flying for anything except necessary assignments.

"Tawtanya, I have known your feelings about the skyplanes and the chemtrails for a long time. Fortunately, I had more than a half-season on my space mission to research the structural plans of the skyplane to determine where the source of the chemicals was being injected and emitted as chemtrails. On my return, I found a chemical generation canister that one of the scientists placed in my skyplane. I also found a way to disarm the apparatus." Khrelyn explained.

"I promise I will talk secretly to trusted pilots in my flight group and ask them to disarm their canisters. I will also ask them to curtail their flights as well to allow the people on Surtees to see a major change in their air quality," Khrelyn finally added."

Khrelyn reward with a warm, sweet smile. "That is all that I can ask of you for the moment," Tawtanya said. The smile faded when she added, "Someday, you will need to take sides. You will either be on the side of Surtees and the inhabitants, or you will be on the side of the Chief Scientist and his mad scheming."

Khrelyn did not answer. A bill was placed before him, and he fumbled in his pocket to find the required trade chips.

Tawtanya got to her feet. "It was nice to see you again, Khrelyn. I need to get back to Myana. We leave in the morning, and we have a small group of leaders to meet with soon."

As they walked out onto the streets together, Tawtanya took Khrelyn's hand. "I think you still have what it takes to participate in the Zrymyr games from what I observed. If you decide to stop piloting, you might consider coaching."

Giving a parting squeeze to Khrelyn's hand, Tawtanya walked away, leaving Khrelyn watching her until she turned a corner and was out of sight. Khrelyn didn't want to scratch seeing Tawtanya off his list of things he wanted to do before leaving Surtees once again. What he wanted to do was to race after her and join her cause. He wanted to be by her side from this day on. Instead, he walked back to his dorm to get ready for his next assignment. He would need to report in the morning to be briefed on where he would be going next.

Falling upon his bed in the officer's dorm, Khrelyn lay back and thought about Tawtanya. He couldn't tell if he was in love since he had nothing to compare it to. He thought about Yyemara. She, too, was beautiful, exotic, and very interesting. It just wasn't the same feelings he had for Tawtanya. Yyemara was reserved and dedicated. Tawtanya was equally dedicated, but she had a fire within her…a passion that Yyemara lacked. Maybe that was what Khrelyn was in love with…Tawtanya's passion.

Khrelyn let his thoughts run towards words Tawtanya used while sitting with him. Destruction of Surtees was a key theme. Khrelyn admitted that he was blinded by his desire to fly. Tawtanya was looking at Surtees through unfiltered eyes. 'Maybe it was time that I do the same,' Khrelyn mumbled to himself before falling asleep.

CHAPTER FORTY-ONE

Noryan felt better than he had in seasons. His once skeletal body was filling out, and his hard-used muscles were even more toned than before. Feeling the salty breeze blowing through his hair made Noryan feel alive. Even the choppy waves did little to affect his good mood.

"Father, watch me," came the voice of Josyah from up above. Noryan extended his neck backward to its full range to watch his son perched on the foremast.

Once Josyah knew he had his father's attention, he jumped from mast to mast as gracefully as his brother Khrelyn had done in the Zrymyr Games. Swinging down from the rigging, Josyah landed lightly on the deck without needing to grab hold of anything to stop his momentum.

"You could compete in the Zrymyr Games right now," Noryan beamed with pride. "I would say all those seasons playing in the barn with your brother has paid off."

Josyah glowed with his father's praise. "I love being on this vessel. The men are good to me, and they are showing me things I never knew how to do before. The food is great. I don't even mind eating fish morning, noon, and night."

Noryan didn't comment, but his mind traveled back to the meals he endured at the internment camp. He only nodded in agreement with his son when he mentioned how great the food was on the ship.

The thunder of footfalls interrupted the conversation between father and son. Soon, the two were surrounded by the other members of the crew. The captain stepped forward and announced that today's training would involve the use of weapons.

Josyah seemed a bit reticent. Noryan pulled Josyah close and briefly hugged his shoulders to let his son know that it was alright. Noryan knew the weapon training would be essential if he were to return to the internment camp to free the other prisoners. Never had Noryan used a weapon. His tools for farming could have been used as weapons he realized as he saw the first of many weapons being demonstrated by the weapons master.

Most of the men on board the ship was trained in many of the weapons before Noryan and Josyah having arrived on board. There were several new weapons that even the seasoned sailors looked at suspiciously.

"Captain, begging your pardon, but I have never seen that weapon before. What is it?" ventured one older man who rubbed his head in puzzlement.

"This, men, is what we will use to fight the Enforcers," the captain said as he held the weapon high for all to see. "It is a specialized recurved bow with an arrow that can penetrate into the bodies of the monsters without us needing to be within their reach."

The captain stopped to look at his men. "This weapon fires arrows that explode on contact. There is no way any Enforcer will survive if the arrow hits its mark. We will be practicing by aiming at the target placed behind our ship on our towed skiff. Please make four lines as I only have four bows at present. I have several shipbuilders making more in secret, so soon, I should have a bow for each of you. We will only fire one explosive arrow so you can see the damage that it can cause. That arrow will be fired by myself at the end of the practice. In the meantime, non-explosive arrows will be placed at the firing line for each of you to use. There are enough arrows for you to shoot ten times. At each line, one sailor who has mastered the use of the recurve bow previously will be assigned to give you pointers. Listen well to what they tell you. Your lives will depend on it."

The captain looked directly at Josyah when he said the last words. Noryan once more gave his son's shoulders a quick reassuring squeeze. Noryan knew the captain wasn't sure Josyah had the stomach to kill.

Noryan stepped up to be one of the first to fire at the target. The skiff bounced in the waves making the target more difficult to sight. Lymson, the training officer, made a few corrections to the stance Noryan had assumed. Physically turning Noryan's torso more to a sideways stance creating a straight line directed at the target, Lymson adjusted Noryan's grip on the bow. When Noryan went to draw the bow into his cheek, the farmer was amazed at how much strength it took to pull the drawstring. Giving Noryan his first arrow, Lymson watched as the farmer nocked the arrow, sighted and released it to miss the target completely. Making a few adjustments with the assistance of the instructor, Noryan released several more arrows, hitting the target solidly each time.

"Move to the back of the line and let your arms rest. You will develop the muscles necessary in time," Lymson said. "You did well for your first try. It isn't like using a pitchfork, is it farmer?"

Noryan moved to the back of the line and rubbed his arm. It did use muscles that were unused while digging through the rock to build a tunnel. Noryan's mind drifted back to his time in the camp and wondered what the tunnel was going to be used for. Never did an Enforcer say a word as to why the men were being forced to dig through the rock. It was difficult for Noryan to even imagine what direction he had been digging. His mind was always on survival. The horrors of watching men die and being dragged out of the tunnel came flooding back. It wasn't until his son came bounding up to him with glee that his mind returned to the present.

"Father, did you see me? Lymson says I am a natural!"

Noryan felt ashamed that he was not watching his son. Not wanting to admit that his mind was in a dark spot, Noryan just grabbed his son in a hug and exclaimed, "You are going to be the best bowman in the entire group."

As the boy beamed, Noryan's dark mood returned. Remembering what Myana and Tawtanya had told him, Noryan thought of his eldest son. Was it true that the boys who disappeared had been turned into Enforcers? Is it possible that he or Josyah might actually need to kill Josyah's oldest brother? Noryan felt his skin crawl at the thought.

Bow and arrow weapons practice continued with the other weapons training for the rest of the month. Josyah made the training into a game and astounded everyone by hanging from the riggings while drawing his bow and shooting at targets. His accuracy was not bested by even the trainers. Laughing, Josyah slid down the sheet at his father's feet. "See if you can do that!"

Noryan only laughed. I would be lucky to even get up that high, let alone hang upside down. You are part furry nedryl, aren't you? I often thought you looked just like one when I would see you hanging from the rafters of the barn. Maybe it is your tail that gave it away."

"Khrelyn always called me a nedryl," Josyah laughed. Pausing, Josyah added, "I wonder which galaxy he is flying to now?"

Both father and son stared up into the evening sky as the first stars started to appear. "Is that what Khrelyn does these days, fly to the stars?" Noryan asked his son while not taking his eyes from the sky.

"I guess he doesn't really fly to the stars. From what he said the last time I saw Khrelyn, he does fly to other planets far from here. In fact, he said he was taking a very important scientist to a planet far away. That was some time ago. He may still be out there since I don't know how long it takes to fly somewhere that far away. I have never even been in a skyplane," Josyah said wistfully.

"I hope that you never need to fly in a skyplane. I would prefer to see you with your feet on the ground…unless you are hanging upside down like a nedryl.

CHAPTER FORTY-TWO

"Ms. Padden, the reporter is here to interview you. Would you like him to come into your office, or would you prefer to meet with him in the conference room?" Ava's secretary asked as she entered the office.

"Here is just fine, thank you, Ginny," came Ava's answer. "Would you mind bringing in a cup of coffee for the man. Oh, what is his name?"

"His name is Peter Rampart. He is British," Ginny answered. "Would you like a cup of coffee as well?"

"No, thank you," replied Ava, who admitted to herself that she could not stand the taste of the beverage. "Maybe a cup of black tea would be nice for the gentleman."

Ginny immediately brought Mr. Rampart into the office and introduced him to her boss. Leaving the door open so she could return with the tea, Ginny smiled, knowing her boss would eat the young man alive.

Ava got to her feet and shook hands with the reporter. Indicating a chair for him to be seated, Ava handed the man a cup of tea when Ginny returned. "Cream or sugar?" Ava asked politely.

Peter Rampart, a tall, slim man with golden hair, took the cup offered but declined the cream or sugar. Setting the cup on the desk, Peter took out a tablet and pen and got right to business.

"Ms. Padden, are you ready to answer my questions for the article I am writing for our business section of the newspaper?" he asked, allowing another quick look at the beautiful face of the lady seated before him.

"What is your first question?" Ava Padden asked without expression.

Peter was trying to figure out a way to soften the woman sitting before him. He noted her erect sitting posture and the stern, serious look on her face. In the past, Peter could soften most any woman with a smile from his handsome face. This woman didn't seem to even notice his good looks. Having spent most of the day in the gym and tanning beds, Peter thought he was a perfect male specimen. He knew this woman would also succumb to his charms in time. Putting on his sweet, boyish grin, he asked the first question.

"How is it that such a young, beautiful woman as yourself has come to lead the largest genetic corporation in the world?" Peter asked, trying hard to be cute.

"Not even cracking a smile, Ava answered. "Are you saying age and looks are relevant to my position?"

Feeling off-balanced by her harsh response, Peter shifted gears and tried again. "I am sorry if I offended you. I didn't mean to imply that you got your position by being young and gorgeous. I was just asking how a young person, like yourself, came to be in a position to purchase a small genetic testing company and then expand it into a significant international business in a short period of time."

"Does intelligence mean anything to you?" Ava quickly and dryly responded.

"Of course, I understand that you must be very intelligent, but that alone won't buy you anything," Peter Rampart said defensively.

"What is it that you don't understand?" Ava asked.

"I guess I am trying to understand how you rose to power so quickly. I mean, I just barely heard of you a month ago," the reporter said, dropping his cute act.

"I can't help that you were uninformed, now can I?" Ava said as she rose to her feet to end the interview. "If you don't mind, I have a business to attend. If you have further questions, I am sure my secretary can answer them for you." Ava got to her feet and opened the door to usher the reporter out of her office.

Peter Rampage closed his tablet and exited the office. The door was closed behind him before he could thank Ava Padden for her time, a courtesy that was drilled into him.

Yyemara sat back down in her office chair and smiled. She liked acting the part of Ava Padden. Already her reputation as a cold-hearted businesswoman was front page on many magazines. She knew her father would be proud that she was not tempted to partake in what this world had to offer. Her time on this planet was going to be limited. Ava needed to set everything in motion quickly. Playing the rich playgirl was out of the question. There was much genetic testing to be done across the planet, and her many companies were now staffed by competent employees who worked around the clock to accomplish what Ananaya needed.

Advertisements and ads were posted for many months now, requesting people from all over the world to take part in genetic testing. Under guises of ancestry composition, family history, genetic counseling, molecular and DNA sequencing, personal wellness, and hereditary susceptibility were employed, with results even more dramatic than expected. People from all walks of life rushed to take part in the research. Yyemara wasn't surprised. Her father calculated the likely reactions from the people of this planet, and once again, he had proven himself to be correct.

Yyemara was not privy to the reasons behind Ananaya wanting this data. Her placement on this planet was to do as instructed like all of his subordinates, and nothing more.

Placing files into her briefcase, Yyemara pressed the intercom button and spoke, "Ginny, I will be gone for a week. Please transfer any calls that you deem important to the New York Office. Please have my driver pull in front of the building. Phone the airport and tell them that I will be ready to leave in one hour."

Ginny, always efficient, replied that she would do as instructed, and the intercom went silent. Yyemara took her briefcase in hand and left the office to take the elevator down to the main floor. She knew the car would be waiting. Her staff was hand-picked by herself. They were excellent, and she wished she could take them back to Surtees with her when she would finally be able to go home.

Looking out at the fluffy white clouds as she exited the building, Yyemara realized that Earth and Surtees were pleasingly different in some ways. The air was cleaner on Earth and the water purer in most cities. She felt a bit of regret that Surtees was a decaying planet. She suspected that Ananaya sent her to Earth so she could escape Surtees, but how Earth fits into his grand plan was not yet evident.

As she slipped into her waiting car, she looked straight ahead until they reached the airport. Observing her private jet from the safety of the car, Yyemara marveled at how advanced the people of Earth seemed to be in comparison to the Surtarians. Skyplanes, the invention of the scientists, was still unavailable to the common people of Surtees. On Earth, even common people owned airplanes.

Almost everyone in the more advanced countries owned automobiles. True, like on Surtees, scientists of Earth manage the space programs. With a feeling of pride, Yyemara realized how much more advanced her father was than any of the scientists on Earth. In fact, one only needed to look at his directives for controlling genetic research on Earth, and his ability to get a spacecraft from Surtees all the way to this planet to prove the fact that her father was pure genius.

Being placed on Earth and no one suspecting she was not what she appeared was both exhilarating and lonely. The fact that she could be placed on this planet and assume an identity that her father created was more than awe-inspiring. However, no one could know who she really was. Keeping herself contained within her hidden identity was also stressful. She must always be on alert to anything that might give her away.

As she boarded the jet to fly to New York to analyze data obtained by her flagship company, Yyemara's thoughts turned to Khrelyn and when he would return. It would be nice to see someone from home. She hoped she would receive communication soon, saying that Khrelyn would meet her at set coordinates.

CHAPTER FORTY-THREE

Kaycee'na received communication that she needed to be packed and at the spaceport in the morning. Her orders were enclosed. Shaking with fear, Kaycee'na packed a few belongings. All the message said was that she would be the head of an ambassadorial committee to another planet. More information would be sent as needed.

Out loud, Kaycee'na grumbled, "My own husband couldn't even come in person to tell me what his plans for me might be. I am getting tired of being treated like I don't matter!"

Even as she continued to complain to herself, she packed in frustration a bit too hastily. If she irritated Ananaya, she feared what the consequences may be. Her shaking was not only because of her rage towards her husband, she feared the unknown of space travel. Rarely had she even traveled by spaceplane. Her life revolved around the lab in the Neuro-Chemical Research Facility. Was Ananaya sending her away because of the failures now becoming obvious as the Enforcers were starting to self-destruct? Was this his way of getting rid of her?

Knowing that the lab members tried hard to cover up their failures, Kaycee'na wondered how Ananaya might have learned of the mistakes. Rarely out in public, Kaycee'na was unaware that most everyone on the streets was seeing the Enforcers becoming weakened. Some of the boldness of the common people came from this obvious visual. Crowds continued to gather in larger and larger assemblies. Their fear lessened, and their voices grew louder as more and more became known of the brutal scientific failures that continued to harm the Surtarians. Ananaya's spies were everywhere. Nothing escaped them, so nothing escaped Ananaya.

As Enforcers became too weakened to do their duties, they were brought back to Kaycee'na's lab. Stupidly, she thought that once back to her lab, no one was the wiser. Her large crematorium removed all evidence of the mistake, or so she thought. Tweaking the process, Kaycee'na created new Enforcers from the boys retrieved from outlying villages.

All her work seemed senseless now that Ananaya intended to ship her out. Her fears mounted at the prospect of leaving the only home she had known. It was difficult enough when Yyemara left. Now, it was her turn.

Entering her cabin aboard the Starcruiser, Kaycee'na wished that she had the luxury offered the other members of the assembled ambassadorial staff. Most of them would be able to sleep during the voyage. Ananaya's directives specified that Kaycee'na use her time wisely aboard the starcruiser. Once in her cabin, the Commander showed her to her monitor where she could review Ananaya's directives. She learned her next months would require more studying than she had done since a student.

First off, Ananaya informed her that she would be going to the planet Aztara. The downloaded data captured by the stealthy probes were available for her to memorize. It would be to her benefit to understand the culture completely to gain their trust. Even though most citizens of Aztara communicated through telepathy, they were capable of speaking and understanding a common language spoken on several inhabited planets. With a sigh of relief, Kaycee'na proceeded on with the directives.

Kaycee'na must win the trust of the citizens of Aztara, offer scientific knowledge and advanced medical facilities in exchange for the land where Ananaya could arrive and continue his work. Ananaya made sure to let Kaycee'na know at this point that he was counting on her, and she should not disappoint him. Kaycee'na knew exactly what the underlying threat would be if she failed.

Now Kaycee'na wondered whether she had enough time to do everything required of her before she landed. With the new agenda looming in front of her, the words of the Commander to secure herself for leaving the gravitation pull of Surtees didn't register the extreme fear she anticipated that it would. Taking a seat and securing herself while staring at the monitor with Ananaya's threat lingering in her mind, she tried to prepare herself for the next phase of her life.

When the Commander of the SSC Starcruiser Elysium announced that she could move about freely, Kaycee'na went to the info-station in her cabin and started to review the cultural aspects of Aztara. The starprobe that orbited Aztara many seasons earlier discovered the inhabitants of Aztara were an easy-going monoculture. Kaycee'na continued to read and found that a mineral called phyrium by the inhabitants was consumed regularly, and it enhanced the people's DNA in interesting ways. The superior changes advanced the 'Longevity Gene' (FOXO3) and the 'Telepathy Gene' (semaphorin 5A) in their DNA.

'No wonder Ananaya is interested in this planet,' Kaycee'na thought without surprise. 'My crazy husband is always looking for ways to live forever. The telepathy gene would be a bonus for him. How he would love to be able to communicate his orders without needing to leave his study or lab.'

Fascinated with this new culture, Kaycee'na discovered that the people did not have an actual leader. It seemed the native people of

Aztara did not have a military or security force of any kind to fend off invaders.

'With such an idyllic world, where everyone can communicate directly across their planet, I doubt there is much friction. Of course, the Aztarians probably don't even know there is life outside of their own planet, so why would they have a military force,' Kaycee'na mused.

Kaycee'na found herself talking out loud. "If there is no leader, who am I supposed to negotiate with? Now, that is going to be an interesting problem. It looks like I am in a no-win situation."

With all the other scientists safely tucked into their containers to sleep through the entire trip, Kaycee'na had no one to discuss the various problems she foresaw when they landed. She was tempted to have one of the scientists *awakened* so she would have someone to share the burden. She knew Ananaya would be furious if she side-stepped his directives by even one small detail and thought better of it.

Kaycee'na couldn't help but wonder what other directives Ananaya may have sent with the other members of the Surtarian committee. A deep-down feeling of dread loomed over the scientists as she worked. Little did she know at that moment in time, that her life would be cut short along with all the women of Aztara.

CHAPTER FORTY-FOUR

Remembering every word on his directives to the crew and the committee heading towards Aztara, Ananaya beamed with joy. He knew his wife would do exactly as he directed out of fear, if not out of loyalty. In just a matter of a season or two, there would be an established spaceport on Aztara for his convenience as well as a stocked lab for his continued work.

The Spaceprobes were priceless. The information gathered from the two planets, Earth and Aztara, was beyond Ananaya's expectations. Ananaya's mouth actually began to water with the thought of what the mineral, phyrium, would do for him. He was already more intelligent than anyone on several planets. If his aging could be stopped or even reversed, as he hoped, Ananaya could rule the universe. The telepathy would be an added bonus for sure.

Comforted by the fact that his daughter was working, almost around the clock, on the planet Earth to find the women with the specific gene on their DNA. Ananaya lovingly called it the 'Warrior Gene,' but his scientist labeled it MAOA being found on the two X chromosomes. With these women that carry the warrior gene, Ananaya could build his army on the planet Aztara without the deterioration that plagued the inferior Surtarian genetically modified adolescent Enforcers.

Rubbing his hands together in glee, the shrunken scientist struggled to get to his feet. His bodyguard stepped forward and assisted Ananaya to the opened window, where he stabilized the decrepit old man while the chief scientist gazed out over the city.

"Others may have failed me on this planet," Ananaya mumbled, "but no one will fail me on Aztara."

Realizing his bodyguard was hanging on each word, Ananaya continued to lay out his plan to the only listening ears available. Knowing his bodyguard was loyal to the death, Ananaya felt embolden to lay out part of his plan in a low voice.

"My Senior Astroscientist in charge of transportation on Aztara will soon be implementing my directives." While the bodyguard gave physical support to the frail old man, Ananaya continued to outline what would happen soon.

"The Astroscientist will be piloting a cloaking skyplane around the populated areas of Aztara. Already in place are chemicals marked XCHROM-6E. This aerosol, when sprayed in the air, will unleash a plague that will kill all the females on Aztara.

"My brilliant daughter, Yyemara, will receive her next directives soon to lock in the location of the women with the warrior gene so necessary for the rest of my plan. Before two seasons are over, I will send Starcruisers to collect the women and take them to Aztara. In one generation, I will have the start of my new army. It will be glorious. With strong, malleable fathers and warrior mothers, add in the longevity gene, and the added bonus of being able to communicate with my army by telepathy, I will not be stopped."

Suddenly feeling exhausted from standing so long and the emotions draining his energy, Ananaya signaled for his bodyguard to help him back to his seat. As Ananaya was settling himself into his seat, the bodyguard asked one question.

"Do you trust the scientists that you will be placing on Aztara to start your work until your arrival?"

"Oh, certainly, I do. I trust implicitly that each scientist will follow my directives. However, there are a couple of them that I don't trust beyond that. I have plans to eliminate them before I arrive." Chuckling, Ananaya started to cough. Once his coughing fit subsided, Ananaya made one more statement to his bodyguard.

"You did notice that I said the plague would kill all women on Aztara. That is not limited to Aztarian women alone if you catch my drift. My incompetent wife, Kaycee'na is female for all practical purposes, isn't she?" Ananaya said with a wicked glint in his clouded eyes.

"I have one more surprise as well. The Senior Astroscientist will not be able to tell anyone what I ordered him to do. I personally placed a special package in his skyplane before they left Surtees for Aztara. On his take-off from the Aztarian Capital Spaceport, the timing mechanism will start, which will detonate upon landing. I can only imagine the flaming, thunderous white-hot fireball that will consume him, the skyplane, and any evidence that I had anything to do with all those females dying on the planet. I will arrive just in time to save their planet with my glorious plan."

Ananaya closed his eyes, and a smile formed on his face. The bodyguard stepped back, knowing the old man had fallen asleep.

CHAPTER FORTY-FIVE

Every chance Khrelyn got while on Surtees after returning from space travel, found him with Tawtanya. He followed her from village to town to city and listened to her speeches. The people of Surtees were inspired by her, and it was obvious that there was a new spirit of life amongst the common people. In the evenings, when Tawtanya was available, Khrelyn would sit and talk with the lovely young woman. They would share food and stories.

"What is it like to be out in space?" Tawtanya asked Khrelyn as she placed a small bite of food into her mouth.

"It is amazing. One can't even put words together to describe the immenseness of space. It is quiet and serene…unless one needs to avoid huge floating obstacles," Khrelyn laughed.

"Is it just one vast darkness, like night?" Tawtanya asked with genuine interest.

"Yes, and no, I guess I would need to say," Khrelyn answered vaguely.

"Well, that was helpful," Tawtanya said huffily.

"Remember, I am not a scientist. I am just a pilot. My understanding is limited to how to get from point one in the universe to point two," Khrelyn said. "I can tell you that space is a hard vacuum. It is full of low-density particles like plasma of hydrogen and helium. It also has electromagnetic radiation, magnetic fields, neutrinos, dust, and cosmic rays. One wouldn't last a moment in space if one were out in it without the protection of the starcruiser or starfreighter."

"What are neutrinos?" Tawtanya continued to press, laughing when Khrelyn's face turned purple from all the questions he could not answer.

Finally, letting Khrelyn off the hook, Tawtanya changed the subject. "Myana and I will be away for a bit on private business. I won't be able to see you for a while."

Tawtanya reached her hand across the table and took Khrelyn's hand in her own. "You said that you have another mission that you must fly that you aren't at liberty to tell me about, so I know you will understand that my business is something that I can't tell you about either."

"Will you be in danger?" Khrelyn asked with concern.

"I doubt that I will be in any more danger than you will be on your next flight."

Somehow that did not relieve Khrelyn for one moment. Space travel always had its share of dangers. What could Tawtanya be doing that was so secretive and possibly dangerous. Khrelyn didn't like Tawtanya to be in danger for even one moment. He knew she had led a protective life this far from the Enforcers, but would that last? At any moment, Ananaya could have her arrested. The puzzlement was why he had not so far.

Parting was mixed emotions for both Tawtanya and Khrelyn. On the one hand, it was hard to know they would not be seeing each other for some time. On the other hand, the known separation approaching caused each to feel an intensity towards the other that was suppressed during the casual time together. Taking Tawtanya into his arms, Khrelyn pressed his lips gently upon hers. A sudden fierceness gripped each, and the kisses became more passionate than ever before. Finally pulling away, Tawtanya raced away down the narrow street to vanish from sight.

Khrelyn, once again, watched the love of his life disappear from view. Slowly, he walked back to the boarding facility. His skyplane was retired to the spaceport at the request of Tawtanya. Knowing she hated the vapor trails, Khrelyn used the method of travel that everyone but the elite used...his feet or rykes. He would have a long walk in the morning to get to his post in time for lift-off.

Catching a ride with a farmer, Khrelyn made it back to the compound in plenty of time. He knew he would be briefed for his next mission the following day. When the time of the briefing arrived, Khrelyn was pleased to discover that he would be taking supplies and new directives to Yyemara. Tucking her doll and some special treats into his belongings, Khrelyn prepared to meet his crew for the flight.

Hoping against odds that someone would be congenial and not put off by his rank, Khrelyn searched the faces for someone familiar that he might be able to relax with on the long journey. Not seeing any familiar faces amongst the officers, Khrelyn knew he would not have anyone to talk with on this trip. That made the destination more anticipated since he and Yyemara would rekindle their friendship.

A quarter season later, reaching the coordinates on Earth, Khrelyn went to the teleport dock to meet Yyemara. Pressing out any wrinkles in his uniform while standing in anticipation of his first meeting with Yyemara in quite a long time, Khrelyn was delighted when she teleported into view.

"Welcome aboard, Yyemara, or should I say, Ava?" Khrelyn said as he reached out his hand to steady her. A slight feeling of dizziness or disorientation always followed teleportation.

Giving Khrelyn a hug, an emotional response reserved for Khrelyn alone, Yyemara sported a huge, uncharacteristic smile. "What did you bring me?" she asked, sounding almost like a young girl.

Khrelyn whipped out the doll Yyemara requested when they last were in each other's presence. "My doll! Oh, thank you. You remembered," Yyemara said with glee.

"That isn't all that I remembered to bring for you," Khrelyn said with a glint in his eyes. "Follow me to your old cabin, and I will show you what else I brought."

The two walked together towards the cabin when Khrelyn noticed the parcel tucked under Yyemara's arm. "What is that?" the commander asked.

"I brought you a change of clothing. You are going to be my guest on Earth for the day. What do you think of that? I am sure you don't need to immediately turn around and return to Surtees, do you?" Yyemara asked with playfulness in her voice.

"I could sure use some time off this cruiser, and time spent with you is exactly what I need," Khrelyn said.

As they approached the cabin, Khrelyn turned Yyemara towards him. "I do have some bad news to share with you," Khrelyn said, hoping his timing was not inappropriate.

"What might that be?" Yyemara asked.

"It seems your mother died on Aztara," Khrelyn said, searching Yyemara's eyes for any sign of grief.

"How did she die?" Yyemara asked as she took a seat in her cabin and invited Khrelyn to do the same.

"From what I understand, there was a plague that killed all the females on Aztara, your mother, and the few other female scientists included," Khrelyn informed Yyemara.

Not seeing any change in her eyes, Khrelyn changed the subject. "There is a directive that is for your eyes only from your father. It is to be destroyed immediately after you read and memorize it."

"Then, let me get right to it. The sooner I receive the information, the sooner you and I can go to Earth and have some fun. Excuse me for the time I need to process the information. I will come and find you when I am ready to leave. In the meantime, try on these Earth clothing to see if they fit. I only had my memories of you to try to size them," Yyemara said as she thrust the bundled clothing with shoes into Khrelyn's hands before closing her door.

Standing in front of the full-length mirror attached to the inside of his cabin door, Khrelyn looked at himself in the Earth-style clothing, and he thought that he looked rather good. The material for the shirt was sleek and soft feeling. He liked how it clung to his muscular body without restricting his movements. The slacks, though snug, were also designed to move with him. The shoes, however, were tight and didn't feel quite right. Removing the slip-on shoes, Khrelyn put on his boots and was happy with the look.

"Tawtanya seems to know what colors will look good on me," Khrelyn said as he continued to look at himself in the mirror at the shiny blue and gray shirt with a hint of mauve and gold showing in the pattern. The utilitarian clothing of Surtees was always drab but functional. "If this style of clothing were indicative of Earth's normal outerwear," Khrelyn said, "then Earth is going to be very colorful."

Khrelyn had barely finished examining himself when there was a knock at his door. Opening it, he found Yyemara standing outside his cabin with a wide grin, which softened her usually severe face.

Once again, Khrelyn's thoughts went to Tawtanya when he looked at Yyemara. 'The resemblance was remarkable when Yyemara smiled,' Khrelyn thought.

"Are you ready to go down to Earth with me for the day? I have lots planned to show you before you must return to the starcruiser," Tawtanya said as she grabbed Khrelyn's hand and dragged him towards the teleport.

"What is Earth-like?" Khrelyn asked out of curiosity.

"I can't show you the whole planet. Today, you will be visiting one of the largest cities on this planet. I wish I could show you more, but your time is limited. I see my father has a timetable, and it involves you commanding a starfreighter, so you need to return. That is all I am allowed to tell you about the directive I just memorized.... Let's go."

As the couple was set on the ground of Earth, Khrelyn looked around with awe. "Is all of Earth this beautiful?"

Khrelyn stood in a lush tree-filled area with manicured lawns and gardens before him. A path could be seen winding through trees and lawn alike. Listening, Khrelyn could hear musical notes and looked to Yyemara in puzzlement.

"We are in a large park in the center of the city. It is beautiful, isn't it? What you are hearing is both birds chirping and some musician playing an instrument further down the path," Yyemara explained.

"A park?" Khrelyn asked.

"Parks are natural land set aside for the people to enjoy. We don't have parks on Surtees. I think it is a wonderful idea. I am going to suggest to father that he makes parks," Yyemara said as she took Khrelyn's hand to move him in the correct direction.

"By the way, you look great in Earth clothing. It suits you. The blue color of your shirt brings out the color of your eyes," Yyemara said and then quickly changed the subject as her face started to show the pink tinge of blush.

"I have picked two restaurants for you to sample Earth foods. Well, I shouldn't say all Earthlings eat this food. The foods are as varied as the nations and people on this planet. Right now, we are in New York City, which is part of a country the Earthlings call the United States of America. I wish I could show you more countries. This world is very diversified. Each country has its own culture, which means the dress and food are quite different. If we were someplace else on Earth, I would have chosen a different style of clothing for you to wear, but this outfit is quite typical of New York City."

As they continued to walk down the path through the park, Khrelyn wasn't sure that Yyemara was correct. Every person he saw seemed to be wearing something totally different. No two people were dressed alike. Puzzled, Khrelyn was about to question what Yyemara had told him when Yyemara interrupted his thoughts with more talk.

"We will be leaving the park soon. If you look over the treetops, you will see skyscrapers. This city is built up so more people can inhabit it. There are more people in this city than on the whole planet of Surtees. It might overwhelm you at first. Be prepared for lots of noise. There are not skyplanes in the city. People move about in automobiles. The streets are crowded with them. You will find the noise deafening at times as the cabbies honk their horns all the time," Yyemara said, trying to prepare Khrelyn for what would come next on her tour.

Stepping out of the park was shocking. Khrelyn watched as the automobiles flew past him. Even more intense than the sound was the smell of fumes from the automobiles exhaust. Khrelyn's thoughts went to Tawtanya's complaints of the vapor trails and the toxins, and he couldn't help but wonder if the automobiles weren't just as bad. Suddenly, there were screeching sounds, and all the automobiles came to an abrupt stop.

"Why did all the automobiles stop moving?" Khrelyn asked as he made the observation.

"Look down the street, and you will see more automobiles moving in the opposite direction. Earth has a system to move as much traffic as possible, giving everyone a chance to get where they want to go. It is rather complicated, but most of the time, it works. Listen to the honking. Right now, someone is blocking the flow of traffic, and it is making another driver angry. People are always angry in this city," Yyemara said without expression.

Yyemara directed Khrelyn to points of interest as they walked to their first destination. "We could take a cab, or I could have called my driver, but I felt you would see more if we walked. I hope your feet aren't hurting."

"They would have been hurting if I wore the shoes you brought for me to wear. They hurt just standing still," Khrelyn said as he looked down at his feet.

"Your boots look rather chic. I am sure Earthlings will want a pair. They are always changing their fashion, "Yyemara commented, leaving Khrelyn to figure out what she was talking about.

"You are about to taste what New Yorkers call pizza. We are entering Lombardi's in a district called Little Italy. Some people eat pizza as their main staple. I hope that you enjoy it. The place has lots of ambiance," Yyemara said as she guided Khrelyn to a table.

The red and white checkered plastic tablecloths were lost on Khrelyn. His eyes went to the large circular trays being carried to the tables by servers. Watching with interest, he saw people pull off wedges of the food with their hands and take massive bites with strings of something hanging from their mouths.

"It is made from cheese, not unlike what we have in Surtees. It has all kinds of ingredients. I think we should have a pizza with everything on it so you can get the full experience. Do you want wine with your pizza?" Yyemara asked.

When the server came to the table, Yyemara went back to her no-nonsense self. She quickly ordered for both of them without a smile or courtesy of any kind towards the server. Khrelyn remembered his first meeting with Yyemara when she entered his starcruiser and shuddered. How Yyemara could be so cold and indifferent to the masses and yet warm and friendly towards him was something Khrelyn was not able to understand.

Khrelyn felt he was the same towards everyone until he stopped and remembered how he must keep his crew at arm's length. He supposed that was all Yyemara was doing, only arm's length extended towards everyone but a select few. Khrelyn felt grateful that he was amongst those select few.

"Are you enjoying the pizza?" Yyemara said after the large tray was set on the table.

"Wow! It is wonderful. People eat this all the time here?" Khrelyn asked as he shoved another large bite into his mouth.

"Not all the time. Later I will take you to another restaurant that is completely different from this one. I want you to have the fullest experience that you can while you are here," Yyemara said as she wiped her mouth with the cloth napkin after taking a sip of her wine.

"I like this wine. What is it made from? We don't have anything like it on Surtees," Khrelyn said.

"No, we don't. I suppose the farmers could make a drink from some of the fruit if they had excess. It would sure make their lives happier if they did have wine. There would be less grumbling for sure," Yyemara remarked.

"You are aware that the people of Surtees are discontent?" Khrelyn asked, having assumed that Yyemara never left her laboratory while she was living on Surtees.

"Occasionally, my father would allow me to accompany him to the Zrymyr Games. I didn't miss the fact that Enforcers were needed to keep the discontent in line. I never understood why they were dissatisfied. My father did so much to make the lives of the common people better," Yyemara said without feeling.

Khrelyn was about to try to explain the common people's point of view when Yyemara announced it was time to continue the tour. Once back in the sunlight, Yyemara hailed a cab.

"You may as well get to ride in an automobile before you return to your command. I think you will find the ride exciting," Yyemara said as she strapped herself into the backseat.

Taking the cue, Khrelyn did the same as the car moved out into traffic with horns honking and fists visibly shaking from the opened window of other cab drivers. Soon their automobile was moving along at the speed of the rest of the cars on the street. Moving from one lane to another brought about more honking and fist-waving from cars behind.

"Is it always like this to move around the city?" Khrelyn asked, feeling fear rising in his stomach.

"Yes, it is always like this. Sometimes, there are accidents, and then the noise gets even worse. I have actually seen the drivers get out and fistfight after one of those accidents. Earth people are very emotional. When they are happy, they laugh and show much joy. When they are angry, they become monsters," Yyemara said.

"Monsters?" Khrelyn asked, not sure what a monster might be.

Yyemara did not respond. She pointed out a large building. "That is my building here in New York City. I have several more buildings and laboratories all over the world. I will be leaving tomorrow to go to another country. I will be very busy from now on with my new directives," Yyemara said casually.

Khrelyn wanted to ask more about the directives, but he knew there was no way Yyemara would answer even the smallest of his questions. Instead, he just marveled at the height of the building Yyemara just pointed out.

"What do all the people do who work for you?" Khrelyn asked, feeling this might be a good lead-in question that would cause Yyemara to reveal more of her father's plan.

"You know that I am a genetic scientist. That is what all my facilities are involved in," Yyemara answered and then let the subject drop leaving Khrelyn's imagination to fill in the gaps.

The afternoon flew by as Yyemara showed Khrelyn one tourist site after another. "I wish we had time to go to a play at the theater. It would reveal to you the creative side of the humans here on Earth. They are quite inventive in ways to occupy their leisure time. However, we only have time for one more meal, and then I must deposit you at the coordinates for you to return to your space cruiser. We will be eating at Keen's Chophouse. It is near the theaters since the restaurant was built for the actors who were in shows here in what was formerly called the Herald Square theater district. You will find the restaurant interesting. The ceilings are lined with pipes where the individuals owned and smoked their pipes when they came to eat. They would leave their pipes for the next time they were in the restaurant. It is quite fascinating."

Khrelyn was about to ask what smoking was when they entered the restaurant, and he saw all the pipes Yyemara mentioned, line after line of pipes on the ceiling. Many of the patrons were smoking but not pipes. Instead, they were smoking small white paper rolled into cylinders. Khrelyn watched in fascination as smoke was blown out of the mouths or noses in some instances.

"Why are these people doing that?" Khrelyn asked.

Yyemara crinkled her forehead, "I don't totally understand. It has something to do with their advertisements and the economy."

Khrelyn wanted to ask more questions since Yyemara's answer made no sense to him when the server arrived. Yyemara ordered for both of them without looking at the menu.

"This restaurant is known for its 2-inch mutton chops. I ordered one for each of us. I hope you will enjoy it."

Khrelyn had no idea what mutton was or why it was chopped. He wanted to ask more questions, but instead, his eyes went towards the ceiling where the various smoking pipes stood in row after row across the ceiling. As his neck became stiff from looking up, he brought his gaze back to Yyemara, who was smiling at his ignorance.

"There is so much that is different here on Earth. I am still surprised by what humans do. Smoking pipes hanging from the ceiling are just one oddity. If you stayed longer, I could show you things that would make your skin crawl," Yyemara laughed.

Chewing contentedly, Khrelyn didn't want to think about things that would make his skin crawl. He wanted to concentrate on the flavors mingling in his mouth. Mutton was still a puzzlement. He wanted to ask more about the food, but his thoughts turned to a lack of affect he sensed in Yyemara's earlier response to his revealing announcement.

Continuing to chat amicably through dinner, Khrelyn risked asking a more personal question. "When I told you that your mother died, you didn't seem to react at all. Were you close to her?"

"Not at all. I was raised by a nanny. I only saw my mother on the few occasions my father felt we should be seen as a family. In those cases, I was to be seen only. Once I was finished with my formal education, I was supervised by my mother at the lab at the Neuro-Chemical Center. She was my supervisor...not, my mother. I am not sure she even thought of me as a daughter," Yyemara answered.

She continued with a question of her own. "Were you close to your mother?"

"Yes, but not as close as I was to my father, "Khrelyn said with a note of sadness in his voice.

"Your father is dead?" Yyemara asked.

"I am assuming that he is. He had my mother take my brother and me away from the farm, and we never heard from him again."

Yyemara's eyes were drawn to the front door where her driver was waving. "Oh, gosh! We are going to need to fly if I am going to get you to the coordinates on time," Yyemara said as she tossed down a bundle of green paper on the table.

"Fly?" Khrelyn said excitedly. He was interested in what skyplanes were like on Earth and was on his feet immediately.

"That is just an expression that Earthlings say. I mean, I will really need to put the *pedal to the metal*," Yyemara said as she took the keys from her driver and rushed towards the convertible silver Porsche parked in front of the restaurant with Khrelyn looking more puzzled than ever. Khrelyn noted as he exited the door, that Yyemara was tying a scarf around her head as she took the driver's seat.

"Get in and fasten your seatbelt. I will need to be driving fast!" Yyemara said as she pulled rapidly from the curb with horns blaring at her sudden intrusion into the traffic flow.

Swerving between cars, Khrelyn held his breath in fear. Cars and buildings blurred as she sped erratically through the streets. Khrelyn was used to speed, but in the skyplane, there was no obstacle that he needed to avoid. Yyemara seemed hell-bent on aiming towards every single one. With the brakes screeching, the car came to a sudden, jerking stop as an old woman with a small pull along cart filled with groceries crossed the street in front of them. Once she barely past the Porsche, Yyemara held her foot to the gas pedal, causing the small sportscar to leap forward and fishtail side to side from the dead stop.

"Do we really need to drive this fast?" Khrelyn managed to ask, with the wind blowing his words into Yyemara's ears.

"If I am going to get you back to your spacecruiser on time, we need to hurry. I am afraid I was having such a nice afternoon that I lost track of time. You will need to stay an extra week if we lose this opportunity. I have a feeling Father would not appreciate the delay," Yyemara said as she looked at Khrelyn.

Khrelyn immediately regretted asking a question when he saw that Yyemara's eyes had left the road, and another obstacle loomed immediately in front of his view. Pointing frantically at the large delivery truck with a sign saying *Meats* on the side that was pulling out into their lane from the curb, Khrelyn was relieved when Yyemara expertly swerved, missing the truck but ending up in on-coming traffic with horns blasting. With a near miss, Yyemara pulled her steering wheel rapidly to get back into her own lane.

Khrelyn didn't relax until New York City was in the rear-view mirror, and the countryside was in front of them. The first thing

Khrelyn noted, besides the trees and flowers, was that his eyes no longer were stinging from all the fumes.

"Why do people live in crowded cities when they could live here in this peaceful countryside?" Khrelyn asked.

"It is all about work. There aren't many jobs here in the country. Some people commute to the city, though. I would guess those people feel like you. Others actually like all the noise and chaos. Earth people are interesting. If I were not a genetic scientist, I would want to be a psychologist or behaviorist and just study this planet's inhabitants," Yyemara said as she pulled off the main road onto a side road.

"We are right on time. I will leave you now. I look forward to the next time you come to Earth. Maybe you will be able to spend another day with me at one of my other facilities. Each one is totally different from the others," Yyemara said as she directed Khrelyn to a spot several yards away from her automobile.

"Thank you again for bringing my doll and for the other treats. Your kindness will always be appreciated," Yyemara said. Before Khrelyn could thank her for an unusual but fun day and ask why the doll was so special, he flickered into oblivion.

CHAPTER FORTY-SIX

Tawtanya and Myana boarded the sailing ship. "All is ready for your inspection," Captain Dyston said formally.

The men and older boys stood at attention. Tawtanya immediately found Noryan and Josyah in the crowd and smiled. Noryan winked back. They looked healthy and strong, and Tawtanya, for a moment, was nervous about what their plight might be on this rescue mission.

"Men, you all know what you will be doing next. Your captain has explained the dangers but also the rewards. If you can rescue the many men and boys being held at the internment camp, your numbers will swell. The army to overtake Surtees will become a reality. I know the dangers involved, and I also know how hard each of you has trained for this event and the war that will follow. We can no longer stand by and let the scientists ruin our planet, or we will have no place to live. This planet is doomed if we don't act now!" Tawtanya said as she had spoken before crowds many times in the past.

Softening her voice, Tawtanya added, "Some of you may die when you encounter the Enforcers. You have trained hard, and you have weapons that should even the odds. I pray that each of you returns to fight another day. Myana and I have been building resistance forces everywhere we go. You are not alone in this fight. You have many brothers and sisters throughout Surtees who have taken up arms. We will win back our planet. We will live good lives again. We will have clean air and water. Our farms will once again yield crops that will nourish and sustain our children. We will never worry again about any of our sons being taken away...."

Tawtanya's eyes were drawn towards Noryan as she let the last words drop. She could see the haunted look in his eyes at the memory of his eldest son's disappearance.

"We will have our revenge!" Tawtanya declared.

The men cheered when Tawtanya stopped talking and stood like a statue, tall and erect. The men were told they could break ranks, and each man went to retrieve their weapons and supplies for the attack on the internment camp.

Earlier, Captain Dyston, Lymson, and Noryan had sat around the captain's table with a map of the internment camp that Noryan had drawn from memory. As Noryan explained the routine of the camp, plans were made for the rescue of the prisoners.

"I usually was awakened before the sun was light in the sky. The small group of men who worked in the tunnels digging out the boulders and breaking them into smaller rocks was about to return home from their long night's work for a short time to sleep before being awakened to help in the fields. My workforce was much larger. There were often as many as one hundred men who were marched out to clear the rubble. We made a steady stream of workers back and forth inside of the tunnel to the outside, where we dumped our loads and returned for more. We rotated digging since only a few could work in the small, cramped area at the end of the tunnel," Noryan explained as he pointed to the tunnel on the map and the approximate distance it was from the main camp.

"How many Enforcers would work on either shift?" Captain Dyston asked as he kept his eyes glued to the map.

"At night, there were usually no more than six to seven Enforcers. In the daytime, the number easily swelled to forty. There were always two Enforcers at the entrance of the tunnel, two at the end to keep the diggers working, and the rest would be stationed at intervals along the tunnel, so no one straggled. The use of trydox prods kept everyone moving swiftly to avoid that excruciating pain," Noryan said, wincing involuntarily at the memory. "In the fields, the Enforcers rely on whips to keep everyone working hard," Noryan added.

"Do any carry stun-blasters or worse?" the captain asked as he mentally calculated the risks his men would be up against.

"The two at the entrance to the tunnel carries them. If anyone tries to escape, the Enforcers usually kill the prisoner instead of trying to recapture them. They are not concerned about losing numbers since a new group of ready and available incarcerated men will be brought in to fill the numbers," Noryan continued to clarify.

"And only men are at this camp, no boys?" Lymson finally gave voice to his concerns.

"No, boys…Tawtanya and Myana have a theory that the missing boys are the Enforcers…." Noryan said and looked to each of his fellow conspirators to catch their reactions.

"That has always been my greatest fear," Captain Dyston said sadly. "We won't tell the others, in case that is true. I don't need any of the men feeling guilty or hesitating to kill for fear they are killing someone's son. They are monsters now, and we need to eliminate them if we are to be free of the scientists' hold on us."

Lymson nodded his head in agreement. Noryan felt sick to his stomach at the thought that one of those hideous creatures could be his son. "Isn't there always a possibility of reversing the effects of genetic programming?"

Tawtanya and Myana walked in on the conversation. "Ananaya is not working on any reversals. He wants Enforcers. He doesn't care about the boys. Exactly who do you think you can talk into working on a cure," Tawtanya asked Noryan. "I understand your fear that your eldest son may be one of the Enforcers, but if he even survived the transformation, he would self-destruct before you could possibly convince a scientist to try to convert him back. There is no possible way we can work on a cure until we have overthrown the scientists. Then what? Do we torture a scientist until he agrees to begin research on the reversal cure?"

Noryan held his hand out to stop Tawtanya's argument. "I can't just kill every Enforcer. One could be my son!"

"We understand your angst," Captain Dyston said empathetically. Changing his tone, he added, "but will you do what must be done when the time comes or will you be frozen with indecision?"

Noryan's thoughts turned to Josyah, realizing he was going to lose his youngest son if he tried to save his eldest. He understood what he must do…what he was being asked…to stop the Enforcers and end the rule of the scientists.

"I really understand now. I will make the right decision. My eldest son is probably already dead. I just wish I could save other people's sons, but I know that is impossible. What we must do is stop any other boy from being turned into an Enforcer. Is there anything more that I can tell you about the camp?"

Having learned all that he could from Noryan's experience at the camp, the five discussed the plan of attack. "I believe it would be in our best interest to attack before the large workforce enters the tunnels. It will be much more difficult to fight the Enforcers in that darkened space with all the prisoners that they can use as shields. Noryan, you will lead the command into the tunnel to take out the six or seven Enforcers and free the night workers. Lymson, I will need your men to be positioned to engage the Enforcers as they march the field workers in place after the sun starts to show in the sky. I will take my men and rout out the Enforcers in the buildings.

There will be some sleeping and some watching the kitchen, latrine, and maintenance crews, so being stealthy will be necessary not to rouse the others to action. Can we count on any of the prisoners to assist us?" the captain asked Noryan one final question.

"Very little, I fear, except for the more recent prisoners brought to the camp. The long-held prisoners are starved and overworked the whole time they have been at the camp. Most are so despondent that they won't even realize they are being rescued for a while. However, the ones who still cling to self-preservation may lend a hand. I know that I barely had the strength to escape, but I did have hope. That is the only thing that got me through the mountains and back to my farmland."

Captain Dyston patted Noryan on his back. "You had something to go home to. Josyah is a fine young man. He will make us both proud this day."

The evening dew was accumulating on the ropes hanging from the masts. This day would be long and hard as the ship sailed around the point but kept just out of view of the camp. Several men scrambled into the smaller skiffs, which would take them to the beaches near the camp. Walls erected to keep prisoners in would be the first obstacle the rescuers would need to breach. Hardened from time aboard the ships, meant the climb would not be difficult as each sailor climbed ropes and riggings many times during their training. Using grappling hooks to direct the ropes to the top of the walls would give the sailors many places to mount their attack.

"Men spread out along the wall. Grapplers, be ready to launch the hooks and knotted ropes to the top," commanded Captain Dyston.

At this time, Noryan knew from experience that most of the prisoners were now being roused to eat a meager morning meal and then would be marched to work in the tunnels, fields, or whatever other jobs needed to be done that day. As the early morning progressed, there would be a very small detail of Enforcers left in the camp to supervise the prisoners who had duties in the kitchen, the latrines, or general work around the camp. The others would be in the tunnel or the adjacent fields overseeing the slave laborers.

Plans made in advance required Noryan's group to leave much earlier to make the distant trip to the tunnel before the night workers would leave, and the day workforce would arrive. Minimal lights would be used to navigate to the end of the tunnel where the workers were based. Only two Enforcers would be posted along the tunnel path to keep the slaves moving. During the night time, the steady stream of slaves would not be needed as the work of digging, crushing rock, and packing carrying poles at the head of the tunnel would take precedence.

An Enforcer or two would be encountered even before entering the tunnel as they were always stationed to make sure no prisoner escaped as they brought out the rocks or burlap bags of soil to be cleared. They were the first obstacle.

Noryan hoped the two Enforcers outside would be Enforcers who were failing. In the past, even the Enforcers who were starting to self-destruct were required to stand guard until the day they died. Noryan almost felt sorry for the Enforcers, realizing that in some ways, they were prisoners of the scientists as well. The only difference was that they did not seem to understand that fact as clearly as Noryan.

As the men cleared the encampment walls, Captain Dyston pointed to the other two groups to separate. One group would clear the fields of Enforcers, headed by Lymson, while another group went to the buildings to make sure all Enforcers were killed. Josyah was to be with the group entering the buildings as the captain did not want Noryan's mind split between watching out for his son and doing his job.

Before progressing with the attack plan, Noryan explained to his group how the tunnel operation worked when he was a prisoner. "Usually, twelve men worked the tunnels. Once large rocks were dug out by two or three workers, three other men would break the large rocks into smaller rocks, which would be carried out on pole carriers by a steady flow of prisoners.

Two Enforcers were stationed to keep the men digging by use of trydox prods when necessary and even when not necessary. Two Enforcers would be stationed in the tunnels to keep the workers from straggling in the tunnels, two other Enforcers were always left at the entrance to supervise the emptying of the rock and soil as well as to keep anyone from escaping. The number of Enforcers usually totaled half of the men supervised, but occasionally, additional Enforcers would accompany the workforce. What I am trying to tell you is that we may encounter six Enforcers or more."

Signaling two men to quietly take to the woods, while the rest fanned out, taking cover as they approached the entrance to the tunnel was the silent order given. The two in the woods were to look for any Enforcer who may be checking the perimeter as well as to fend off any Enforcers who may come late to the party.

As they continued their forward movement, hidden by the cover of trees or boulders, Noryan signaled a halt. As was the normal routine, two Enforcers were at the mouth of the tunnel talking. As one prisoner came out of the tunnel loaded down with heavy boulders on his carrying pole, the Enforcer closest to the entrance, intentionally tripped the man, causing him to fall, knocking out his front teeth on the large rock he was carrying.

Laughter erupted from the other Enforcer. Enraged, Noryan nocked his arrow and let it fly into the chest of the maniacally amused giant, who stood wavering on his feet before falling to the ground. Before the second Enforcer could give the alarm, another sailor's dead aim, took that Enforcer to the ground as well.

Racing to the fallen prisoner, Noryan silently warned him not to yell out for fear there might be Enforcers in the woods. Seeing the relief on the fallen prisoner's face as he suddenly recognized him made Noryan feel as though his life suddenly had meaning.

"Gyson, old buddy," Noryan whispered. "We are going to get you out of here. Are you able to stand?"

Starting to talk in a normal voice, Noryan cautioned him with a finger to his lips. "Whisper."

Gyson indicated that his legs were not broken, only his front teeth, as he winced in pain from the air, hitting the exposed nerves as he talked. Noryan gave him his kerchief to clean the blood off his face and directed Gyson to go to the woods and remain hidden.

"Shouldn't I go back to camp?" Gyson asked in a hushed voice.

"No, fighting is taking place there now, and I don't want you caught in the cross-fire. There are two of our men in the woods. I am sure they have seen what has happened from their concealed place and will meet you as you walk into the woods. Go now," Noryan directed.

Waving his fellow rescuers forward, the small band entered the tunnel. When the light from the entrance faded to dim light, the men halted to allow their eyes to adjust. Noryan directed half to ignite their light sources to give them a chance to see where they were going. Noryan's hearing heightened with only a dim source of light, heard the shuffling noise of another worker coming close.

Noryan knew this would be a tricky moment. The worker being surprised may call out in alarm, and his voice would echo down the tunnel to the ears of the Enforcers. The element of surprise would be taken away. Calling out softly was the only way he could think to handle the situation.

"It is me...Noryan. Please don't call out."

As the shuffling noise became louder, a voice whispered back. "Noryan, is that really you?"

Immediately, Noryan recognized Jaspyn's voice. He laid next to this man on the floor for seasons. They often whispered in the dark to encourage each other. Knowing if he used the man's name, Jaspyn would relax and follow his orders. Noryan said quietly, "Jaspyn, we are here to rescue everyone at the camp. I want you to go outside and go into the woods. One of our men will find you and help you hide."

Placing his carrying pole on the ground, Jaspyn grasped Noryan and hugged him fiercely. Noryan could feel every bone in his friend's arms and back, and a feeling of rage from seasons of abuse overcame him.

"You have become fat, my friend," Jaspyn said with a quiet chuckle.

"And you are still as lean as when I left," Noryan said as he bent over to pick up the man's burden at his feet. "I need to ask you to carry this burden one last time. I don't want any of my men to trip over the rocks. I need each one to be able to fight, so an injury now would complicate matters," Noryan said as he handed the large, heavy pole carrier back to his friend. "We will meet again soon. Go now and find a safe place to hide," Noryan said as he guided Jaspyn along the line of rebels.

The tunnel, wide enough for four men to walk side by side, had been intentionally enlarged to allow for the small cart to have access for the future plans that Noryan was not privy. He still had no idea where the tunnel was to lead, but he knew that it progressed significantly since his own escape. With the tunnel now longer, the Enforcers would not miss the two men who had escaped for quite some time. Eventually, Noryan figured one Enforcer would be sent to find out what the delay may be for the return of the two prisoners.

The rebels would continue to walk in relative darkness. The floor was smooth from seasons of prisoners shuffling along the path, and the ceiling was high enough for the tallest Enforcer to walk down the center without bumping his head. Noryan knew his men were uneasy being so deep into the tunnel with very little light, but being prudent was necessary at this time.

Quietly moving along the tunnel, Noryan estimated that they were now six k-rods along into the tunnel. As he predicted, the heavy footfalls of an advancing Enforcer could be heard. Noryan directed his men to stagger themselves with several kneeling to allow others to shoot over them and to extinguish the lights at this time.

Whispering a fast directive, Noryan told his men that he would ignite a light source just before the Enforcer was directly in front of them. "Don't waste arrows. In fact, Stymly, take the shot and make sure your aim is true. We have limited blast arrows, and we may need the rest to fight the way out of the internment camp. The rest of you be ready just in case Stymly misses."

Seconds later, Noryan lit his light source as the Enforcer's grotesque facial features were displayed prominently in the glow. A look of horror crossed the Enforcer's narrowed eyes as he saw the band of men before him with bows drawn and eyes intent to kill. Grabbing his only weapon, the trydox prod, the Enforcer growled in rage and advanced upon the kneeling first row of archers but did not make contact as Stymly's arrow exploded in the Enforcer's chest, causing a deep gash with the smell of burnt rotten flesh lingering in the dank tunnel air.

Dragging the dead Enforcer to the far-left side of the tunnel walls, the group continued quietly deeper into the gut of the mountain. "How much further do you think this tunnel may go?" One man whispered.

"No talking," came Noryan's harsh whisper back. With only one-fourth of the men igniting their light sources again, the path was barely illuminated. Noryan did not want the Enforcers at the end of the tunnel to see their approach.

Halting his group of men, Noryan listened carefully. He could just barely make out the clinking sounds of tools hitting rocks. He knew they were almost to their end destination. Spreading the men out to fill the entire width of the tunnel as best as they could with the curve of the ceiling, the line formed was three men deep. The men already knew once they got to the point where they could see the Enforcers that the front line would kneel as before to allow the middle line to shoot their arrows if the first line missed. The light sources were extinguished.

Walking as quietly as possible, the band of rescuers advanced until they could make out the images of the prisoners digging and the three Enforcers standing guard. With a signal from Noryan to let loose the first line of arrows, the Enforcers barely had time to turn to see their attackers before they lie dead.

The stunned workers cowered in the tunnels until Noryan spoke. "Don't be afraid. We are here to rescue you from this torment. It is me, Noryan. I used to be one of you."

One bedraggled man got to his feet. "I remember you. I thought you were dead. I was sure the Enforcers hunted you down and killed you."

"You were wrong. I made it out, and now I am here so that you can be free." Noryan said with glee in his voice. His announcement was answered with sobs and tears of first--disbelief, then relief and finally something more...hope.

"We have a long walk back through the tunnel. Our work here is not yet done. We will need to join our comrades and continue the fight above ground," Noryan said as some of his men came forward to assist the bewildered men from the cavernous tunnel.

CHAPTER FORTY-SEVEN

While still dark, Lymson's men found hiding places near the cultivated fields. Having been cleared for growing food to feed the Enforcers, and occasionally the prisoners, there were few places of concealment. Doing the best that they could to hide behind stalks that would soon be ready to harvest was the only good hiding place available.

Simultaneously, Captain Dyston and his men would be attacking the sleeping quarters of the Enforcers. Better to thin out the enemy before the real fighting began, was his theory. If Noryan's intel was correct, Captain Dyston knew which building would contain the sleeping giants. A quick arrow through the chest would eliminate them from the fight.

Leaving the majority of his me outside to engage any Enforcers that might come out of the buildings, Captain Dyston and a smaller band of men went quietly into the dorms. Before entering, the captain told Josyah, "the other groups should be at their positions, we must act quickly, take to the rafters inside the main building now." From Josyah's perch on the rafters high above, the captain hoped that Josyah would be able to see any Enforcer that might sneak up on his band of men.

Hearing the loud snores of only a few sleeping Enforcers, Captain Dyston knew most of the other Enforcers were already rousing the prisoners or eating a morning meal. Disappointed that fewer

Enforcers would be dealt a killing blow first thing, the captain knew his men would end up encountering more than a fair share of Enforcers, for which he didn't have an alternative plan. Fear crept into his mind at the thought of losing even one of his men. Pushing that thought from his mind, he gave the signal to extinguish the lives of the thirty sleeping Enforcers lying before him.

Arrows rang out through the sleeping quarter, and Enforcers never awoke. From above, Josyah let an arrow fly from his bow at an Enforcer who opened another door waking the sleeping giants inside. A stunned loud and long cry was emitted from the Enforcer before he died, which Captain Dyston suddenly realized their surprise attack was over, and many more Enforcers would be alerted.

"Get to cover! We are going to have company!" the captain yelled.

Josyah scampered across the beams of the rafter as agile as any nedryl to find a better-protected perch from which to shoot. Barely in place, Josyah saw the door filled by Enforcers attempting to push through, shoulder-to-shoulder, to combat the intruders. Not realizing their stupidity in fighting each other to get through the narrow door, the jammed Enforcers were easy targets for the men firing their stealthy arrows.

Silence followed as the Enforcers realized their mistake. A new plan was developing, and Captain Dyston feared it might involve explosive devices. Calling a retreat, he told his men to get out of the building and take cover outside with the other sailors.

Josyah, hearing the call for retreat, held his ground. As the sailors ran out the door leading to the outside, an Enforcer stood inside the doorway with a device in his hand. As he pulled his arm back to lob the device at the retreating men, Josyah let loose an arrow, causing the monster to fall back into the arms of fellow Enforcers who stood behind him. The device went off, killing more than a handful of Enforcers.

Josyah scrambled across the rafters to find a new place of concealment. The crossbeams of the rafters were large and bulky, which gave him the cover he needed. Ducking behind, he missed the Enforcer, whose eyes scanned the beams for the enemy who fired the last arrow. Seeing nothing, the Enforcer stepped over the dead, and with many more Enforcers charging behind, they left the building to fight the men on the outside.

Captain Dyston's men were scrambling to take cover in the encampment. Finding spots to conceal themselves, they each nocked their arrows into their bows to meet the charge of the Enforcers. As the giants ran outside, the first many were dropped with arrows. The rush of more Enforcers didn't give the men time to nock another arrow, so many retreated further to give themselves more time while other sailors drew their long knives in preparation for hand-to-hand combat.

Many of the Enforcers carried trydox prods and whips, while others rushed out with only their long arms and huge muscles as their defense. Even without weapons, the Enforcers would be formidable and nearly impossible for one man to bring down alone.

Seeing targets, the Enforcers ran straight for the men who were either without arrows, having spent them on previous targets, or being caught unprepared. As sailors realized they must depend on their superior agility to stay alive, individual fights became frenzied.

Captain Dyston kept his arrow nocked and ready to take down any Enforcer who was winning the battle on the ground. Letting his arrow fly at one target or another from his concealment, he gave many of his men time to recover and fight again.

Josyah took to the rooftops and did the same. His high position gave him an advantage that his captain was denied. As men he had grown to admire and care about were knocked senseless by the prods, Josyah would send a blast arrow into the back or chest of the attacking Enforcer. Unable to assist the fallen men to their feet, Josyah would look for the next Enforcer to kill.

The sounds of battle caught the ears of the Enforcers who were marching prisoners to the fields. Knowing there was no escape for the prisoners, they abandoned them to run to the compound to fight the intruders.

As more Enforcers were seen to pour into the gates from the fields, Captain Dyston began to lose hope. Many of his men lay stunned or maybe dead from blows given by the Enforcers. Blood could be seen on several where the leather whips broke their skin viciously. Captain Dyston spotted one of his men with limbs twisted in unnatural positions, where an Enforcer obviously crushed the life out of him.

Snapping himself out of despondency, Captain Dyston reached for another arrow and realized it was his last. Seeing a fallen member of his party lying on the ground, Captain Dyston ran to retrieve the fallen man's quiver with several arrows visible. As he almost reached his goal, his eye caught sight of an Enforcer barreling down on him.

Making a sliding grab for the quiver, Captain Dyston tried to reach for an arrow and nock it while still rolling on the ground. As he turned onto his back to make his aim, the Enforcer's chest blew open from a blast arrow driven deep into his body. Blood splattered, and chunks of rotting flesh flew across the captain. Quickly rolling further away, Captain Dyston was barely able to get out of the way of the falling body.

From his advantage point, flat on his back, his sight was directed upwards to the rooftop where a smiling Josyah raised his bow in salute. Getting rapidly to his feet, Captain Dyston returned the salute.

Cheers were heard from his men as Lymson's team entered the walled encampment through the open gates. Drawing their bows on the run, the men let fly multiple arrows dropping Enforcers in the process of maiming the ship's men. Some of Noryan's men also arrived, having heard the battle from their return from the tunnels. Captain Dyston now felt hope that the odds were more even, and his men may have a chance to destroy the remaining Enforcers if they could fight from concealment, instead of battling with their long knives.

Shouting an order for the new arrivals to take cover and continue the fight, Captain Dyston did the same. It seemed there was still an unsurmountable number of Enforcers, and the odds were not quite in their favor. Many of his men were out of arrows, and the newest arrivals to the battle were using their arrows rapidly. Still, many Enforcers remained standing with weapons of their own choosing.

Once again, the Captain's men were driven to fight hand-to-hand. This time, the men joined forces and fought two against one Enforcer to even the odds. One man would strike from the back and move quickly out of the way as his team member would viciously strike a blow, either aiming at the hamstrings to drop the monsters to their knees, or to give another disabling blow to a vital organ. Even fighting as teams, men were being slaughtered.

Captain Dyston no longer had time to yell out orders. He was fighting for his own life along with his men. Screams of pain were constant to his ears as he side-stepped to avoid prods or whips. Keeping out of the reach of the huge muscular arms of the Enforcers was imperative. If allowed to be grabbed, most men found themselves crushed or worse. Captain Dyston danced out of reach many times, but he was feeling his body fatiguing to the point where his muscles were no longer responding to his brain's orders to move.

Falling to the ground, Captain Dyston found himself vulnerable once again. Josyah, from this rooftop perch, reached for his last arrow and let it fly to once again save his captain. Now the young lad had no idea what he should do. He was too small to take on an Enforcer even with the help of a team member. His valor would not allow himself to stay on the rooftop while the other men were fighting for their lives. Before climbing down from the roof, Josyah saw the prisoners in the fields running towards the gate with the tools in hand used to work the crops. Their defiant screams could be heard as they entered the gates and ran to help their liberators.

Swinging their long-handled tools with sharpened curved metal blades as weapons, the prisoners, enraged by seasons of torment and abuse, savaged the Enforcers as a mob, chopping and tearing the flesh of any Enforcer within their reach. All that could be seen were a ring of skeletal backs with tools hailing down onto a bloody mass in the center.

Shivering, that any man could become so vicious, Captain Dyston still was grateful for the help from the prisoners. Them jumping into the foray was turning the battle into his favor. Few Enforcers remained on their feet, but the few were still causing damage to the men. As Noryan entered with the remaining prisoners freed from the tunnels and his team carrying two of their dead prisoners, Captain Dyston knew they had won. The few remaining Enforcers were quickly destroyed by the arrows of Noryan and his team.

The administrative personnel walked out with hands overhead and didn't offer any resistance when swarmed by the now liberated prisoners. Knowing any command he gave to stop the savage beating of the human prison wardens would not be listened to, Captain Dyston turned his attention to his surroundings.

Captain Dyston looked at the carnage with mixed emotions. What his men had set out to do was accomplished, but he felt no joy at seeing the results. All the Enforcers were dead or dying. Many of his own men were also dead or dying. The scene before him seemed surreal. Littered bodies, some crushed and lying on the ground in distorted shapes was too ghastly to look upon for more than a glance. He averted his eyes to the men remaining on their feet. Each looked dazed and exhausted. The prisoners slumped to the ground, overwhelmed by what they did. Captain Dyston felt he must say something.

"Men, we have accomplished what we set out to do at great cost. Sadness is in all of our hearts at seeing our brave men who gave their lives for this cause. We must go forth and carry their sacrifices as a torch to rid Surtees of all the hideous monsters...including the scientists. You men who have slaved here for seasons are now free. We will send more ships for you to return to your homes and family, but we request that once you are back to your normal health that you rejoin us to continue the fight," Captain Dyston said at the top of his voice so all could hear.

Cheers erupted from the prisoners when it sunk in that they truly were free and safe from their tormentors. Some got to their feet and raised their tools high in the air as they continued to chant. "Free Surtees! Free Surtees! Free Surtees!"

As the crowd settled, Captain Dyston gave orders for the dead Enforcers to be gathered, and their bodies burned. The injured men were taken to the dorms, and their fallen comrades were to be taken to the ships for burial at sea. Food from the storerooms was cooked, and the prisoners had their first real meal for seasons.

Noryan and Josyah's reunion was joyful and flooded with relief that both were safe and uninjured. Each told the other their tale from the battle. Noryan's tale entailed how once they were on their way to the encampment, thinking they were safe, Enforcers who were patrolling the perimeter fell upon the rescued prisoners and the few men of Noryan's who lagged behind to help in the battle.

"We were moving slowly. The men who were working in the tunnel all night long were exhausted. I fear I had become lax. My mind was spinning and reliving the events that took place to free the men in my charge when all of a sudden, there was an Enforcer in front of us and two behind. They had stun-blasters, and we had arrows. My quick-thinking men nocked their arrows into the bows and released them, but not before two of the prisoners were lying dead from the blasts. My heart sank. I assured each and every one of the prisoners that they were now safe and free...."

Feeling despondent for a moment, Noryan thoughts went to all the men who were just rescued, and his heart was lightened momentarily. The couple men that he lost would weigh heavy on his mind for many seasons to come if not for the rest of his life.

Captain Dyston told his men to be ready to return to the ships after the bodies of the dead Enforcers were burned. Noryan made up his mind to stay with the rescued prisoners until the next ship arrived to carry the men to safety. Josyah, too, would stay with his father to help with caring for the debilitated men. With good food, rest, and exercise, all the men were expected to make a full recovery. The injured would be taken to the ship immediately for the ship's physician aboard to treat. All was taken care of as the captain commanded, and the sailors headed for the skiffs with the injured. The gates were left wide open with the prisoners cheering their liberators as they boarded the skiffs that were bouncing gently in the waves.

"Tell Tawtanya and Myana that we will rejoin them soon," hollered Noryan as the men started to row towards the waiting ship. "We will join her in the Capital City!"

Raising his hand in a salute, Captain Dyston assured Noryan that his message would be delivered. A gathering stood on the beach and watched the skiffs glide through the open water. Slowly, men returned to the dorms to rest.

CHAPTER FORTY-EIGHT

The communication from Surtees indicated that there would be little rest or recuperation for Khrelyn or his men. It seemed that soon after they touched down, and Khrelyn would assume command of the Starfreighter SSF Ganymede. The destination was not included in the directives.

Khrelyn knew he must see Tawtanya one more time before leaving no matter what. The logistics were yet to be planned, but Khrelyn had some time yet before the space cruiser's return to Surtees. There would only be a short time to find Tawtanya and see her, and that was only if she was in the Capital City. If she were in a more remote part of Surtees, he would only be able to leave a note for her with her mother.

The return trip was agony. Khrelyn planned and re-planned how he would best be able to get away for a short time to find Tawtanya. When they finally entered the gravitational pull of Surtees, Khrelyn was in a sweat.

Quickly disembarking from the starcruiser at the Surtees' spaceport, Khrelyn dropped his flight logs off at the flight control center and rushed out before they could ask him any questions. Finding a skyplane available, even knowing Tawtanya would not approve, Khrelyn disabled the chemical tank and headed for the center of the Capital City, where he hoped to find Tawtanya.

Asking around for where she might be, Khrelyn learned to his joy that she would be holding a rally in the main square.

A large crowd was already gathering in the capital city of Surtees's main square. Khrelyn opened the door to the meeting room, where Tawtanya gathered with an elite group of fellow protestors. "Can I speak to you a moment in private?" Khrelyn asked as he stepped into the room.

Tawtanya's face brightened when she looked up and saw it was Khrelyn speaking. "Of course, my fellow activists were just leaving to circulate amongst the crowd before I speak. I have very little time." Tawtanya nodded to the others to vacate the room.

"I will be leaving to explore another galaxy and planet today. I needed to see you before I left. I won't be back for several months. I wanted to let you know how much I admire your passion for your cause…"

Before Khrelyn could tell Tawtanya how much he enjoyed the evenings with her and that he thought he was falling in love with her, Tawtanya interrupted, feeling on fire with her passion for the cause. She was anxious and stirred to a feverish pitch, thinking about the speech she would be giving to the waiting crowd.

"I also admire you. If it weren't for your time and efforts, many more skyplanes would still be dumping chemicals into our air. I just wish that we had met seasons earlier. The children wouldn't be sick right now if we had.

I can't believe all the awful things the scientists have done to our planet disguising their ruse as progress. The robot UberBugs have destroyed our crops, and the children are malnourished as we speak. The adults are showing symptoms of dementia even before they are elderly. Even more frightening is the fact that whole populations of people have disappeared from our cities. Many of our male children have disappeared. Any child with a disability is taken away to institutions where they supposedly are being helped. The elderly are hidden away in convalescent hospitals, and we aren't allowed to visit any of them. It is more than odd. It feels like a conspiracy gone really bad to me. I know the scientists are behind every evil thing that has happened to our planet and is currently happening as well.

"I know you are employed by the malicious criminal Hoygazor, the Chief Astroscientist. I also know you still feel some loyalty to him, but I can see you are starting to realize I am right. All the scientists are bad. Ananaya, their leader, is pure evil!"

A knock at the door caused Tawtanya to stop her diatribe. Poking his head barely inside the opened door, one of her lead activists told Tawtanya it was time for her to step onto the podium. Nodding her head and saying she would be right there, Tawtanya turned to Khrelyn. Suddenly, feeling guilty she had spent the last few moments she would have with Khrelyn for months by lecturing him, impulsively, she flew into his arms. "I have to go. I am sorry I got so carried away. Please hurry back. I will miss you, dreadfully." With a quick kiss, Tawtanya rushed out the door.

"I love you," Khrelyn said to the closed door.

****

Public unrest spread through the entire planet of Surtees, like a wildfire through a field of dry grass. The Surtarian citizens were furious with the scientists. Citizens in every city and town throughout the planet protested publicly. Woodworkers built soapbox stages in every town center throughout the planet. Farmers, workers, and important individuals spoke to the gathering crowds about their outrage. Large groups of citizens were both verbally and physically confronting the scientists with their fervent hatred when the scientists entered or exited their Science Centers.

In the Science Center headquarters at the Capital City of Surtees, Ananaya, the Chief Scientist, stood resolutely on the center stage of the meeting hall within the sterile white science building. He spoke for the first time in many seasons, with hundreds of his senior scientists seated at different levels around him. Ardently he commanded in as loud a voice as his weakened lungs allowed, "The time has finally come...we have been preparing for the inevitable for many seasons now...we must immediately leave Surtees and join our exploration team of scientists and guards at our new home on Aztara. The citizens...of Surtees no longer believe...we are here to do them no harm."

Just then, as if on cue, a large cubed screen lowered, at center stage, from the Science Center's meeting hall ceiling. The screen displayed an athletic-looking individual, dressed in all black, declaring her anger while standing on one of the soapbox stages in the capital city's town square. Surrounded by stucco white buildings and thousands of villagers stomping on limestone pavers, yelling in unison. "NO MORE SCIENCE...NO MORE SCIENTISTS!"

Tawtanya, a well-known sports champion, addressed a growing crowd. "The scientists on Surtees are out of control; they worked for generations on covert programs intended to re-engineer our genetics," she shouted. "They contaminated our water for many seasons with botched anti-aging chemicals. Our air is polluted with the chemicals in the skyplane's vapor trails. This causes another problem, a rapid advance in ozone depletion. Our bodies are slowly changing generation by generation with genetically modified food products and the required annual vaccines."

The crowd roared in unison again, "NO MORE SCIENCE...NO MORE SCIENTISTS!"

Ananaya interrupted the scene going on outside in the town square. Speaking directly to his scientists, "Men of science...the citizens of Surtees...do not understand we always held their best interest at heart. Our intentions were simple...prolong and improve their lives."

Most of the scientists knew the real truth was always about Ananaya's own health; he was becoming old and weak...sooner than he liked. The scientists had become increasingly aware that the experiments Ananaya directed them to do over many seasons to conduct specific chemical tests on the water, air, and food were not for the betterment of the citizens. In fact, the citizens of Surtees became his lab specimens. The ultimate goal, if successful, would provide Ananaya with a long healthy life. If the citizens benefited from his genius, all the better, they would appreciate his brilliance in the end.

Unfortunately, under extreme pressure from Ananaya's orders to meet impossible time schedules, the project scientists botched their tests again and again. Through these many unsuccessful tests, these project scientists ultimately failed to safeguard the citizens of Surtees. Ananaya repeatedly showed his displeasure in their failures by exiling the incompetent project leaders to re-education camps in the mountainous region of Surtees. The scientists remaining were always fearful that they would be next to be exiled if they displeased Ananaya.

Ananaya and the team of scientists, in the meeting hall, returned their attention to the center stage screen. As the crowd outside grew much larger, they quieted again when Tawtanya repeated her claims, gesturing with her graceful arms. "The scientists have dumped chemicals into our water system, a supposed anti-aging chemical, for two generations now. Many of our children and grandchildren suffer from gross distortions, osteo-generative changes, and neurodevelopmental disorders."

Tawtanya's right hand rose upwards with her finger poking at the sky. "The Astroscientists created numerous chemical vapor trails with their skyplanes. The chemical vapor trails linger, where intense ultraviolet light transforms the vapor." Violently jabbing her finger repeatedly at the sky, she continued with emphasis. "This interaction releases chlorides and bromines that deplete our protective ozone layer at a rapid rate. Soon our children will be unable to walk or play outside without serious damage to their skin. The pollution the chemical compound creates, in the air, we breathe, is changing our genetics!"

The scientists continued to watch the verbal wrath on the screen with apprehension. With each new condemnation, Tawtanya spoke louder, becoming increasingly animated. "THE SCIENTISTS," she bellowed, "supplied our farmers with genetically modified seeds. THE SCIENTISTS persuaded the farmers that these seeds would be more resistant to insects and drought, increasing their yields and profits." Speaking louder, "What we know now, the crops grown from these seeds are unusable for our food production. Besides the crops, the seeds also grow thorny ugly weeds throughout the fields. Sadly, the bread we make and the vegetables we eat from these crops have no nutritional value.

Then the scientists created Robot UberBugs...bugs that were designed by scientists to eat the weeds. Instead, they ravage all our crops, including our heritage crops." In tears with her voice quivering, "our children grow ravenous from the lack of good nutritional non-genetically modified food products, and our fields are overrun with these ravenous Robot UberBugs."

Tawtanya's voice rising with spittle emitting out of her mouth, "Another interesting point...WHAT HAS BECOME of the male children they abducted over the past generation? It makes you wonder? Where did they go? Why don't the scientists respond to our requests for more information? They continually lie or deny what really happened.

"The crowd suddenly erupted as one loud voice, "NO MORE SCIENCE...NO MORE SCIENTISTS!"

With the brash female in the town center sharing more of what the Ananaya perceived as fake messages, he and his entourage left the meeting hall. The large group of scientists remaining in the meeting hall still fixated on the center screen hardly noticed the departure of their Chief Scientist. The remaining scientists sat mesmerized by Tawtanya's animated impassioned entreaties.

Tawtanya blared louder, "THE SCIENTISTS...THESE SCIENTISTS convinced us that every person from pre-pubescent to adulthood needs a seasonal vaccine for improving our immune systems. Unfortunately, one generation too late, we are numb with grief over the elderlies increased dementia problems from these vaccines. We all know once they diagnose a person with dementia, the scientists place that individual in supposed homes for the aging." Now with rage, "NEVER TO BE SEEN AGAIN." Distraught, she continued, "We are losing entire generations of our citizens to this terrible disease. Why is this happening? It is happening because the scientists do not want the insight and wisdom that our parents and grandparents provide to educate and guide the younger generation's decisions."

Tawtanya's last statement provided clarity. The crowd understood now that the project scientists cast out the disfigured children and the senile elderly. What the crowd did not know, is the project scientists were hiding these and many more failures.

Once out of sight of the larger group of scientists in the meeting hall, Ananaya spoke with his personal entourage of senior scientists. "Before this reckless creature's speech is over, each of you must pass along my directives to all of the scientists in the meeting hall." He continued, pointing at each of the senior associates. "The remaining scientists in the main hall must immediately gather their notes, belongings, and necessary instruments. Make sure to stress that they are required to return these items to the meeting hall for delivery to the Starfreighter, SSF Ganymede, waiting at the Spaceport."

Ananaya continued, "Once that is completed, guide everyone safely from the Science Center to the Spaceport through our newly built underground tunnel system."

Having said this...Ananaya turned to one of his associates and told him to discreetly capture Tawtanya and bring her to his Starcruiser, the SSC Cydonian, without haste. He asked another one of his key associates to double-check and make sure the entire database from the various science centers on Surtees is uploaded to the computers waiting on the starfreighter.

Ananaya pulled aside three of his top senior scientists. Hoygazor, Senior Astroscientist (air); Eyutho, Senior Marine Scientist (water) and; Doyfear Senior Agriculture Scientist (food). Ananaya directed these senior scientists to gather twenty of their best scientists and move lab equipment and data to the re-education center in the mountains. He added that they will find further directives once they arrive at the re-education center. Ananaya told them he would be in touch with them soon.

Ananaya screamed at the rest of his team, "DON'T JUST STAND THERE, GET MOVING."

Grabbing Hoygazor, the Senior Astroscientist, Ananaya directed him to send two starcruisers and two starfreighters to the Science Center's Spaceport that his late wife, Kaycee'na and her team acquired and built on Aztara. He commanded him to send a dozen skyplanes and fifty Enforcers with each starfreighter.

Finally, he told Hoygazor, to take the rest of our starcrafts from around the planet to the Spaceport at the re-education center in the mountainous region. Also, take twenty of your best Astroscientists and fifty Enforcers to the re-education center as well.

The crowd outside in the town square was becoming impatient. Tawtanya could tell it was time for a call to action. "Join me in stopping the scientists from using these hideous chemicals in our water systems. Join me by banning the Astroscientists flights in our atmosphere so that the skyplanes stop dumping the chemicals into their vapor trails. Join me in burning all genetically modified crops and weeds. Join me in building simple yet effective Robot UberBug traps. It may take a few seasons…we will eradicate those Robot UberBugs from our planet. Join me in replanting new crops with the good heritage seeds we secreted away in hiding.

Finally, join me in saying…NO…to these dreadful vaccines."

The crowd shouted again, "NO MORE SCIENCE…NO MORE SCIENTISTS!"

A few of the newer naïve scientists were not paying much attention to Ananaya's directives given to them by his associates. Bravely, they walked out of the front entrance of the Capital City Science Center with the hope of convincing the crowd to be more patient. Their inexperience with Ananaya's regime left them hopeful that they could make changes to benefit the people of Surtees.

Seeing these younger scientists at the front entrance of the Science Center, one side of the crowd began yelling, "There! There they are now! They are leaving! GO AFTER THEM!" Roused to a frenzy, the crowd turned into an unruly mob, hell-bent on ripping apart the scientists on the Science Center steps.

The distraction of the crowd-turned-mob allowed Ananaya's close associates, now dressed in street clothing, to capture Tawtanya. No one took notice of the celebrity struggling to get away from her captors.

Ananaya arrived at his Starcruiser, the SSC Cydonian, in time to see the last of the scientific notes and instruments loaded onto the starfreighter next to his starcruiser. Once aboard the SSC Cydonian, Tawtanya broke free of her captors' grasp. Rapidly approaching Ananaya, she grabbed his tunic and spat in his face, yelling, "You foul decrepit old man. Look what you have done to our planet, our people and our children. Is there no compassion left in you? You are sick and evil!"

Furiously, wiping the spittle from his face with the corner of his sleeve, Ananaya commanded his guards to lock her up in the cargo space. "Maybe the cold environment down there will cool her off during our trip to Aztara.... "

Once Tawtanya and her guards were out of sight, Ananaya barked another order, "Direct Commander Khrelyn to launch his starfreighter immediately. Let him know we will be leaving once he passes out of Surtees gravitational pull."

Receiving his orders, Commander Khrelyn, on the Starfreighter SSF Ganymede, departed Surtees's atmosphere gradually until he entered the outer rings of space. Totally unaware of everything that was happening on Surtees, Khrelyn focused on the control panel, readying his spacefreighter for the hyperluminal jump to Aztara.

The flight control center of the Starcruiser SSC Cydonian, with Ananaya aboard, was massive. Besides the control panels surrounding the oval-shaped control center; a curved multi-dimension screen enclosed the entire front area of the flight control center. The commander of the SSC Cydonian quietly spoke with Ananaya, letting him know they were awaiting his command to depart Surtees. Ananaya asked if all his directives were in place.

The commander said, "Yes, Syr!"

"Then let's depart," said Ananaya. "Put the rear camera view on the screen...show the image in multi-dimension."

As the outline of Surtees was moving further and further away on the screen in front of them, Ananaya told the SSC Cydonian commander to put the final directive into action. The commander reached across the control panel with his right hand and pressed a red and yellow cross-hatched button. Just then, as if on cue, the screen came alive as detonations became visible across the planet, Surtees.

Commander Khrelyn viewed the explosions on Surtees from the SSF Ganymede and became immediately disturbed and fearful for Tawtanya and her many friends' lives. A burning feeling in the pit of his stomach was rising in his heart, after each new explosion. He feared Tawtanya and her fellow protestors might be lost forever. Khrelyn could not imagine never seeing Tawtanya again. He admitted he fell in love with Tawtanya and her dichotomous, rebellious, and loving ways.

Staring down at Surtees, Khrelyn was in shock. His mind raced in confusion with what just happened. Who set off the explosions? How many people might have been killed? Was Tawtanya alive or not? Would he ever see her again? Should I turn this spacefreighter around and go find her?

A loud voice broke through his confusion, "Syr! Our orders are to go to hyperluminal speed now. Do I have your permission?"

Not even aware of the nod of his head, Khrelyn continued to stare down at his beloved planet until it blinked out of sight.

Back on SSC Cydonian, Ananaya, having anticipated the Project Scientists' deception, he was exhilarated by the pre-planned detonations. Ananaya exacted his revenge on those that repeatedly failed to complete his directive perfectly and those that conspired to betray. Smiling with smug self-satisfaction, Ananaya thought to himself how this time everything would be perfect. Aztara would be where he would achieve all his dreams.

CHAPTER FORTY-NINE

Hoygazor watched the select team leave with Ananaya to the tunnels to prepare to depart Surtees. Hoygazor found himself no longer teetering between sides. He was now a Surtarian, and he would remain a Surtarian. Looking to his team, he ordered, "Go to the tunnels and collect any equipment left behind. Then quickly disarm as many of the explosives set by the Enforcers. You have very little time. Go and move fast!"

His men departed with a sense of urgency as Hoygazor himself sprinted for the Spaceport to retrieve as many skyplanes as the remaining pilots could operate. Ananaya would see this as one of his directives being carried out and would be less suspicious of what Hoygazor was preparing to do.

On the streets, Myana was frantically searching for Tawtanya. No one had seen her since her speech. One person in the crowd said he thought he saw Tawtanya being dragged away by two men, but with all the riotous actions happening, he was not certain.

If Tawtanya was taken to a re-education camp, they would find her. Myana knew she needed to take charge if she was not going to let Tawtanya down. Surtees must be saved.

Eyutho, never one to willingly follow Ananaya, except for self-preservation, delighted in the fact that the Chief Scientist was leaving the planet. There was so much that needed to be undone. The seas were still intact since Ananaya had not directed any chemicals to be placed in the largest body of water. However, the lakes and reservoirs would be a challenge. Finding compounds that would counter-act the anti-aging chemicals would take time. The challenge of making the rebels understand that he was working on their behalf would not be easy. He and the other scientists were seen as the enemy. He knew Tawtanya was the Champion of the People, but would she give him safe passage to discuss what he might be able to do? He was not entirely sure he would be met with anything but suspicion. However, he needed to try and soon.

Noryan and Josyah, having enlisted the men from the internment camp, were forming a militia along with the sailors back at the Marine Science Center. Enforcers still stood in the way of freeing men from other internment camps. It was the new militias' duty to stomp out the Enforcers, find where Enforcers were being created, and end the tyranny of the Chief Scientist's army.

Without notice, explosion-after-explosion erupted; panic ensued in the villages and cities. People ran for cover as many science buildings fell to the ground in complete destruction. Once people realized that only science buildings were being destroyed, cheers erupted. Thinking the rebels were at work, many people on the streets took up arms to fight off Enforcers.

Onboard the departing starcruiser and starfreighter, the explosions were seen as large fireballs, and mixed emotions were being felt. Joy was seen on Ananaya's face and abject horror was seen on Commander Khrelyn's. Neither knew that what they thought they saw…was not what really happened.

CHAPTER FIFTY

Aztara, an otherwise quiet planet, was now a planet of immense sadness. With the unexplained plague that only killed the females, men and boys alike were left to mourn with cries of despair and woe. After a time of mourning, meetings were called in every village, town, and city. Connecting with their minds telepathically, questions were asked as to what this would mean to the planet and what was their recourse.

'Our planet is doomed!' thundered a thought throughout the minds of all the citizens who were able to attend the meetings. Many men were still home with young and infant boys, too preoccupied to allow their minds to be distracted to tune into the thoughts at the meetings.

'Without women, there is no future for this planet," was the consensus of most of the Aztarian. Tears were seen appearing in more than one man's eyes as the weight of the horror was relived.

No one was thinking about the team of scientists on this date. The arrival of the aliens was met with mixed emotions. The citizens from the southeast welcomed them as it brought prosperity to their village. Others were less excited for the alien humans arriving from an unknown planet and could not help feeling that their arrival spelled doom for their small, peaceful planet.

At the Aztarian Capital City meeting hall, Byrett, a Surtarian genetic scientist, could only see the concern and fear in the Aztarian men's faces as they continued to communicate with their minds. Byrett asked for permission to speak, "If you will reach out with your mind to your fellow Aztarians and convey what I am about to propose as a solution, I will be grateful."

With permission granted, Byrett proceeded, "Soon, Ananaya, the Chief Scientist of Surtees, will arrive. He learned of your fate from my staff when he learned of his wife's death from the horrible plague. Ananaya implemented an emergency plan to help Aztara to flourish and grow as a planet. A renowned scientist from the planet called Earth discovered a group of women whose genetic composition is compatible with the men of Aztara. With their arrival, your lives can continue as before this horrible plague destroyed your world as you know it. Have hope. While I do not have exact timing, your new wives will be arriving before the end of next season. Go home now and grieve, as we are also doing for the loss of our female scientists, including Ananaya's own wife, Kaycee'na."

The gravelly voice of the shop owner choked out a question to be answered by Byrett. "How do we know that they will want to be part of our world?"

"That is a good question. The genetic scientists on Earth completed an extensive process to find women who are totally compatible with each and every one of you. You will find the merging of lives to be easy and comfortable for everyone," Byrett said, knowing his words were being telecommunicated to every part of the planet.

Answering a few more questions from near and far, Byrett left the meeting to return to the Southern Science Center on Aztara. He knew Ananaya was waiting on his starcruiser to hear how the men of Aztara received the plans the Chief Scientist laid out many seasons before the plague.

"All went as you said it would," Byrett said to the Chief Scientist on interspace hyper-link.

"No one was the least bit suspicious?" Ananaya asked.

"Not in the least. The men are so weighed down by grief that I doubt any could think beyond what is happening in their lives at present. I believe that everything is proceeding as you prescribed. The women will start to arrive soon, even before your arrival, as per your directives," Byrett said.

"Wonderful," Ananaya said enthusiastically, "our good fortune is yet before us. This time everything will work out as planned. Aztara is our future. Send new orders to the commanders of our starcruisers, to leave immediately for Earth. I want no delays in the continued arrival of the earth women."

To be continued...on Aztara, A Galactic Love Story, Volume II

AZTARIAN SERIES
GLOSSARY OF TERM

Ananaya *(ann-a-na'-a)* – The main protagonist in the Aztarian Book Series. Ananaya is an obsessive-compulsive Surtarian Chief Scientist. Ananaya nearly destroys his home planet of Surtees in his attempts to develop longevity for his own desires. Through one of many space probes, he discovers that the planet of Aztara has the Longevity Gene provided by the multi-purpose mineral phyrium. This is precisely what he was trying to create on the planet Surtees with a bonus – Telepathy. Finally achieving longevity, Ananaya realizes that telepathy will provide an enigmatic advantage against his enemies.

Astro Scientist – A Surtarian scientist and intergalactic pilot.

Ava Padden – Yyemara's earthbound name.

Aztara *(az-tare-a)* – The purple planet in the Ursa Draconis Galaxy.

Aztarian *(az-tare-e-an)* – Refers to the original inhabitants of the planet Aztara and the offspring of the interspecies Aztarian males and Earthling females.

Biogerontology *(bio-jare-on-tology)* – Attempts to answer the question of why and how we age, and how to possibly slow the aging process. Unlike gerontology, biogerontology focuses on the biological reasons behind aging.

Capital City Spaceport – An intergalactic port for spacecraft built by the Surtarian scientists near the capital city of Aztara.

Captain Dyston – *(die- stun)* – Sea Captain that lead the raid on the internment camps with Noryan.

Chief Scientist – Ananaya, the head scientist from Surtees.

Cloaking Skyplane – A planet-bound plane that is used for undetectable intra-planet travel.

ComProbe – A stationary super-luminal communication probe that is dispersed by a Starcraft at intervals as it travels intergalactically between planets. The ComProbes are retrieved on the Starcrafts return.

D'Hantin *(dan'-tin)* – The father of Tymorian, son of Morsian, and inventor of many items, including the SoundBlaster.

Doyfear *(doy-fear)* – (FOOD) Head Agriculture Scientist Responsible for all Agricultural Scientists, Aquaponic Scientists, and farmers.

Earth *(er-th)* – Third planet from the sun in Milky Way Galaxy. Earth is in one of the spiral arms of the Milky Way (called the Orion Arm), which lies about two-thirds of the way out from the center of the Galaxy. Earth is part of a Solar System - a group of eight planets, numerous comets, asteroids and dwarf planets which orbit their Sun.

Earthlings *(er-th-lings)* – Refers to Inhabitants of the planet Earth and the females that were abducted and sent to the planet Aztara.

Enforcers *(in-for-cers)* – Genetically modified and enhanced guards of the scientists.

Entayta *(in-tay-ta)* – Robotic Scientist responsible for the UberBug robots.

Eyorkie *(ee-yor-key)* – Sutarian word for a shout of delight or satisfaction when one finds or discovers something unexpected.

Eyutho *(ee-u-tho)* – (WATER) Lead Marine Scientist responsible for all Marine Biologist', Fisherman, oceans, rivers, lakes, and fisheries.

Fyyenen *(Fie-in-en)* – Experienced genetic scientist that spent much time tutoring Yyemara at an early age.

Genetic Scientists – Genetic scientists analyze DNA characteristics to genetically engineer new drugs or splicing techniques to modify ones' DNA.

Giants – Another term for the Enforcers.

Guyzar *(guy-zar)* – Ananaya's devoted assistant.

Hexyeb – *(hex-yeb)* – Head Scientist for the Center for Genetic Studies.

Hoygazor *(hoy-gay-zoor)* – (AIR) Senior Astro-Scientist responsible all Starcraft, Astro-Scientists, Pilots, and Flight Crews. and Meteorologists.

Inter-Galactic Starprobes – An un-manned, relatively small, Surtarian spacecraft designed to travel long distances at very high speeds exceeding 2-3 times the speed of light. This Starcraft examines scientific, genetic, biological, and historical information on various planets and their continents throughout the Universe. The information is then transmitted in short data packets, superluminally, from one stationary ComProbe to another until it reaches its destination.

Josyah *(joos-ya)* – Sutarian born farmer and rebellion fighter. Merlynn and Noryan are his parents. Khrelyn is his brother.

Kaycee'na *(kay-c-na)* – Female Neurochemist, wife of Ananaya and mother to the twins, Yyemara and Tawtanya. Died in the plague that killed all females on Aztara.

Khrelyn *(kray-linn)* – Sutarian born Starfreighter and Starcruiser Pilot, Astro Scientist. Merlynn and Noryan are his parents. Josyah is his brother.

K-rod *(kay-rod)* – A unit of distance measurement equaling 3.125 miles or 5 kilometers.

'Longevity Gene' (FOXO3) – This gene plays a significant role in the aging process. When the mineral phyrium is consumed, it diminishes the aging process by many folds.

Lylan *(lee-lan)* – Zrymyr games spectator

Lymson *(lim-son)* – Armament training officer.

Lyryca *(lear-e-ca)* – lady friend of Merlynn.

Merlynn *(mer-lynn)* – Farmer. Noryan's wife and Khrelyn and Josyah's mother.

Mind-Voice – Inter-species telepathic communication.

Monochloride – Chemical compound that is oxidized and sprayed into the skyplanes vapor trails creating chemical trails for the benefits of anti-aging. Generally sprayed with nucuobromine.

Neurochemist – Kaycee'na, a neuro-chemist, studied the human brain and nervous system, including the understanding of human thoughts, emotions, and behavior. While on the planet Surtees, Kaycee'na focused her research on the possibility of improving longevity. On the planet Aztara

Kaycee'na oversaw the Genetic Engineering of the Warrior in the DNA of the first generation Aztarian/Earthling boys. Kaycee'na died in the plague that killed all the females on Aztara.

Noryan *(nor-yan)* – Farmer, prisoner, and one of the rebellion leaders. Merlynn's husband and Khrelyn and Josyah's father.

Nucuobromine – Chemical compound that is oxidized and sprayed into the skyplanes vapor trails creating chemical trails for the benefits of anti-aging. Generally sprayed with monochloride.

OXPHOS – Ananaya's goal is for genetically modified food crops would enhance Microchondrial metabolism.

Phyrium *(phy-ree-um)* – A mineral only found on the Planet Aztara. This mined mineral enhances the 'Longevity Gene' (FOXO3) and the 'Telepathy Gene' (semaphorin 5A). It decreases aging while allowing telepathic communication between humans, creatures, and building structures, and machinery.

Pi-Gau *(pie-ga-owe)* – Is a laser generator inside of the electromagnetic drive for Starcraft propulsion.

Pulse or Pulsed – A short quick inter-species telepathic message.

Robotic UberBug – A super robotic artificial intelligent bug. Created by Doyfear and his team of Agricultural Scientists. They eat the weeds created by the genetically modified seeds the scientists created in the hopes of finding a genetic solution for longevity.

Rod – A unit of distance measurement equaling 3.3 feet or 1 meter.

Ryke (*rye-ke*) – A wooden wheeled cart with a wooden bed for carrying farm goods to market. Usually, pulled by a trydox

Ryndor *(ren-dor)* – Ananaya's narcissistic father. Ryndor brought his family and scientific team from a dying planet to Surtees. Ryndor and Ananaya's specialty was Biogerontology.

Science Center – Surtarian centers for scientific research. Found in every city and town on the planet Surtees.

Science Compound – Surtarian center for scientific research. Located in the southern region of the main continent on the planet Aztara.

Science Compound Spaceport – An intergalactic port for spacecraft built by the Surtarian scientist near the Science Compound in the southern region of the main continent on the planet Aztara.

Spaceport – a port that is purpose-built for the landing and departure of spacecraft, people, data, and freight.

Starcruiser, SSC Cydonian – A Surtarian spacecraft designed to travel long distances at speeds greater than the speed of light. Ananaya's personal Starcruiser.

Starcruiser, SSC Elysium – A Surtarian spacecraft designed to travel long distances at speeds greater than the speed of light. The second Surtarian Starcraft to enter the Aztarian airspace. The initial Spaceprobe sent by Ananaya was the first. Kaycee'na was the first Surtarian scientist to set foot on Aztara.

Starcruiser, SSC Emissary – A Surtarian spacecraft designed to travel long distances at speeds greater than the speed of light. Khrelyn's command Starcraft. Khrelyn traveled between

Surtees and Earth to support Yyemara and her genetic engineering duties. Khrelyn brought the first abducted Earthing women to Aztara to replace the women that died in the Aztarian plague.

Starfreighter, SSF Ganymede – A Surtarian spacecraft designed to travel moderate distances at speeds approaching the speed of light. The Star Freighter can carry a considerable amount of weight and data.

Starfreighter, SSF Legacy – A Surtarian spacecraft designed to travel moderate distances at speeds approaching the speed of light. The Star Freighter can carry a considerable amount of weight and data.

Surtees *(sur'-tees)* – A puce color planet in the Porphyrion Galaxy. Home of the scientists, Ananaya, Yyemara, Khrelyn, Kaycee'na. Also, the home of Tawtanya a renowned Surtarian athletic celebrity and activist.

Surtarian *(sur'-tare-e-un)* – Inhabitants of Surtees.

Syonne *(see-on-nay)* – Kaycee'na's delivery nurse. Tawtanya's childhood nurse and adopted mother.

Syr *(sir)* – Used as a polite or respectful way of addressing a man.

Tawtanya *(tah-tahn-ya)* – Renowned Surtarian female athlete and activist. Daughter of Ananaya and Kaycee'na, twin sister of Yyemara. Her love interest is Khrelyn.

'Telepathy Gene,' (semaphorin 5A) – The Telepathy Gene increases one's ability to communicate telepathically with another being, species, or even a compatible machine or building. The gene allows one to transmit, receive, block, speed up, or slow down the delivery or acceptance of images and information. The consumption of phyrium enhances this sixth sense.

Teleetheric *(tell-la-eth-ric)* – Is the ultimate form of the telepathy gene involving our entire spiritual being, encompassing our mind, body, and soul.

Toybyn *(toy-bin)* – Old sea captain. Friend of Myana and Tawtanya. Resistance leader.

Transporter – Uses a super-diamagnetic torsional gravity system made from phyrium. This transporter was invented by Ty's grandfather Morsian and built by Ty's Father, D'Hantin, and his engineers in a factory east of the capital city of Aztara.

Trydox *(try-dox)* – Massive oxen enlisted for pull rykes or working the farm fields.

UberBugs *(uber-bugs)* – Robot designed to destroy heritage crops and pests.

UberBugs *(uber-bugs)* – Robot designed to destroy heritage crops and pests.

V'zeyuk *(v-za-yuk)* – Mean, spoiled, masculistic rich boy that participated in the Zrymyr games.

'Warrior Gene' (MAOA gene) – Women have 2 X chromosomes where men have 1 X and 1 Y. This gene is carried on the X chromosome, so women can either have it 1) not at all, 2) on only 1 X (therefore making them a carrier), or 3) on both X's (exhibiting the trait themselves). Warrior Gene causes increased risk-taking and aggressive behavior.

Wylmer *(while-mer)* – Surtarian farmer. Friend of Noryan.

XCHROM-6E – a Genetically engineered virus that Ananaya created for the plague on Aztara.

Yyemara *(yee-mar-a)* – Surtarian female Genetic Scientist, daughter of Ananaya and Kaycee'na, twin sister to Tawtanya.

XTTPL – xanthothinphyll chemical additive for water. XTTPL provides vitamins and antioxidants for drinking water and irrigation of the genetically modified plant seeds.

Zoolyol *(zool-yool)* – Ananaya's childhood nurse. Yyemara's childhood nurse.

Zrymyr *(zrr-mear)* – Zrymyr games are the most important inter-science center games on the planet. The games are based on difficult obstacles

Zyla *(za-eye-la)* – Wife of Ryndor, mother to Ananaya.

Carole Walker Carter

Starting life in a small town in Nebraska, Carole and her family frequently moved across the USA, Carole met many fascinating personalities that inspired characters for her many stories. With a vivid imagination, Carole expressed her love of story-telling in Children's Literature, Mystery, Science Fiction, and Fantasy books as platforms for her expressive writing.

Carole lives presently in the Pacific Northwest with her husband, Don, her childhood sweetheart and partner, their pet dogs, several chickens, and a few fish. Carole's career involved working with children from pre-school through high school, dealing with special needs, and "at-risk'" children as an Occupational Therapy Assistant and Educational Assistant.

Aztara, Mastel Kingdom, the prequel to the *Aztarian Series*, providing insight into the lore of the creatures on Aztara. Surtees, Science Rules, the first volume in the *Aztarian Series* describes the narcissistic protagonist that abused both Surtarians and Aztarians for his own personal needs. Aztara, A Galactic Love Story, is the first published book and the second volume in the *Aztarian Series*. Aztara, Secrets Revealed, the revolt where Aztarians take their planet back. Carole announced in the summer of 2017 a mystery book series, *Evers and McFarlan Detective Series*. Final Alumni, Shadowy Faces, and Nine Points of a Circle all are available today. Carole also started a *Fantasy Series* in the fall of 2017 for young people. Little Dragon is the first book in the *Child Rowanda Series*, Return to Arolsen, The Underworld and the Dragon Princess will be available in the winter of 2019/2020. Please watch for additional volumes in the *Aztarian Series*, *Evers and McFarlan Detective Series*, *The Child Rowanda*, Series, and Carole's many children stories on her website www.walkercarter.com and www.amazon.com.

Aztara, The Mastel Kingdom
By
Carole Walker Carter

Aztara, The Mastel Kingdom, tells the background story of the mastels before entering into a bonding relationship with the miners of Aztara. The setting for this book is two generations before the plague that killed all the Aztarian women during the time frame for Vol II *Aztara, A Galactic Love Story.*

Idyllic as it might seem, the mastels are nomadic, dependent upon the weather and growing cycles for the food they eat.

The bond between the griswells and mastels seems destined to failure, until Morsian, an inventor from the eastern factory villages, creates a symbiotic relationship that will change everything on Aztara...forever.

Explore the early world of Aztara and enjoy Mastel's unique story.

This book will be available on Amazon, Kindle, Nook, and Barnes & Noble in the winter of 2019/2020.

Surtees, Science Rules
By
Carole Walker Carter

Surtees, Science Rules is the First book in *Aztarian Series.* In Surtees, Science Rules, we discover how ruthless a utopian society can be when the ruling power is Scientists.

Ananaya's family are the Oligarchs in this society. His father and mother are obsessed with increasing longevity to keep their power and wealth. Ryndor, Ananaya's father, set up several of his senior scientists as the leaders of scientific research centers.

Hoygazor became the leader of the Astro-Scientists that travel the universe. Eyutho lead research into Marine Science. Doyfear founded the Agricultural research centers. Kaycee'na, wife of Ananaya, developed Neurochemistry research.

Ananaya's sinister plans will become known as he maneuvers his way through the Oligarchy.

This book will be available on Amazon, Kindle, Nook, and Barnes & Noble in the winter of 2019/2020

AZTARA, A Galactic Love Story
By
Carole Walker Carter

In <u>AZTARA, A Galactic Love Story, the
second book in the</u> *Aztarian Series* centers on
two main characters and their magical
creatures that they share a unique bond. The
two main characters are caught up in their
own personal grief.

Shayla, an Earth woman, who finds life on
Earth hardly worth living after being deceived by her husband, and
having her only son die, is close to suicide.

Ty, having lived through a plague that killed all the females on his
planet, finds refuge in his work, mining a mineral instrumental to all
aspects of life on Aztara, including telepathy, longevity, and levitation.

Scientists from Surtees, a dying planet, relocate to Aztara to receive the
benefits of phyrium. In their attempt to rebuild the Aztarian
population, they import Earth women who carry a specific gene, the
warrior gene, to mate with the Aztarian men.

The story is about finding love, trust, and internal strength as well as
romance, intrigue, and thrills while the two main characters come to
grips with a situation, not of their own choosing.

Find this book on Amazon, Kindle, Nook, and Barnes & Noble Now!!

AZTARA, Secrets Revealed
By
Carole Walker Carter

AZTARA, Secrets Revealed, the third book in the Aztarian Series, opens with Shayla's and Ty's love for their twins, Nayela and Kestle. Nayela, the only interspecies girl who communicates telepathically with a mastel, finds others her age calling her a freak. Kestle has his hands full with being a gang member.

A tragic event occurs that changes everything for Kestle. Self-banished to the Wildlands leaves Kestle bitter, depressed, and alone to deal with situations he has never encountered. Going deeper into the Wildlands, in search of food and water, brings Kestle to the dreaded Orange River. Saving a young runaway girl, Sinaka, from certain death, Kestle's loneliness ends, but he discovers there is more to this young girl than he first thought. Sinaka finds it is her turn to save Kestle when he is wounded by a monster. With unexpected help from a beautiful creature and Sinaka's psychic and empathic powers, Kestle finds healing.

The Surtarian Chief Scientist, Ananaya, accelerates his plan to genetically modify the Aztarian/Earthling boys' Warrior Genes, with performance-enhancing injections. Ananaya's plot is to create a daunting army of new Enforcers.

All hell breaks loose when the usually passive Aztarians decide to fight to get their boys back.

Find this book on Amazon, Kindle, Nook, and Barnes & Noble Now!!

Final Alumni
By
Carole Walker Carter

The Final Alumni is the first book in the *Evers and McFarlan Detective Series.* This series follows two high school best friends who join forces to solve multiple cases. Tish, haunted by a childhood experience, enables herself with many disciplines of martial arts, while Scotty falls back on his sharpshooter training and physical prowess as a football hero. Together they make an unstoppable team.

Now living in Chicago, Illinois, and mentored by a well-respected couple who owns a detective agency, Tish and Scotty are enlisted to assist Aileen and Patrick Jamieson in solving cases in Chicago while pursuing a series of unsolved murders in their own hometown as well.

Find this book on Amazon, Kindle, Nook, and Barnes & Noble Now!!

Shadowy Faces
By
Carole Walker Carter

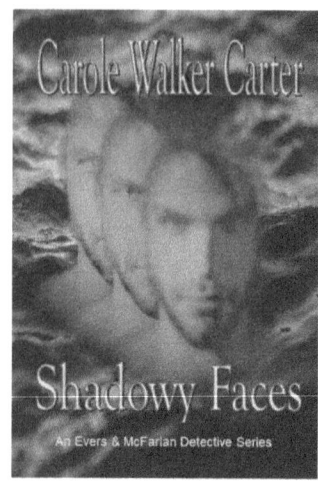

Shadowy Faces is the second book in *the Evers and McFarlan Detective Series*. In Shadowy Faces, Tish and Scotty are confronted with the lives of three young women who have been ruined. Each young woman deals with lost weekends where all they can recall are vague faces tormenting them. These shadowy faces become the focus of the investigation of Evers and McFarlan along with the Jamiesons and the Chicago Police. The team works methodically to discover what happened to each of the women to bring the criminals to justice.

Tish has to lean on a discipline her Grand-Master taught her even with the warning of what could happen to her if anyone should learn of her new martial arts fighting technique. Scotty also faces the threat of losing the love of his life

Find this book on Amazon, Kindle, Nook, and Barnes & Noble Now!!

Nine Points of a Circle
By
Carole Walker Carter

Carole Walker Carter

Nine Points of a Circle is the third book in the *Evers & McFarlan Detective Series.* In Nine Points of a Circle, Tish and Scotty are now husband and wife, owners, and licensed detectives in the Evers & McFarlan Agency. Even though the Jamison's are retired, they will continue to consult with Scotty and Tish.

Nine Points of a Circle

Evers and McFarlan Detective Series

Captain Jones hires the Evers and McFarlan Agency for what appears to be a serial killer. Four deaths have occurred over the past two years, and the bodies were dumped on different streets in downtown Chicago. At the same time, Tish and Scotty are approached by a well-known Chicago business executive regarding his missing daughter.

Both cases will take all of Scotty's technical expertise and Tish's detective skills to solve. Follow them as they delve into the seedy depths of the Chicago underworld.

This book will be available on Amazon, Kindle, Nook, and Barnes & Noble in the summer of 2018.

The Child Rowanda, Little Dragon
By
Carole Walker Carter

Twelve-year-old Rowanda lives with her mother in the lush garden country of Neslora. Seemingly an idyllic world with endlessly blooming flowers, buzzing bees, and birds chirping, Rowanda and her friends are confronted with the horror of the abduction of their mothers.

Rowanda finds herself confronted with the daunting task of finding and rescue her mother and the mothers of her friends. A tyrant king abducted and transported the mothers to a desert world where they are being held as slaves.

Armed only with four talismans, chosen from many by mystical means, Rowanda goes through a portal to Arolsen where her fate is intermingled with two desert dwellers. Together they join forces to brave the desert, defending themselves from nomads, terrible creatures, and scorching desert days and frigid desert nights to rescue Rowanda's mother.

The Palace City reveals the true identities of Rowanda's traveling companions and the reasons they accompanied her on her quest.

Find this book on Amazon, Kindle, Nook, and Barnes & Noble Now!!

The Child Rowanda, Return to Arolsen
By
Carole Walker Carter

When Rowanda and the Elder Sorceresses become aware that the charms left in Arolsen are causing destruction in Neslora, Rowanda, her best friend, Nalivia, as well as Beirimor, Rowanda's father and his mother, the Elder Sorceress, must return to Arolsen to set things right. Many adventures await all four of the Neslorians. Boultori, the wicked king's brother, is being held captive in the palace prison. The Neslorians plan is to rescue Boultori and place him on the throne so he can make Arolsen a safe, flourishing, and blissful world…

Rowanda finds Arolsen more fascinating as two new talismans chose Rowanda. A tiger's eye and an animal's tooth manifest their magic by controlling the most feared creatures of Arolsen. These creature's aide Rowanda on her quest for justice.

Nalivia, a new and untrained sorceress and Rowanda's childhood best friend, joins this adventure as she is tasked to find charms that will aide Boultori when he battles his evil brother, King Nashua. With help from Anarigar, a young goat herder, the two youth finds themselves in trouble.

Magic abounds in this second book of the Child Rowanda series as good battles evil to rescue a world from slavery and hardship and to keep Neslora from the same predicament.

Find this book on Amazon, Kindle, Nook, and Barnes & Noble Now!!

The Child Rowanda, Underworld

By
Carole Walker Carter

Trying to rid the world of Neslora of the evil wizard, Nashua, Rowanda finds herself dragged into the Underworld with the evil sorcerer.

Navigating the terrifying darkness of this new world, Rowanda finds a mysterious and mystical guide who reveals that Rowanda can only exit the Underworld the same way she came in, with the evil sorcerer at her side. However, Nashua must be truly repentant of his depravities before he is allowed to leave, which means Rowanda cannot leave if he does not repent.

Trying to find Nashua in the darkness and convince him to repent, becomes a difficult process. Making matters worse are the demons, intent on making both Nashua and Rowanda one of them that would mean living an eternity in the Underworld in agony.

Find this book on Amazon, Kindle, Nook, and Barnes & Noble Now!!

The Child Rowanda, Dragon Princess
By
Carole Walker Carter

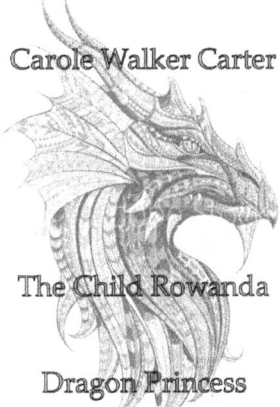

Leaving the Underworld through another portal, Rowanda finds that she has not returned to her home-world of Neslora but finds herself on another parallel world with the devious Nashua, where she is elevated to a princess.

Friends and members of her family are in this world, but they are not as they should be. They are doubles with a different personality and…no recollection of Rowanda.

Rowanda finds herself at odds with her look-alike parents, the king, and queen of Soleran.

Rowanda's magical talent of charming animals allows Rowanda to help the enslaved citizens of this world by joining the rebel army in opposition to the king and queen.

Wanting nothing more than to return to her own world, Rowanda seeks the aid of a fire-breathing dragon.

Find this book on Amazon, Kindle, Nook, and Barnes & Noble Now!!

Childhood Stories my Dad Told Me
By
Carole Walker Carter

Growing up on a farm in Nebraska during the Great Depression was difficult, but for two young boys, it was also filled with fun and adventures.

These stories tell about the amusing antics that my father and his younger brother found themselves in during these hard times.

The stories are filled with insights about rural schools, country social events, and harvest time, as well as the day-to-day chores of a working farm.

Find this book on Amazon, Kindle, Nook, and Barnes & Noble Now!!

www.ingramcontent.com/pod-product-compliance
Lightning Source LLC
Chambersburg PA
CBHW070808180626
46818CB00001B/154